★

"We have the body of one of the missing boys."

"Which one?"

"The last one to go missing, the ten-year-old from Percy Street."

"He has been identified?"

"Yes, by his father. We have his body." Archie Young hesitated. "And parts of another."

"How was he found?"

"In a wooded area, by a young couple…looking for somewhere quiet and dark."

"How did you come to find the body…was it buried?"

"Yes, but working free from the soil and leaves…they didn't see it themselves at first, but they saw a man with his dog staring at something among the trees. Or seemed to be—the dog was in the bushes. He said to them that there was something funny that they ought to look at. The young man did so while the man stood back. He soon saw it was a body, saw the feet, he says…he had his mobile with him and telephoned the police."

"And the man?"

"He disappeared into the dark."

★

GWENDOLINE BUTLER

A GRAVE COFFIN

W🌐RLDWIDE®

TORONTO • NEW YORK • LONDON
AMSTERDAM • PARIS • SYDNEY • HAMBURG
STOCKHOLM • ATHENS • TOKYO • MILAN
MADRID • WARSAW • BUDAPEST • AUCKLAND

With my thanks to Dr. Colin Fink for
all his help on scientific and
medical matters.

A GRAVE COFFIN

A Worldwide Mystery/August 2001

First published by St. Martin's Press, Incorporated.

ISBN 0-373-26392-9

Printed in U.S.A.

Author's Note

One evening in April 1988, I sat in Toynbee Hall in the East End of London, near to Docklands, listening to Dr. David Owen (now Lord Owen) give that year's Barnett Memorial Lecture. In it, he suggested the creation of a Second City of London, to be spun off from the first, to aid the economic and social regeneration of the Docklands.

The idea fascinated me and I have made use of it to create a world for detective John Coffin, to whom I gave the tricky task of keeping there the Queen's Peace.

*A brief calendar of the life and career
of John Coffin, Chief Commander of the
Second City of London Police.*

John Coffin is a Londoner by birth, his father is unknown and his mother was a difficult lady of many careers and different lives who abandoned him in infancy to be looked after by a woman who may have been a relative of his father and who seems to have acted as his mother's dresser when she was on the stage. He kept in touch with this lady, whom he called Mother, lodged with her in his early career and looked after her until she died.

After serving briefly in the army, he joined the Metropolitan Police, soon transferring to the plain-clothes branch as a detective.

He became a sergeant and was very quickly promoted to inspector a year later. Ten years later, he was a superintendent and then chief superintendent.

There was a bad patch in his career about which he is reluctant to talk. His difficult family background has complicated his life and possibly accounts for an unhappy period when, as he admits, his career went down a black hole. His first marriage split apart at this time and his only child died.

From this dark period he was resurrected by a spell in a secret, dangerous undercover operation about which even now not much is known. But the esteem he won then was recognized when the Second City of London was being formed and he became Chief Commander of its police force. He has married again, an old love, Stella Pinero, who is herself a very successful actress. He has also discovered two siblings, a much younger sister and brother.

ONE

THE ROOM HAD a view of St Paul's Cathedral if you looked hard over the rooftops. To get into this room, you were required to press the red button on the door before entering; inside there was the distinct impression you were photographed from every angle and possibly microwaved as well. To the nervous it felt that way.

The air itself was not fresh but filtered through a silent air conditioner which somehow made its presence felt so that even air and breathing were controlled in this room.

John Coffin liked the view but was not sure of the company. He had got back the night before from a visit to Los Angeles where he had left his wife on business of her own, collected the dog from the kennels and found an urgent message from a high authority.

'Wait until you see the body,' said Edward Saxon. 'Then tell me you cannot help me.' He looked into John Coffin's eyes, so blue, cold and clear. 'Or study this photograph just to give you an idea.' He pushed the photograph across the table.

Coffin bent his head to look. 'Jesus.'

'Yes. Look, I know we were never pals, but we got on well enough, we worked together for long enough. So did Harry Blyth, you worked with him.' He tapped the photograph. 'That's Harry Seton now. Or was.'

'You hit hard.'

'So? What about it? Will you help?'

Coffin still kept quiet.

'It's not just me, you know, I am not asking this as a favour...it's important for all of us.' He looked Coffin straight in the eye. 'You might die because of what is going on, someone you love might die. It's certain that many have died al-

ready. Or been impaired, mentally and physically.' He went on:
'These are frontline pharmaceuticals for life-threatening,
serious illness. Some are coming in legally through parallel
importing, where a manufacturer finds they can make a drug
more cheaply in Taiwan than West Middlesex—these are all
right, because the quality, strength and the release of the drug
in the patient will be the same. Sometimes there is counterfeiting, this has been an increasing problem first noticed on a
professional production level in the late eighties. The cardboard
covers and packaging are printed exactly the same, but the
drugs inside might have been made in a backyard in Taiwan
so that the activity in the patient, purity and contamination, all
vary from the kosher production runs by legitimate producers.
They might be no more than coloured starch, but unscrupulous
pharmacy importers buy them, accept the false serial numbers
without checking and offer them to none-too-fussy pharmacists
at reduced prices. Big money and big chances for corruption.'

Coffin sat taking it all in. 'What powers will I have?'

'As much as I can give you...' Quickly, he added, 'All you
want.'

'Access to the production date and all papers and files?'

'The lot.'

'Freedom to interview all the characters that I want to?'

Was there a pause, a hint of reservation? 'Yes,' agreed Ed
Saxon.

'Right, then. It's on.'

Edward Saxon drew a deep breath, whether of relief or pain
was not clear to Coffin. It might be a mixture of the two. Rumours of Saxon's ill health had reached him, but rumours, of
course, often lied.

'I will have to fit my investigations into my other duties.'

'That's understood.'

Coffin let his thoughts go back to the years when he, as a
detective sergeant, had worked with Saxon in that remote area
of South London where Kentish men and Men of Kent had
once vied with each before the Great Wen had swallowed them
both up.

He had worked with Edward Saxon, admired the man's tenacity, but had sensed a reserve behind the good manners. That was all right, a man was entitled to his own secrets; Coffin had his own. Although he had noticed that the passing years peeled them away. Marriage, the passing of time, seemed to take off the surface through which a few artefacts you had buried came to the surface, as in an archaeological dig. His own wife Stella knew most things about him now, life had disgorged them before her, one way and another. Probably she still had a few secrets. He smiled at the thought, which he almost found endearing.

He wondered about Saxon's wife.

'How's Laurie?' he asked.

'Not too well. No, she hasn't been well...she's away at present.' He added, as an afterthought, 'How's Stella?'

'She's away too. In Los Angeles, looking at scripts.' Among other things.

'They still film in Los Angeles? I thought it was all over the place, never in Hollywood now.' It was an idle comment, he did not really know or care.

'They do film in Los Angeles in this film. And on location, later.'

He smiled. Stella had complained that she would be filming in the winter in the wilder reaches of the Bronx. If the film got that far, always a question. Stella, anyway, had other plans for herself before filming started. She would be in Los Angeles, attending to scripts and other more personal matters.

'It's an English company, anyway,' she had said, 'filming a short story of Scott Fitzgerald.'

It was, as he knew, an avant-garde company, more interested in winning prizes than money. Stella had accepted a part because, so she said, it would do her image good. But Coffin had an insight into one of Stella's secrets and how her image would be improved: she planned to have cosmetic surgery in Los Angeles because American doctors were good at that sort of thing. 'So much custom, you see, they are at it all the time. Makes the prices higher but the noses better. But I have arranged a prix fixe.'

'Like in a cheap hotel,' he had said.

'You needn't have said that, darling.'

But I did need, he thought, and it slipped out.

'Laurie's with her mother.'

Coffin looked down again at the hideous photograph of Harry Seton's dead body. 'He was married, I suppose.'

'Yes, I want you to talk to Mary.'

Coffin looked up and raised an eyebrow.

'Not just a sympathy talk,' said Saxon. 'She may know something that helps. I think she does.'

'I want to know all the details of what is facing me first.'

Saxon hesitated. 'I expect we seem a small and unimportant unit to you.'

Coffin looked around the room, and he laughed. 'Oh, I assure you, you do not. I have taken in where this unit works, and the security measures you run. On the contrary, you look important and influential to me.'

'We have enemies.' Saxon spoke quietly but with conviction. 'Inevitably in this trade. Which is why we have the neutral name of TRANSPORT A. We do need and use transport, but that is not our purpose. We watch transport, for that matter.'

'Drugs,' said Coffin thoughtfully, 'but not the usual sort: heroin, crack and so on, not them. They don't come into it from what you have told me already. I've got that much.'

'No, always possible, but not what we are at present investigating.'

'Go over it again for me, please.'

Saxon nodded. 'Pharmaceuticals. Antibiotics, drugs that can cure, or not in some cases. Legitimate drugs, manufactured here or abroad...Hong Kong, Singapore, watered-down, weakened, adulterated one way and another, packed up with fake packing, to look genuine. Sold sometimes to honest outfits that don't realize what they've got but, no, it is cheaper than their usual supplier; more often to firms that know exactly what they want and want them cheap. Big profits all round and never mind the deaths. We have been monitoring them for some time, of course.'

Coffin nodded.

'Nothing new, been going on for decades, and various units have been investigating it. We are the latest, it was hoped we would be more effective, we are national, cover all areas.' He turned to look Coffin hard in the face. 'Don't tell me you don't know about this.'

'Not in the way you are telling it. Go on.'

'We are small in numbers, but regional: Mercia, Wessex, Deira, Anglia...all old-English groupings, and of course, the headquarters in London. In Mercia, my head man is Tim Kelso...you won't know him, he's young and new, but good. In Wessex, I have Peter Chard; in Deira—the ancient name, I chose it because I liked the sound but it is the Newcastle area, in fact—there is Joe Weir; in Anglia I chose Felicity Fox, who is very good. There is also Susy Miller, who shoots around as wanted. And I mustn't forget Leonie Thrupp, also in Coventry, that's Mercia territory.'

'And where was Harry Seton based?'

'London, with me. He was my back-up.'

There was a pause.

Coffin felt he had to prod, so he said: 'But that was only a cover from what you say. He was that and more. His real job was quite other.'

Another pause, then Saxon sighed. 'Yes, three or four months ago, March it was, we began to notice that investigations initiated in all good faith were failing as if the word had got round. False drugs were going round the country and into the shops, sometimes through genuine if gullible traders, sometimes through outlets that knew exactly what they were doing and knew it before we did. As a unit, we were not only failing to do our job but failing radically. We looked around for a reason, and found only one: corruption from within.'

'Was it a shock?'

Saxon said, honestly, 'Yes and no. It's always something to

look out for in this sort of operation. So I put Harry in to investigate… On the quiet, no one to know what he was doing.'

'Do secrets like that hold?' In Coffin's experience they did not, perhaps should not.

'No, probably not, or not for long. But I thought Harry would clear it up quickly.'

'Was there any reason why you should think that?'

'Money does show up as a rule, and I thought Harry would sniff out the man who was living above his income. I mean, if you are corruptible, you want to enjoy the fruits, it goes with the crime.'

Saxon started to fiddle with the papers in front of him, moving his hands quickly away as if they were hot. Perhaps to him, they were.

'So, he made progress?'

'He said he was "getting into things", whatever that meant.'

'How did he report?'

'Nothing in writing…we met in a pub for a drink. Not always the same one, but the sort of pub we might have gone to naturally in a friendly kind of way. He talked but never gave names. That was in character, partly why I gave him the job; I knew I could trust a discreet tongue.'

'And he didn't talk to you either?'

'No, I didn't want it particularly when it was still in the air. I had to meet these people, act normal, not show suspicion. I am not a good actor, I would have given signs, which could be dangerous.'

Not too bad an actor, Coffin thought. I remember you in the past, Ed Saxon, you could act a bit then. Remember the Billy Trout murder in the late seventies…1978, was it? You capered around then like magic. I used to think I would see you in panto, but I was never sure as what: Buttons, the Clown, the Wicked Stepmother, or even, Ed, one of the Ugly Sisters… I knew about that side of you, Ed. The one part I never gave you was the Good Fairy, and I am not giving it to you now.

Ed's eyes flicked away.

Whatever you really want from me is going to be good for

you and maybe not so good for me, thought Coffin, seeing the look.

'So you have no idea what he was working up to? There was something? He wasn't just null and void?'

Sunlight was pouring into the room. Saxon got up to pull down the blinds, cutting out the sun, but making the room even more closed and private than before. Wasn't there an animal that hid from the sun, Coffin asked himself, and was it a nice animal or a nasty one?

'The sun doesn't worry me,' he said politely.

Saxon said briefly: 'Don't like it on my face.'

But that's life, almost what life is: shining a light in your face that you don't want. Happens the minute you are born. Perhaps Saxon had preferred the womb. Not what you could say to him, though. 'So what had Seton got to say?'

'On our last meeting, in the Rose Revived in Harters Lane...do you know it?'

'Remember it.' A big pub with dark corners. Like my mind, Coffin passed judgement on himself. I am afraid that I have got one or two dark corners where you are concerned, Ed, my lad. As you will have for me.

'So what did he say then?'

'That he had found three people who seemed to have a higher standard of living than he had expected.'

Coffin considered this: 'He said people? Did you think that an odd word to use? Did he mean that a woman might be included in his list.'

'I do have some women officers in the unit, as I said before.'

'How many?'

'Several. And a few whom you might call helpers.'

'I'll bear them in mind, pay special attention just in case.'

'You shall have their names. I will take care you have all the records. Where they are based and all that.'

'And Harry kept to your quiet agreement not to name names to you?'

'He did.'

Coffin sat silent, then said, 'And you believe him? Believed he was making progress?'

'He could tell lies,' said Saxon, 'I knew that, but they were always what you might call political lies—they pushed a job forward. So, yes, I believed him: three people, sex ambiguous.'

'Did he seem nervous? As if he thought he might be attacked?'

'No, not Harry. He never showed nerves. I'm not saying he didn't know when to be cautious, of course he did, or he wouldn't have survived...' He stopped.

'As long as he did,' Coffin said for him. 'Because he didn't survive, did he? He is dead.' He stared again at the photograph. 'Terribly dead.'

'I didn't see him again. No one heard from him, not even his wife, but he was working underground in a way, so there was no worry.'

'Not even from his wife?'

'No, she said she was used to silence when he was on a case. He might make the odd phone call, this time he didn't.'

'Pity she didn't scream for action.'

'It wouldn't have made any difference, Harry was long dead. He could have been killed soon after we met at the Rose Revived. So the medics think.'

Coffin got out the photographs of Harry's dead body, all five of them, and shuffled them in order round the table. There were five photographs because Harry had been cut into five bits.

Coffin arranged them in the order he thought right: head first, the torso second, the arms next, and one leg...the other leg had disappeared. You had to remember that where this body was found in Deptford Park there were urban foxes.

'How was he killed?'

Painfully, Ed Saxon said: 'By degrees.'

'I don't think so, even if it looks like it, I don't think death gropes for you; one bite and you're gone, that's how I see it.'

Saxon shrugged, as if he did not care for this way of talking, it might even be meant to be a joke. 'If you say so.'

'Where was the body found?'

'In the bandstand in the park—it is partly boarded in. He may have been killed there, there was enough blood.' Saxon gave the files another push towards Coffin. 'It's all here, medical reports and the forensic stuff, you can read it all up.'

'I might want to ask the pathologist and the forensic chaps questions.'

'Sure. You will find names and places in the files, you may know some of the team from when you were in the Met.'

'Probably younger than I am.'

'Oh, they stay with us a long time in this business.'

Coffin considered: 'So you decided that he must have been getting close to the corrupt officer and therefore killed, in this particularly revolting way?'

Saxon stirred in his seat. 'I had one reason which I have not yet mentioned... We had established a hotline so that he could talk to me. He never did use it except to set up meets. I had hoped it would be more use to us, he wasn't much of a talker, Harry. It had its good and bad sides. But two days before he probably died he rang, asking me to turn up at the Fisher's Arms off the Strand. I did and he did not.'

'Did it worry you?'

'From then on, I worried.'

'You didn't do anything even then?'

'No. I sat and waited. About the worst thing I could have done. I just left it.' He added: 'I had a lot on my mind at the time; there's never just one worry, is there?'

'No.' Probably not, we both have a lot of experience on those lines.

Ed Saxon suddenly clenched his hands and banged on the table. 'Bloody, bloody business.'

Coffin studied Saxon's face, tight and drawn: you are full of anger.

Saxon pushed a small bunch of keys across the table. 'Harry had a room here, but he hired a special place, just off Fleet Street; three, Humper Place. Top floor. These are the keys.'

'Thanks. Right.'

'The forensic boys have been there, of course, couldn't keep them out, but they were required to leave everything as they found it... They got nothing out of it, by the way. You may do better.'

Coffin drew the files on the table towards him. 'What have I got here?'

'Apart from the forensic and medical stuff, which I mentioned, you have a complete list of all the people in the unit, whether based in the Wessex, Mercian, Newcastle and Anglian teams. With it comes the evidence of corruption and why I thought it came from the unit. Read it for yourself and make up your mind.'

'I will do, of course.'

'You may find Harry had left records in his office in Humper Place, nothing in his room here, and he did his own typing.'

Bet it was a word processor, thought Coffin, the days of penpushing and typing are gone. Harry might have been vulnerable if his machine could be read.

In Saxon's face, he read the same thought. 'I'll check the computer.'

'I miss the old days when I wrote a report, typed it out and then someone lost it in the files forever. Suited me. Now you know the words are there forever, even if you had deleted them.'

Ed Saxon was still uneasy. 'And what will you say you are doing here today? You will be noticed.'

Coffin smiled. 'Never apologize and never explain.'

'Good.' Saxon was still uneasy.

'Now, in my turn, a question: why did you pick on me for this job?' This tiresome, probably dangerous, bloody job?

'I knew you were safe, which is more than I can say for all my colleagues... We always did call you the pea-green incorruptible.'

'Sea-green, I think. And it was from Thomas Stearns Carlisle, and he was writing about Robespierre.'

'Oh.' Saxon nodded. He never had read much, Coffin remembered. But someone in his circle must have done... Jason

Hull, Coffin suddenly remembered the man, he'd been a reader. Where was he now? Retired, dead?

'How's Jason Hull?' he asked. 'Do you ever see him?'

'Dead. Lung cancer, he always did smoke too much. Good man, though.'

'So, what other reason did you have? There was one, wasn't there?'

'Sharp of you. Yes. In that file of papers, you will find a note in Harry's own writing. He wrote, capital letters: ASK COFFIN. So I have asked you.'

'And how long have I got?'

'I could say: As long as you need. In fact, hurry, please, we are under pressure.' He moved his hands together as if washing. 'Just get a whiff, we will do the rest…and don't forget you will have back-up from the Met. Well, in theory, anyway,' he ended doubtfully.

Coffin picked up the files on the table. 'Right. I'll take these, see what I make of it. Then I will come back to you.' He held out his hand. 'Goodbye, Ed.'

Ed Saxon watched him go, then sat down at his table, and stared at his hands.

COFFIN WALKED OUT into the sunlight. What do you make of all that, Coffin, my boy?

And how much of it did you believe?

Ed Saxon wants something from me, and somehow I don't think it is just who killed Harry Seton. A difficult character, old Ed, I was never quite sure when I was with him when we worked together, and I don't feel any more sure now. An ambitious and successful man. He had been successful himself, head now of the police in the Second City of London. Married to a well-known actress and as happy as it was in his nature to be.

What Stella would say when she heard was: Why was he doing it?

Why had he accepted the investigation into corruption, which might involve old colleagues? He had already recognized a few names in a first quick run-through of the list before he left.

Just curiosity, he told himself. Not a complete answer, but it would do for now. He had also, although he was not sure if Ed Saxon knew this, received a request, order really, from on high to undertake what he was asked to do. This he had queried.

'Why, sir, why me?'

'It does seem a relatively unimportant job...I say relatively, as it has its own importance,' the voice had said smoothly. They were talking on Coffin's private line. Untapped as far as he knew. 'But we want you to do it.'

'Don't think about that now,' he told himself. 'Enjoy the walk.'

He was walking, just walking, enjoying the air and the sun. He was on Waterloo Bridge, walking south before he realized it. He loved the view down the river and up the river, he even enjoyed the massive block of the National Theatre. His own Second City had some good views of old docklands but nothing to compare with this.

Coffin stood for a moment looking at the water running fast beneath him. The Thames was supposed to be a clean river now, but it seemed pretty murky to him. It must be several millennia since it had been a clear, leaping stream. Perhaps the Romans had seen it that way, but it must have been changing even then. The same river ran through his Second City of London, but his London, once bombed and battered, was now full of old warehouses containing new businesses of the sort that was not dreamt of when St Paul's was built: computers, mobile phones and video recorders for midget television sets. There were health farms, slimming clinics and teachers of Chinese medicine, as well as small factories which were busy one day and gone the next. Life moved on in the Second City.

He had cut short his visit to Stella, and the reason for this was that he had his own problems back home in the Second City. In particular, a number of missing children. Four now. There was no rest for anyone in the Second City till the children were found. Dead or alive.

And what about the children who aren't missing but who must be sheltered from the knowledge of this?

He had pointed out this investigation in the Second City to the man from the Home Office when he was requested to agree to what Ed Saxon would be asking of him, and had been told to get on with it. Deal with both investigations, he could have what help he needed.

Coffin got an ironic pleasure in discovering he was *persona grata* in the highest circles, when in the past he had been such an unorthodox, troublesome, unloved policeman. Time and its whirligigs bringing in its revenges, as Shakespeare had remarked.

He put his hand in his pocket, where he felt the bunch of keys that Ed Saxon had passed over to him. On impulse, he put his hand up for a passing taxi.

'Three, Humper Place, off Fleet Street,' he said.

'I know, gov,' said the driver, slight reproof from one who knew his Knowledge.

He could have walked from where he was, but he wanted a space to think while the taxi crawled through the London traffic.

A right into Fleet Street, another right and there was Humper Place.

'Doesn't look good, gov,' said the cabby, breaking into his thoughts.

Two red fire engines and a police car blocked the way.

Coffin paid the cab off and walked forward.

Number three, Humper Place was smouldering.

The fire seemed to light up something in his mind: Wait a minute, he told himself, supposing I am being asked to investigate this corruption business because the Second City is involved?

TWO

A SMALL CROWD of people stood at the kerb, with the air of having fled from the building in a hurry, but even as he looked they were disappearing into a small bar at the end of the cul-de-sac. The Queen's Arms, it proclaimed itself, with a large portrait of a crowned lady who might have been Queen Victoria or Mary, Queen of Scots, since she was long since faded into a gentle blur. You could see the crown, however.

Coffin walked towards the police constable stationed at the door of the building. He did not identify himself.

'Can I get in there?'

'No, sir, sorry, no chance.' The constable was young, blue-eyed and with red hair.

Coffin stared up at the building. It looked to him as though the fire was out, the flames had died down.

'I need to get in urgently.'

Coffin was still assessing the scene. It might have had the making of a nasty fire, but it had been controlled and the building looked solid still. There was an outer fire staircase which could be used. He nodded towards it. 'I could go up there. It's mostly smoke now, isn't it?'

'You can have a word with the Chief Fire Officer, that's him over there.' The constable nodded to a large, uniformed man standing by a car. 'I can't give permission, out of my power.'

'Yes, I understand that. Where did it start?'

'Top floor. Or so I've been told.' The fire was certainly damped down, but there was still smoke and heat. Coffin was both curious and anxious. Had the flat to which he had the keys been damaged?

If so, was it by a genuine accident or by deliberate attempt?

If it was arson he was very interested indeed.

He strolled towards the Chief Fire Officer. The man glanced towards him without interest, then turned away to speak to one of the firemen. It was then that Coffin realized the disadvantage of being anonymous. For years now, he had had quick attention to his questions, he was not used to being ignored. In short, he had grown into being the Chief Commissioner of his force and was now going to have to shrink back in size.

He stood there thinking the problem out: a certain duplicitous honesty was his best line. If the fire had not happened, then he would have slipped in and out with no one noticing. If anyone had asked, just one of the forensic team. But no one would have asked.

Slowly he advanced to the Chief Fire Officer, who went on talking, then finally addressed him over his shoulder.

'That your car there?'

Coffin looked towards a car parked at the kerb. Before he could speak, the Chief Fire Officer said: 'Move it. Shouldn't be there.'

Coffin bit back the comment that the car appeared to be perfectly parked and in no one's way, but contented himself with saying politely that it was not his car. He could, however, see someone sitting in it, but decided not to mention this.

'Is it safe to get into the building yet?'

'No.' A blunt refusal.

Coffin nodded. 'Right,' he said peaceably. 'So when?' Tomorrow, next week, he would have to accept it, and hope that the firemen had not destroyed too much.

'Can't say.'

'I need to get into flat twelve.' He held up the keys, swinging them a little.

'You the tenant? You rent the place?'

Smooth, taking manners, thought Coffin, charming fellow. 'I am part of a police forensic team that has been examining the place.' It seemed safe enough to say this much. It might easily be common knowledge, passed around the other tenants.

He needn't have worried. It cut no ice.

'You can get in with the others when it is safe. Can't say when yet.'

Reluctantly, Coffin faced the fact that he had got used to being speeded through any obstacles back home in the Second City and that life was tougher outside.

He walked down the road to the pub into which he had seen the rest of the tenants disappear. He noticed that the car was now empty and a figure was walking into the pub. To his surprise, it was a woman.

The Queen's Arms was old and small and dark, it could have been there since the Great Fire of London in 1666, or even have survived it. Certainly it had survived the Blitz and all the rest of the bombs that particular war had thrown at it. Now it had a large notice advising customers to watch untended bags because of IRA bombs.

Inside it was crowded. Coffin stood at the door, wondering if he could work out who were the tenants who had fled from their offices.

He ordered a drink, which he stood by the bar drinking while he let his eyes study the crowd.

Well, he knew the woman: the back disappearing down the road had been wearing a black coat. So there she was with a drink in her hand at a table in the window.

And oddly enough, she was looking at him. Looking at him looking at her.

He stared down at his drink to break the link, but he could still see her in his mind's eye: she looked lean, intellectual and sophisticated. She was dressed in black, but not dead black, there was a gleam of leather and the hint of silk at the throat. In other words, she looked expensive. Life with Stella had at least taught Coffin what good clothes cost.

Around him, the crowd of the dispossessed were drinking and shouting at each other.

'I blame the chap on the top floor.' This was a stout man in a check suit. 'We never had anything till he moved in, and then we had the police, and now the fire brigade. And where is he now? It's him.'

'It did start there, damn it. I ought to know as I was near it. But I don't think he's there any more. I never see him now.' A pretty, slight girl in the shortest skirt and with the longest hair that Coffin had lately seen walking around London. ('On the way out, that Loopy Lu look,' Stella had told him. 'And it's time the wearers knew it, but it's got to be a uniform for them and they really don't see themselves. They will be dinosaurs before they notice it.') 'I think he's gone. They weren't police you saw, they were debt collectors.'

'Didn't look like debt collectors to me,' said Check Suit, 'more official. And they locked the door.'

'Trust you to notice that.'

'They didn't set fire to anything, though.'

'Wonder who did? I hope my notes on the report I am writing for Lord Herrington on fiscal controls and the EU aren't too kippered. I couldn't bear to do it again, he's so stupid you have to make it easy.'

This was Miss Miniskirt, so she was the intellectual heavyweight of the two? She was a lawyer, he guessed, so what was Check Suit? Another lawyer? No, a businessman of some sort. Probably he imported or exported something, handbags or lacy knickers.

'Lord H. is always kippered himself, isn't he, the way he drinks and smokes? I will say this for the fire people, they got there fast and put the fire out damn quickly. I don't think I will have lost anything.'

'The smell of smoke on everything is bad enough,' grumbled the young woman. 'And that foam stuff they use as well as water...' But she didn't sound too worried. Lord Herrington would have to put up with his smoked report.

The two of them turned away to talk to the rest of the homeless.

While listening to all this, and trying to assess what it told him about Harry Seton's activities, Coffin had been watching the woman in the window.

The second sense that all long-time coppers develop told him that she was watching him while listening to the man and woman, just as he was.

That told him something.

He met her eyes and this time, she smiled and nodded at him. The moment was flooded over by a burst of laughter from the dispossessed to his right.

Coffin got up, walked across and stood looking at her; he said nothing.

She held out her hand. 'I know who you are: John Coffin. My husband had a photograph of you. He was in it too.' Still she kept her hand extended. 'Mary Seton.'

Coffin took her hand, noting the softness and the shining tinted nails, not what you expected somehow from a copper's wife, although heaven knew, his own wife Stella was typical of nothing, not even the stage.

'Mary Beaton, Mary Seton, Mary Carmichael and I...'

The line from the old Scots ballad ran through his mind; he could not remember who 'I' was, but he did know that she came to a bad end. On the scaffold, having killed...whom? Her lover or her bastard child?

'I think we are expected to meet to talk about my husband. Ed Saxon told me you would be around.'

'I was going to call. But today I wanted to have a look round his office.'

'The one that someone tried to burn? Yes, I wanted to see it too. We picked the wrong day, didn't we? Sit down, do. You make me nervous standing there.'

Coffin put his glass on the table, then sat down opposite her. He doubted if he could make Mary Seton nervous.

'You know, I had no idea the office existed until Harry died... I only learnt then by accident. Wives are supposed to be kept from too much knowledge, painful knowledge, that is. Or that's Ed Saxon's philosophy.'

Are you sure, thought Coffin cynically, wondering if he could believe her ignorant. I think he doles out the painful bits as it suits him, and if he let you know about this office then it suited him.

He was, he feared, a natural cynic where Ed Saxon was concerned.

He nodded his head. 'I know Ed has his ways.'

'I came today to look round. I didn't have a key but I thought I could get in. I would have done too.'

Coffin believed her.

She made a gesture with her hands. 'Well, you saw...when I got here there was the fire brigade and the police.' She nodded towards the talkers and drinkers near the bar. 'So I followed this lot in here.'

She had sat in the car watching, Coffin commented to himself, a careful, cautious woman. He liked the way she used her hands. Stella would have approved of that: what you do with your hands on the stage is so important, they give you character or take it away. Never walk on the stage without knowing what to do with your hands and never let them droop.

He could see that Mary Seton would never walk on to her stage with drooping hands.

She must have picked up his thoughts. 'I know you are married, I have seen your wife act. I admired her.'

'Stella's in Los Angeles at the moment.'

'You must miss her.'

'I do, of course, but we agreed when we married that she must be free to follow'——he paused——'well, whatever the theatre demands. I wouldn't want her to lose by being married.'

'It applies to you too.' She sipped her sherry. 'But men don't expect to lose by getting married, it's just an extra, nothing to get in their way.'

Coffin gave her a cautious look.

'I don't think most policemen's wives have happy marriages,' she went on. 'Stella is lucky.'

Coffin thought that Stella was not so much lucky as good at fighting her battles, probably he would have been as selfish and demanding as any, but Stella had not allowed it.

'She deserves it,' went on Mary Seton. 'She is so talented.'

'I think so,' said Coffin, glad to be on solid ground at last.

'I made my own career—I own a small chain of fashion

shops, I don't think Harry minded, or if he did it didn't show. It meant he didn't see so much of me as he might have done...I have to travel a bit.'

The noise from the group at the bar interrupted them; loud laughter and a small bit of horseplay with Miss Miniskirt doing most of the pushing; she was not one to overlook, Coffin decided.

'Jolly, aren't they? They aren't worried about the fire, or why it was started. Harry was destroyed and now someone has had a go at destroying what he was working on.' She turned her head towards the window; Coffin saw the glint of tears on her lashes.

'We don't know that it was arson.'

'Oh, we do...it started on the top floor, Harry's floor.'

Coffin had been looking out of the window, from where he could see that the fire engines were drawing away. He would probably be able to get into the building quite soon, if the top floor was not too hot. Or wet.

'I want to have a look round myself, so I am hoping that it may not have been destroyed.'

She looked at him and shook her head.

'They didn't let me see Harry's body. Just his face, so I could identify him, the rest was wrapped in sheets.' There was no mistaking the tears on her cheeks now. 'So I suppose they had a reason.'

You insensitive ox, Coffin told himself, all this bitter talk she's been throwing at you is because she is bloody unhappy. She loved the man.

There was another burst of laughter, and Miss Miniskirt swept past. 'Going to inspect the ruins,' she called out.

Mary watched her go; through her tears, she said: 'She spent a lot on that suit but she wasted her money: it doesn't fit her. Didn't you notice the sleeves?'

Coffin shook his head, he had not noticed the sleeves. All right, he had thought the black suit expensive, so he got that right.

'You think I'm a bad-tempered cow, all right?'

'No, I think you are a very unhappy woman.'

There was a pause. 'I loved him. I didn't always like him, but I loved him.'

There was silence.

She stood up. 'I'm going to follow that woman. See if I can get into the building? Are you coming too?'

'Yes, but I don't know what our chances are.'

'I am going to get in, I saw a fire escape. I shall go up that.'

'I saw it too.'

'I was working it all out as I sat in the car.'

'Why are you so anxious to see Harry's office here?'

Mary slowed her pace, they could both see the woman in the miniskirt arguing with the police constable now on solitary duty.

'Because Ed Saxon didn't want me to. I only got the address because I read it upside down on his desk. What about you?'

'Work,' said Coffin evasively. 'An investigation.'

'Are you working on Harry's death?'

'No, the Met are handling that, of course...' This was true, although he would be privy to what they turned up and in return they would want to look at anything he got. A strange position to be in, he thought, never happened before. It made him feel two-headed.

Mary looked at him sceptically, but she said nothing, moving ahead of him towards the office block. The woman in the mini-skirt was still talking to the police constable. She seemed to be arguing fiercely.

Both of them had their backs to Coffin and Mary Seton. Without a word, Mary put her foot on the bottom rung of the fire escape, gave Coffin a meaning look, and ran up, leaping from step to step.

Coffin followed her. He was agile himself but she was nimbler. Good mind too, Harry Seton had been a lucky man. Only his luck had ended. Older than Mary. Hadn't there been a first wife? He had memories of hearing of one called Elsa. Elsa he had never met, but he was willing to admit that she had been pretty and lively and clever, as with Mary. Did one always marry the same woman? What had happened to Elsa? Had she dropped Harry or the other way round?

These questions flashed through his mind with speed as he went up the staircase. He was at the top before he remembered the answer: Elsa was dead.

Curious thing, the mind, why had he just remembered Elsa and her death?

Mary was looking through the glass door, it was darkened, stained by smoke. 'A bit kippered, but you can see through.'

Coffin was feeling in his pocket. 'Got a key?'

'No. I haven't a key. Harry never gave me one, I wasn't told about this place, remember? I only found out when he was dead, and Ed Saxon certainly wasn't about to give me a key. Keep wives out is embroidered on his chest, that one. I was going to break in if I could. So I was always coming up this way.' She looked down at her feet, 'I was going to knock my way through the glass with a heel.'

Coffin was sorting through the bunch of keys. 'You'd have a job breaking this glass without a wound or two. Good thing you met me.' He wasn't sure how much he believed her, but she had a beguiling way with words. 'Are you sure you weren't going to bribe your way in?'

She grinned. 'Somehow, somehow. Maybe, maybe. But I found you. Come on, let's get in.'

The lock turned easily enough but the door was stiff; it gave way, though, before his shoulder.

'Here we are. In.'

Harry's office had not been burnt to bits, or flooded with water. It smelt of smoke and was untidy, but that might have been Harry, not the firemen.

His files had been in metal cabinets, but some drawers had been opened and the papers were on the floor. They were scorched but not destroyed.

'If they were after Harry's work, it was a shitty job,' said Mary.

'Maybe not, maybe just a warning…to you or to me. How do you know about where the fire started?'

'I was listening to that workshy crowd who had evacuated the building. All full of joy and even accusing each other of doing the job.' She had advanced into the middle of the room, and was looking around her. 'No, you are right...it's a warning only.'

'You ought to work for the CID,' said Coffin, who had also heard the conversation, with admiration. 'Are you sure you didn't start it yourself?'

'I didn't hate Harry and his work that much...' She was still looking round the room. 'But you are quite right: there were times when he was alive... All wives hate their husbands in patches.'

'Thanks for that,' said Coffin, wondering if he had better watch Stella for one of those patches.

'I might well have burnt his office down, but not now he is dead.' Then she said: 'He had a period in a clinic when he had a kind of breakdown...did you know that?'

'No.'

'Drink, mostly. Usually is with coppers, isn't it?'

'I can see you admire us.' But he couldn't say no, because he had been down that road himself. It was likely that Mary Seton knew it, too.

Coffin looked round the room. It was dampened down by a spray of water from a fireman's hose, but was not damaged. He was pulling open the drawers of the desk...still warm, but there was stuff inside. Not much but something. He thought that Harry probably hadn't kept much stuff there anyway. Wise fellow. Not that it had availed him much in the long run.

There was also the computer on a table against the wall, perhaps he was more of a computer man.

It was not a comfortable room, probably the smallest and cheapest (no lift to it) in the building, but Harry had tried for a personal touch: there was a pot plant, now dead, on the desk.

'Wonder who gave Harry that plant?' said Mary. 'Not me. Some fool thought it would cheer the room up.' She touched the soil. 'I see he never watered it.'

He may not have had much chance, thought Coffin. Mary read his face.

'Yes, all right, he died.'

Coffin began to gather up the files from the desk, then those on the floor. He could see traces of the forensic efforts, with pale powder marks distributed freely over almost every surface, desk top, drawers, and the files inside.

Not as many files as he had expected, he would have to ask a few searching questions about what, if anything, had been carried away. No doubt every document had been photocopied. He scooped them up, wishing he had a bag to put them in. Then he saw a carrier bag in the wastebasket. It was from a shop in Birmingham: FOOD GALORE, Reform Street. So someone had been in Birmingham.

Then he turned to the word processor.

Mary, who had stopped prowling round the room, watched him. 'Harry wasn't much good at that. I ought to know as I had to teach him what he had to know—the basics, anyhow.'

'I'm not much good myself,' said Coffin, 'but I know how to switch it on.'

The screen glowed blue.

'The fire doesn't seem to have hurt it, you can never tell with these things.'

'It's on battery,' Mary pointed out. 'He travelled around with it. It wouldn't be touched by any power loss.'

He pressed a key and a list of files came up. They were numbered, not names, so Harry must have kept a key or relied on memory.

He pressed the key for Number One. The first page came up. In big capital letters, he read:

WE'VE HAD A LOOK AT THESE.
WE KNOW YOU WILL BE LOOKING TOO.
HA HA.

'Ha ha to you,' said Coffin, pressing on to page two of File Number One.

It was blank. Someone, possibly Harry, had wiped it clean. A quick glance through the next three files showed these to be blank also.

Frowning, Coffin turned off the machine. Mary, who had been watching over his shoulder, said nothing. 'I'll just pack this up and take it with me.' He looked around for the carrying satchel which was on the floor. 'Right, that's it.' For the moment; he would be back and without Mary Seton. 'Seen all you want?'

'Yes, nothing to see really. Hasn't given me much idea about Harry's last days. If you learn anything you can tell me, will you?'

Coffin nodded. 'I will.'

She smiled at him. 'Of course, I know what that means, you being a policeman. Can I give you a lift?'

'To the Tower terminus of the Docklands Railway? That'll see me into my territory. Thank you.'

They were both silent on the short drive; Mary Seton drove efficiently through the traffic, delivering him near the entrance to the Docklands Light Railway, already known by regular users as the Dockers' Delight.

'How long does the battery last at full strength on this machine?' He tapped the computer.

Mary shrugged. 'About two and a half to three hours when used.'

'And unused?'

'I don't know. Just guessing, I should say about a week or a little more.'

Coffin considered this; the machine he had on his lap registered two hours' working time left. So it had been plugged into a socket and the power stepped up.

By whom? Also why?

He occupied his mind with this question as Mary drove.

'Thanks for the lift.' Coffin opened the car door.

Mary leaned forward then kissed him lightly on the cheek. 'Thank you. You helped me through a bad patch.'

COFFIN WAS THOUGHTFUL as he let the train swing its way through old Docklands. It was a journey he usually enjoyed because it provided a perfect example of the whirligig of time bringing in its revenges: the former run-down, working-class area was now full of smart and expensive flats powered by the new businesses which had moved in. He was satisfied to see history being made. His own Second City partook of both elements, a good deal of it still solid working class with a new dash of upmarket chic in converted factories and warehouses. Crime was about equal in both communities.

But he wondered about Mary Seton. A kiss is just a kiss. Of course, but why me, he asked himself.

The train stopped at the Spinnergate station which was where he had parked his car on the journey in. His car was still there; he checked to see if all the wheels plus wheel hubs were in place, as you were well advised to do in Spinnergate if you left your car alone for any length of time. All present and correct. His force's pressure on the petty criminal must be paying off.

At last, he thought, as he got in the car to drive home. No joy there without Stella, though, without her it didn't seem like a home. Even the dog, Augustus, seemed low spirited, but that was probably due to overeating because Coffin just fed when he asked, which in Gus's case was often.

Gus appeared to greet him with a wagging tail and a small bark of complaint.

'No, I couldn't take you with me today. Not today, Gus. Grow up, you are a big dog now and must learn to live alone.'

Gus barked again. He had no intention of learning anything which did not suit him. But he meant to be guileful, since if he was too difficult he remembered that Coffin would get Phoebe Astley to look after him. The chief inspector was not gentle and persuasive like Stella Pinero, nor absent-minded and kind like his master, Coffin. No, Phoebe was firm, and strict, leaving a dog with not much freedom.

Coffin fed the dog from a tin of his chosen meat, then he went to see if he had any message from Stella, either faxed or on the answerphone.

The big sitting room was cold and dark. He turned on a light before drawing the curtains at the large window. If he looked out of this window, he could just see the roofs of the University Hospital, where a talk with the head of the pharmaceutical department was something he meant to take. He knew Perry Curtis slightly, but well enough to value his insight and judgement.

Nothing from Stella, but a message from his own office.

'Paul Masters, here, sir. Could you ring back as soon as possible, please?'

The inspector's voice sounded tense. Paul Masters administered the Chief Commander's office with calm skill. He did not readily show strain.

Coffin picked up the telephone and dialled the number that rang straight through to the phone on Paul Masters's desk.

'Coffin here. You wanted me?'

'Ah, yes indeed. Chief Superintendent Young wanted to talk to you… As it happens, he is here now.'

Archie Young spoke quickly. 'We have the body of one of the missing boys.'

'Which one?'

'The last to go missing, the ten-year-old from Percy Street.'

'He has been identified?'

'Yes, by his father. We have his body.' Archie Young hesitated. 'And parts of another.'

'How was he found?'

'In a wooded area by a young couple…looking for somewhere quiet and dark.'

'How did they come to find the body…was it buried?'

'Yes, but working free from the soil and leaves…they didn't see it themselves at first, but they saw a man with his dog staring at something among the trees. He was holding back the dog. Or seemed to be, the dog was in the bushes. He said to them that there was something funny that they ought to look at. The young man did so while the man stood back. He soon saw it was a body, saw the feet, he says…he had his mobile with him and telephoned the police.'

'And the man?'

'He disappeared into the dark.'

Coffin put the telephone down slowly. 'I'll be in,' he muttered. 'We will talk it over then.'

WHEN ONE QUESTION bothers you, there is always another one weighing on your mind.

There was one way of getting an answer to one problem.

He rang the Home Office man who had urged him so persuasively to investigate the pharmaceutical problem for Ed Saxon.

'Tell me straight: why was I picked for the job?'

There was some silence. 'You stand high, Chief Commander, you have a great reputation.' Then he added carefully: 'And of course, we both know Humphrey Gillow.'

'Did Ed Saxon want me?'

'He was very glad to get you.' That came quickly. 'You'd worked together before. In fact, he said that Harry Seton had named you as a good person in trouble.'

Oh yes, old friends. 'Had he got a choice? I mean, did you have a list of suitable names?'

Silence again. An answer probably brewing up there, but taking its time.

'So it was just me?' And wasn't I lucky with Harry naming me and everything. 'But there was a special reason. So let me guess: something to do with the Second City.'

'Yes, there is reason to believe that an important connection of this outfit is in the Second City.'

One question answered brings another right out. 'So why did you not tell me straightaway.'

'We wanted you to approach it unbiased, with an open mind.'

So it wasn't me that was so wanted, it was the place I came from. I knew Ed Saxon wasn't being straight with me. I could tell it in his eyes.

There was something else too; I shall find out.

He put Augustus on his leash, and set out to walk with him through to his own office in the police headquarters not far from Spinnergate tube station.

THE SECOND CITY, created out of old dockland London, with a long history behind it, a town before the Romans came, a city to greet the Normans, so large and rich by the time Napoleon was defeated that the Prussian General Blucher cried out in envy: 'What a city to sack.' Hitler thought it might fall to him too, but was disappointed in his turn.

Now the Second City, its four districts of Spinnergate, Swinehouse, Leathergate and East Hythe had clung on to its character while absorbing banks and newspapers, watching old warehouses converted into expensive flats and eighteenth-century dock houses become cherished dwelling places again. Meanwhile, the indigenous population resisted rehousing in tower blocks as far as it could, preferring, with an obstinacy that had served them well in the past, to live in the old terraces of houses that had survived the bombs.

There were bombs sometimes now, although planted overnight or delivered in person by hand or mortar and not dropped from the air, but these bombs too the Second City could cope with and survive.

Coffin was most familiar with Spinnergate because this was where he lived in the tower of the old St Luke's Church, now secularized to provide him a home, as well as being the site of St Luke's Theatre complex. His wife, Stella Pinero, was the theatrical brain behind the theatre, while his half-sister, Letty Bingham, a much-married wealthy banker and lawyer, helped on the money side.

Dog and man strode through Spinnergate, companionable and silent. Augustus encouraged his master to walk as much as possible on the grounds of health and pleasure: he was thinking of himself, but he had noticed that master (not a word Augustus accepted, food giver, walker, protector, these were how he thought of Coffin in a wordless way) needed little persuasion.

Augustus had a few words: his own name, walks, dinner, these sounds he recognized, more complex emotions were known but not given labels.

But Augustus recognized the route they were taking and felt a tinge of depression, he was going to the 'other place', this being how he sensed Coffin's office. It was a kind of home to him, he was welcomed, he had a warm corner, there was a bowl of water, even food on occasion, but that said, he was ignored. This obliged him to plant himself across Coffin's feet to remind the man of his existence.

Coffin strode in, was greeted politely at the door, and took the lift to his offices. In the outer office, were two secretaries who changed constantly, usually through a career move or a baby. One woman, the tall, well-dressed Sheila, had been with him for some time now and he had hopes she would stay. Coffin valued constancy in his relationships.

He nodded and spoke to Sheila, then looked across to the corner of the room where his valued assistant, Inspector Paul Masters, had created a kind of personal territory.

Paul got up and came across. 'Good afternoon, sir. Letters and messages as usual on your desk.'

'Right.' Coffin was already walking towards his own quarters while Augustus was sidling across to Sheila, a known and secret source of chocolate. 'Anything special?'

Paul Masters hesitated. 'You've spoken to the chief superintendent…I don't know more than he will have told you then.'

'He told me a boy had been found, dead, and identified by his father. One of the missing boys. And parts from another.'

'That's right, sir. It's all that's known at the moment. The chief superintendent was off to see the father, but he wanted to get in touch with you first.'

Coffin advanced to look at his desk where Paul Masters had arranged a display of files and papers. He had an aesthetic sense, Coffin always felt, so that papers, although grouped logically, were fanned out in a neat presentation. He even managed to control the faxes, while keeping them in a separate group.

All the same, they represented work, work and work, and there was always a special collection marked URGENT.

'He will be in to see you, sir, after he has seen the father.'

'Who is running the investigation?'

'The chief superintendent is in overall charge, of course—he's keeping a watching eye on things.'

'And who's running the investigation?' he asked again. He was shuffling the papers on his desk as he spoke. All the information he was asking for would be there, but it was quicker to get it out of Paul Masters, who might also oblige with a few case histories of the officers concerned, and how well they were doing the job. This was done tactfully, but Coffin knew how to read between the lines.

'Inspector Paddy Devlin is the senior officer in charge, with Sergeant Tony Tittleton...they are both very experienced in dealing with children.'

'Experienced children-watchers?'

'That's it, sir. Paddy Devlin, whom I know quite well, sir, I trained with her, handled the paedophile case in East Hythe last year. She is very, very competent.' Due for promotion too, and hopeful of getting it.

Red-haired and handsome too, but he did not mention this fact.

'Yes, I remember now. Nasty case. Is there reckoned to be any connection with this lot?'

'Could be, but I haven't heard it said.' One of Paul Masters's assets to Coffin was that he heard all the gossip that got held back from Coffin. It worked both ways, because if there was anything an officer wanted Coffin to know then he would take care to let Paul Masters know. 'But it is one of the things they will be looking out for, of course.'

Coffin handed over to him the computer in its case, and the bag of documents.

'Get this computer to John Armstrong and ask him to get back, if he can, all wiped documents. It's urgent.'

'Yes, sir.'

'And the documents in the bag: I want them photocopied. I

will think about the next step when that is done. They are confidential.'

'I'll do them myself.'

'Good.'

Paul Masters disappeared tactfully while Coffin turned to the papers on his desk. He did not dislike the task as much as he sometimes let people think; there was satisfaction in running a tidy, tight ship.

He read and signed letters, initialled reports, reflecting as he did so that the end product of a career as an ambitious and successful detective was to be an administrator.

However, with some skill and some luck, he had kept his hand in as a detective. Just as well, he considered, in view of the job now handed to him by Ed Saxon.

As to that matter, he had no idea where to start, and the very clear idea that it seemed stupid to separate what he was asked to do from the investigation into the death of Harry Seton.

Not that he intended to do that himself; he would be thinking about Harry's death with every move he made. And the note found on Harry's PC suggested that the Met team would be thinking about him.

Maybe they should meet.

The sound of voices in the outer office disturbed him; Paul Masters knocked and put his head round the door.

'Chief Superintendent Young is here, sir.'

It gave Coffin pleasure that it had been he who had promoted his old friend and fellow worker to this rank, but Archie deserved it. A tall, still thin man (his wife kept an eye on his diet) with a kind heart and a shrewd brain. An invaluable comrade and friend.

Now the man looked sober. 'Not good news, I'm afraid. You know the outline of the case: over a period of two months, four boys have gone missing.'

Coffin nodded.

'Three still missing and one found,' said Archie Young heavily. 'And the leg of another child, possibly one of those missing.'

Coffin had a list:

Matthew Baker, aged eight years and three months.
Archie Chinner, ten years old and one month.
Dick Neville, eleven years old and a week.
Charles Rick, ten years old and four months.

'And which one has been found?'

Archie Young's voice was still quiet and sombre. 'Archie Chinner was the boy whose body was found. He was hidden in the bushes on that bit of scrubland where the Delaware Factory once was. It's due for redevelopment but nothing much has happened yet. As I told you, a courting couple found him last night.'

'Who interviewed the couple?'

'Devlin. And I spoke to them as well. It's all on tape, but I have given you the gist.'

'Have to try and get hold of the man who pointed out the body.'

'Devlin is organizing it, using the local media to ask him to come forward, but she's not hopeful, he would have stayed around if he had meant to be helpful.'

'What was he like?'

'Just a man with a dog to the couple. They were surprised to see him, not usually anyone around up there. He left the dirty work to them, they found the body and it shook them up. I have looked into them, just what they seem to be.' His voice was heavy.

'And his father identified the boy?'

'Yes, he had been dead a few days but he was recognizable. Easily.'

'How did you know which father to call in?'

'We had photographs of all the boys. All four of them went to the same school, the Junior School of the Royal Road Comprehensive—the Clement Attlee School is the full name, and the parents supplied photographs.'

Coffin waited, he could tell that Archie was quietly making his way up to what he wanted to say.

'So he was identified easily enough,' Archie went on. 'No trouble there…the only thing is…' And here he paused.

Coffin waited. You didn't hurry Archie when he was taking his time.

'His father said that the clothes he was wearing were not his own… Not a stitch he had on was his.'

'Any idea where the clothes came from?'

Archie shook his head. 'They look newish, may not have been worn much but not shop-fresh. Some boy has worn them.'

'That may help.'

'May do… But there was blood on them.'

'Much blood?'

'Quite a bit…but the interesting thing is that preliminary tests on the blood groups suggest blood from two people: one the boy's and the other from an unknown person.'

'From one of the other boys?'

'Could be… Or from the murderer.'

'How was the boy killed?'

'Can't be sure until the PM. Smothered, possibly.'

'So where did his blood come from?'

'Probably from the anus…he had been sexually assaulted. Pretty badly, too.'

Coffin tightened his lips. This was a horrible business. 'That may be why he was smothered: he was too badly hurt to send him back into the world.'

'And he may have known his abuser.'

Coffin was starting at the list of names. 'Wait a minute, Chinner…not a usual name. Is the father…?' He stopped, letting the query rest on the air.

'Yes, he's one of ours. A police surgeon, Dr Geoffrey Chinner, a local GP as well.'

'I know him, he worked on a case that interested me.'

One of the many, thought Archie Young.

'We kept that information quiet when the boy went missing

because we weren't sure how it would touch his chances of survival. The media found out but went along with us.

'That is not all: every one of the missing boys had a parent who was one of ours.'

'Why didn't you tell me?'

'I was coming to you with it.'

Coffin was silent. Ed Saxon's call had come in yesterday, he had been preoccupied with other problems, there was always something urgent.

'I am supposed to know that sort of thing.'

'I am sorry, sir.'

'Before anyone else.'

Archie Young was silent.

'All right,' said Coffin grouchily. 'I was in Los Angeles.'

Coffin got up. 'I want to see where the boy was found. Then I want to see his body.'

'I'll drive you.' Archie Young was still prickly with apology, while feeling that he had been unfairly treated: the Chief Commander had been in Los Angeles, a holiday, God knows he rarely took one, and there had been a silent feeling that this break should be respected.

In the car for the drive across Spinnergate to East Hythe, they talked.

Coffin stared about him at the streets as they drove. There was a good deal of traffic, buses and many private cars. His eye was caught by a flash of yellow, red and green in a shop window. Great glass bottles full of colour and underneath a more sober display of packets. 'What shop's that?' They were going down what had once been the main shopping street of old East Hythe and was still the High Street. A memory of the shop stirred inside Coffin. He ought to remember more.

Archie Young took a quick look. 'Oh, that's old Mr Barley's chemist's shop, he keeps it old-fashioned like that. You should see inside. Doubt if he does much trade, but tourists love it.'

He gave a nod to the west: 'And you can just see the roof of the school the boys went to. We are trying to keep it from the children—it's mixed, of course—as much as possible.

There's the Junior School attached.' The lost boys had gone there, sent by hopeful parents because it had a good reputation.

He drove on quietly, the traffic was heavy here.

'Miss the old trams,' Archie Young was concentrating on weaving his way through the traffic.

'No, you're too young. Tell me about the parents of the boys.'

He sounds a bit better, thought Archie with relief, he's loosening up

'Not all the parents are officers: the Neville lad's mother works in the canteen at the Leathergate substation, the Rick lad's father is a DC in Spinnergate, and Matthew Baker's dad is a CID sergeant in Spinnergate.'

Coffin looked at him. 'Archie Chinner?'

The chief superintendent looked away, out of the window. 'Yes, the boy's my godson. His father is a police surgeon as I said.'

'Sorry.' There was a pause. 'Would you like to withdraw from any interest in the case?'

Young shook his head. 'No, I couldn't. In any case, Paddy Devlin is really handling it for all practical purposes, and she's good.'

'So I have heard.' They were passing through a large council estate, the Attlee Estate, which provided plenty of work for the Second City force. The press blamed youth unemployment, but Coffin wondered.

'From different districts but, you say, all four boys went to the same school?'

'It's a very big comprehensive, good academically so parents are pleased if their kid goes there, got an Oxford scholarship last year. A bus goes round picking up the pupils to ferry them there.'

'It's worth thinking about the school,' said Coffin thoughtfully.

'You can bet we are. Going over the place with a fine comb, nobody missed out.'

The road wound up a hill crested with trees and open land. 'Plans to turn this into a park, but nothing has come of it yet.'

There were several police cars parked at the kerb, and a uniformed constable talking to a TV camera team. Coffin and Archie Young drove past the group fast.

At the top of the hill there was a thick belt of trees and bushes. Here an area was marked off by tape.

'He was found buried there.' Archie Young nodded to where the grass was already dug up. 'A shallow grave; the couple that found him noticed the flies buzzing around... And the smell,' he added. 'Then they saw the top of a shoe...trainer, the sort kids wear all the time now.'

Coffin walked over to look at the grave where white-coated forensic workers were still going over the ground. Other men were slowly searching the little patch of woodland.

'Looking for anything,' said Archie Young. 'Not much to go on so far...'

'Except the bloody clothes. And the other limb.'

'Already in the lab being gone over.'

A tall woman appeared through the bushes. ''Afternoon, sir.'

Coffin smiled and held out his hand. 'Inspector Devlin. I believe I saw you at a party my wife gave in the theatre.'

'I'm one of her fans, go to nearly everything she does—I think she's brilliant. And I was in the audience for you, sir, when you talked to us about advances in communication-techniques crime.'

'You've got a nasty one here,' said Coffin.

Paddy Devlin gave Archie Young a quick look. 'Yes,' she said to Coffin. 'We are giving of our best, I can promise you.'

'I just wanted to come and look.'

'Glad you did, sir.'

He looked up the slope of the hill. 'How was the body brought here? Or was he killed on the spot?'

'No, it looks as though he had been dead a day or two before he was buried here. As for being brought here...' She shrugged. 'You could park a car on the road up there, it's very deserted at night, then carry the body down, or use a market trolley.

You wouldn't have to pinch one, plenty of them left around the streets.'

Coffin took a few paces through the trees, looking towards the road. 'I think you are right. There will be traces left.'

'Forensic think they have found some...marks on the ground, broken branches on the bushes.'

'Good.' He looked from Inspector Devlin to Archie Young. 'I would like to speak to the boy's father myself. All right?'

'I think Dr Chinner went back to work... It's a one-man practice and he felt he must do. On the Attlee Estate, no one else will work there.'

'I'll drive you,' said Archie.

Coffin still had his eyes on Inspector Devlin as they drove away. 'I hope she's up to it.'

'She certainly is.' Archie spoke out loud and clear. 'One of the best we've got. I can't say what state Chinner will be in; he had himself under control but it may not have lasted...and I wouldn't blame him.'

'What about the mother?'

'She's dead. Geoff and I knew each other at school, and we were neighbours...he always had this missionary, must-help-the-public, spirit, that's why he works in the Attlee bunker. It is that...metal grilles on the windows, special locks on the door...broken into about once a week even then.'

'I can imagine.'

Archie Young drove efficiently towards the Attlee Estate, straight up to the surgery which did indeed have an embattled air, but where the outside windows were newly painted and there was a flower in a pot on the outer windowsill.

'I hope he's got that geranium nailed down,' said Archie as he parked. 'Or perhaps he takes it home at night.'

'He doesn't live over the shop?'

'No, would you? Got a nice house round the corner from me in Oakwood Drive...but neglected since his wife died.'

'Keeps this place up, though,' said Coffin, getting out of the car.

Archie did not answer, he was already striding forward to Dr Chinner's surgery.

The waiting room was not crowded: an old man with a stick and bent back, a woman with a baby on her lap, and a dog that seemed to have come in for attention on his own—he had a bandaged leg.

'Thank God I haven't got Gus with me, he'd probably join the queue.' He knew, as any dog owner does, that dogs are terrible hypochondriacs.

Dr Chinner appeared, ushering out the last patient, a woman with her child. 'There's that dog again,' he said. 'Why can't he go home. Hop it, Jason.'

Jason did not.

'He thinks he's your dog, you see, Doctor,' volunteered the old man.

'I expect he will be in the end,' said the doctor. He looked at Archie and Coffin, gave them a nod, and said that they could have five minutes and no more.

Coffin thought that he had never seen a man holding the pressure inside him down more strongly and dangerously: he might explode any minute... You'd think a doctor would know, he said silently. Dr Chinner was a short man with a crest of red hair and bright-blue eyes. Normally he must have looked friendly and approachable. No mean feat as a professional working on the Attlee Estate.

'I will tell you anything I can, answer any questions, but get on with it, please.'

Coffin hesitated. 'I don't have a question, Doctor. I just came to offer my sympathy. I am very, very, sorry. We will do all we can to get the man who did it.'

'Thank you. Thank you.' There was a bare admission in his tone that he recognized it for an act of kindness, and that he knew the Chief Commander.

He had not asked them to sit down, nor did he now. He had never even quite closed the door to his surgery.

Coffin looked at Archie, who went forward and patted his

friend on the shoulder. 'I'll come round to see you later. Or you can come to us...what about a meal?'

Dr Chinner nodded, but it was not exactly a yes, or a no. 'Thanks for coming. I think I am better on my own just at the moment, Archie.'

He held the door for them, and as they went out, he said: 'Next patient.' And the dog got up and trotted in.

'So what did you make of that?' asked Archie as they drove away. He had sensed a query behind Coffin's polite goodbye.

'Well, he's good with dogs.'

'Seriously.'

Coffin shook his head. 'I know we start with the family, but I don't think he killed his son.'

'No,' said Archie fiercely. 'So?'

'But don't let friendship blind you—I think he knows something.'

Archie said nothing as he sat hunched over the driving wheel. 'Drive you back, sir, shall I?'

They parted with not much more said. Archie was disconcerted, angry and uneasy.

At the school, the Royal Road Comprehensive, the day had ended, but small groups hung around the playground, skateboarding, rollerblading, or just talking and scuffling in the dust with a football. It was not encouraged that they should do this, but not forbidden either.

One group were skateboarding but coming back together to talk. Just a quick comment, they were not into long conversations, dialogue was an adult skill not altogether mastered. This group was well informed, picking up scraps of information and assessing them. To be well informed, you have to be interested, and this group, four boys and two girls, were very interested.

'We have to be,' said one to another. 'It's up to us. And we ought to do something.'

'What?' said his friend, the same age more or less, but female.

'I'm thinking.'

'My parents stop talking when I come into the room,' the girl said, and she laughed.

'Tell you what,' her companion said: 'We ought to get someone to say something.'

COFFIN WENT TO HIS office, and collected Augustus. 'You missed something, pal,' he said. 'You could have had your leg bandaged.'

There was a message from the wizard, John Armstrong, an old friend, who was looking into Harry's computer. 'I think I ought to be able to get most of the deletions back, they were not deleted by an expert. But I can't promise. If you don't hear from me then it is, No.

'One left alive, anyway, and I think you ought to know of it.

'It is a file on you, complete dossier of life and career, with present address.

'It lists strengths—pertinacity, imagination, sharp mind.

'Weaknesses: likes to be right.

'I don't know who put this together or why,' went on John Armstrong, 'but someone doesn't like you.'

Coffin dialled his friend, his answerphone was on also, so the Chief Commander left a message:

'Fax me that file, please. And to my home.'

His friend must have got back to his desk very speedily, (if indeed he had been away and not just sat there listening as the message came through) because the fax was waiting for Coffin when he got back to St Luke's.

He flipped through it quickly, noting without pleasure that Harry had left something else.

There was a short, accurate profile of his wife, Stella Pinero, including the fact that she was now in Los Angeles.

Somehow, he did not like it.

But then he remembered the sort of man Harry had been and what he had said once.

A bit drunk, words spilling out, he had said: 'I want to get all I can on you, Coffin, because you hide a lot, you've got plenty going on that I would like to know about. Your past career, too. You've been in trouble, but look at you now. Yes, you are worth a study. And that lovely wife of yours. To know her is to know you.'

Coffin shook his head. That was Harry. Friend or enemy, who knew which?

Did Harry know himself?

But what Coffin knew was that he would always protect Stella.

THREE

AN OLD SCHOOLMASTER of John Coffin, who had had a great deal of influence on him although Coffin never liked to admit it, had been in the habit of pronouncing: Life is real, life is earnest. He usually said this at exam time, which was perhaps why Coffin geared himself up grimly and got good marks. He wasn't an exam man, they were not things he thought about often, but just the word 'Life', pronounced the right way, could spur him into action even now.

But at the moment he did not need it: the juxtaposition of two cases, their lifelines crossing, was enough to make him only too aware of the seriousness of life. His life in particular at the moment, and without Stella here to laugh and ease him into happiness, it was going to be bad.

Without Stella, he thought, so why was she figured in the file on Harry Seton's PC? Not good news. So perhaps it was as well she was safely out of the way across the Atlantic. He felt like going back there himself, but life over here had a firm grip on him. It had a firm grip on Archie Young, too.

What was more important: the mission wished on him by Ed Saxon (and others higher in the chain of command), and apparently suggested by Harry himself with the words 'Ask Coffin', to find out who was doing the dirt in the pharmaceutical world, with special reference to Ed Saxon's outfit, or the murder enquiry on a child in his own Second City.

All policemen get used to dealing with two cases, or more, at once. In his time, Coffin had handled as many as ten, carrying all the details in his mind and yet keeping them distinct, so why was he getting the feeling that there were parallel lines here which converged in the distance?

Of course, Harry had been murdered too, but that was the

Met's job, and if the message on the word processor was from them, they were not too pleased to have him walking on their ground.

Territory, there was a lot of territorial feeling in this job. Always had been and always would be. Probably Sir John Fielding's officers in those distant days in the mid eighteenth century when he invented their force had had strong feelings about where they operated and who might interfere with them. The Peelers of a century later had carried on the tradition, because Dickens's portrayal of Inspector Bucket did not suggest a man who would welcome intruders.

Coffin took a deep breath and pulled towards him the files he had brought down from London, already photocopied by the industrious Paul Masters.

He now had two stacks of files: the photocopies and the originals. Now why did I want copies, he asked himself, and came swiftly back with the answer that he wanted them in case there was another fire.

Or the equivalent—theft. Whoever had killed Harry, had tried to get the files destroyed. True, the Met had had a look at them first, and might have been coming back for more, but someone had tried, not too efficiently, to burn the lot.

He looked from the photocopies to the scorched originals.

In the outer office, Paul was packing up to go home; he worked a long day, getting in before the Chief Commander, rarely taking a lunch break, and usually still at work when John Coffin left. Coffin saluted an ambitious man. But tonight, Paul was leaving early since he was off to the opera. Coffin suspected he had a new girlfriend who liked Mozart. Or his wife, there was one, but who knew what went on in Masters's private and somewhat secret life?

Inspector Masters put his head round the door. 'Want me to take the dog for a walk before I go, sir?'

Augustus looked up and wagged his tail hopefully. He got up and shook his body, he was a shrewd psychologist and knew how you did it. Generations of his ancestors had wagged their way into comfort and pleasure, and the genes were still working.

'Go on with you, then,' said Coffin, and to Paul Masters: 'Thank you.'

When the pair had gone, he turned back to his papers. The photocopied files were offering sparse information.

There was a map of Coventry with some street names marked in pencil. One area had a ring drawn round it. Attached to this were some scribbled notes which seemed to be of times and routes. It looked as though Harry had set off early and driven there.

Against the name H. Pennyfeather, he had put a query. And Coffin had a question mark in his own mind there. Did he know that name or not? Half a dozen further names were just recorded and given a tick.

Did this mean they were passed as all clear, whereas Pennyfeather was not? Or did the tick mean that they had been interviewed and Pennyfeather had not been at home.

Or did it mean something else altogether? Coffin ground his teeth and worked on.

A photograph was attached to one of the pages. It was the photograph of a woman.

It was not a photograph of Mary.

He saw a youngish, smiling face, with a smart, short haircut and large earrings. The woman was wearing a dark business suit. It was not a posed, studio photograph, but appeared to have been taken at a meeting of some sort, since he could see figures in the background. M.G. was written there.

Coffin worked through the papers, assessing them quickly. There was a similar group with a map of Oxford, and another of Newcastle. In each case, the map was marked, and it came with a list of names, some ticked and one or two with a question mark.

Thrupp in Coventry, and Weir in Newcastle, each had a question mark, as had Fox in Cambridge and H. Pennyfeather, but with no place name. So that made four in all. Sex not clear, but Ed Saxon had said he had a few women working for him. Possibly M.G. was one of them, although he hadn't named her.

He sat thinking about TRANSPORT A and its problems which high authority thought stemmed from the Second City, curse it. Thus was I lumbered, he thought.

When the phone rang, he had a premonition it was going to be Ed Saxon, and so it was.

'How are you getting on?'

'I haven't got far yet.' Not anywhere, really. 'It looks as though I'll have to go to Coventry first... You know about the fire?'

Ed Saxon admitted he knew about the fire. 'I had Mary in here.'

'What did she want?'

'She said she'd met you. You seem to have made an impression. Not easy on that one, she's a hard case. What she wanted was what you'd expect, to find how near we were to getting Harry's killer. Not too near, I had to tell her. She didn't take it well.'

'I can't blame her.'

'Who's talking about blame? But she was casting plenty of it around, she blames me in particular. And she isn't far wrong. After all, I chose him for the job.'

'It may have nothing to do with that, you know.'

'You've got an idea? What? What is it?'

There was silence. Coffin could hear Ed striking a match for a cigarette, the man was in a pressured state.

'Have you any idea, something you're not telling me?'

'No, Ed. And the Met are investigating Harry's death, remember? Not me. But I shall have to make contact with them.'

'Yes,' said Ed, as if the idea did not please him.

'I am beginning to get the feeling that Harry knew he was about to be killed.'

'Oh God, is that your great thought for the day?'

'It's a start.'

'Where did you get it from? Out of the air, I suppose?'

'No. From you.'

'Don't get you.'

'Oh, come on, Ed. I've known you a long time and you don't change. I think he told you he was frightened, that he knew there was a threat. And he knew who it was from; it was from the figure in your outfit who is profiting from the sale of phoney medicines and drugs. That was why you wanted an outsider like me to carry on the enquiry.' There was another reason, of course, why I actually got the job, but you may not know of it. The Second City is involved.

Wouldn't Ed know this? Why did he not know? Perhaps he was not fully trusted himself. Wheels within wheels, he didn't like. Touch dirt and you get dirty, he thought.

Ed was staying silent.

'And perhaps you thought my investigating skills might have got rusty with the years and I wouldn't turn up what you feared.'

There was still no answer from Ed.

'Who was it he suspected? Not you, by any chance, Ed?'

'No, of course not.'

'Come on, Ed.'

'He was just guessing, in my opinion…there was a woman…she had been working for us, not in a high capacity, but on this pharmaceutical case—she was investigating likely medical contacts, she'd been a nurse and knew the language. He suspected her. Called her bad. I said, "Don't go Gothic on me, Harry."'

The one in the photograph, Coffin thought.

'He thought she was dangerous, I thought he was wrong.'

'Does she have a name, this woman?'

'Margaret Grayle. You might as well know…we had an affair. Over now, of course.'

'Of course,' said Coffin, half ironically. In his experience, whenever anyone, man or woman, admitted to an affair it was always claimed to be over. It might be or it might not. It was in his mind to be wary and sceptical of this lady. 'You had better give me her address.'

'Oxford. But you should find it in Harry's papers.'

'In case I don't.'

A sigh came across the line. 'If she's still there, it was Owls House, Raven Road, Oxford.'

Not sure if I believe that address, thought Coffin, but he wrote it down.

'And have you told the Met about Miss Margaret Grayle?'

'Did I say Miss? She is married. And no, I haven't said anything. The Met have good men on the case, they will find Harry's killer. And it won't be Margaret.'

Not in person, Coffin thought, but she might have hired someone. Or been pressured to help get rid of him by associates she might have in the pharmaceutical racket. The body cut into five pieces, that sounded like a professional job.

'Was Harry having an affair with her too?'

'Not as far as I know,' said Ed gloomily.

'We'd better meet sometime and you can tell me what it is you do know.' Coffin tried to keep the irony out of his voice. 'Meanwhile, I have a very nasty murder on my hands here in the Second City, so I can't give your affair all my attention.'

Then he moved the conversation back a step. 'Wait a minute...you said as far as you know, Margaret was not having an affair with Harry... Does that mean you think she was but can't prove it?'

'It was just an idea I had, can't put it any stronger, and it could have been wrong at that.'

'And did Mary know?'

Silence for a minute. 'She might have done.'

'You mean you know she did,' said Coffin bluntly.

'She might have guessed...she's a clever woman.'

'Don't tell me you are having an affair with her too?'

'As soon have an affair with a piranha fish,' said Ed bitterly.

Perhaps both women had joined together to kill Harry. Now that was a picture.

Let me read myself a scenario, thought Coffin. Mary got to know about Margaret, who didn't love Harry so much after all. (Or had a lot to hide and wanted him out of the way.) So she got together with his wife and they did the job. Wasn't there a

French film with that theme? Was it *Les Diaboliques?* He had seen it with Stella. But the body being cut into five bits still worried him. It didn't sound like a female killing.

Still, it wouldn't do to be sexist.

He must find out if it was physically possible for the two women to have done it. Check on the physical force required, check on where they were at the relevant times. It would explain Mary's strange need to get into her dead husband's office. She might want to know what was there that could incriminate either of them.

Not a bad scenario; it needed working on, though.

Wait a minute, he told himself, this is the Met's job, not yours.

The telephone was bleating away. 'Are you still there?' Ed was saying.

'Yes, I'm still here.'

'You'd gone dead quiet. I thought I was talking to myself.'

'No, I was listening.' Didn't hear a word, however. 'Tell me, who is in charge of the investigation?'

'Larry Davenport. That was what I was telling you. Nice chap, he'll get in touch,' said Ed gloomily. 'Although some of his juniors are a pushy lot.' Could have been one of those who left me the rude message on the computer, thought Coffin. 'He remembers you.'

Paths do cross, Coffin admitted to himself, sometimes to your advantage and sometimes not.

'He says he grew up in East Hythe and his sister still lives there.' He added with relish. 'He's a useful chap, he's one that knows where all the bodies are buried.'

Coffin thought that he knew the burial sites of more than a few bodies himself. He pointed this out to Ed Saxon. 'I've always had thoughts about the Cassington murder and what happened to Maisie Deeds...I bet you have too.'

'Yeah.' The sound was almost a wince. 'Well, keep in touch. You're off to Coventry, did you say? It's a Tim Kelso there, remember.' He wanted to get away.

'Hang on,' said Coffin. 'What are the names of the women you have working in this organization?'

'Felicity Fox in Cambridge, Leonie Thrupp in Coventry and Margaret Grayle is what I call a mobile…lives in Oxford, works where required.' Ed Saxon put the receiver down hard.

Two of those names had earned a question mark: Fox and Thrupp.

Coffin heard the bang. 'I hit a nerve there. Can't be the Cassington lad or Maisie, so what?' he asked himself. 'He's hiding something, I'm sure of it, and it isn't just a tumble in bed that his wife doesn't know about.' He considered what Saxon had said. 'I must take a look at Thrupp in Coventry. Then there was a question mark for Fox in Cambridge which was the centre for the Anglia outfit of TRANSPORT A. So one of the ancient university towns had a question hanging over it. Ancient but not innocent?

He thought for a moment about Stella, perhaps even then undergoing surgery. Hope she doesn't have her nose altered. I like that nose.

He looked at his diary. He could go to Coventry almost at once. It would mean a shuffling of appointments, but Paul Masters would do that for him, and he could spend some of the time beforehand studying the records left behind by Harry, which would not be a long job.

He could tell already that either Harry had not kept many or he had destroyed them.

The names of those with question marks were made a note of and he would be checking on them. In Coventry he would be seeing Leonie Thrupp and the man operating in that area. What was it now? He turned back to his own notes:

Tim Kelso in Coventry.

Peter Chard in Oxford.

Felicity Fox in Cambridge, which was the East Anglia area.

Joe Weir in Newcastle, which Ed Saxon, more romantic than Coffin could have guessed, had wanted to call by the area's old-English name of Deira.

He did not know any of them, but none had won a question mark, whatever it might mean, good or bad, from Harry.

Just as he was thinking that he ought to get in touch with Inspector Larry Davenport, who was investigating the murder of Harry, the man himself was on the telephone.

'Hello, sir. Remember me, Larry Davenport...Inspector, CID now.'

Ed Saxon must have telepathy, Coffin told himself, or else he knew you were about to ring.

'We both have an interest in Harry Seton.'

'So we do.' Coffin was brief. Let Davenport be expansive if he liked.

'Thought we ought to get in touch, sir.' You help me, I'll help you, the breezy voice hinted. 'We've got East Hythe in common, too, sir. Nasty business about the boy.'

'It is. Not too good about Harry Seton. How are you getting on?' Bet you won't tell me.

Neither did he. 'Not much to say, unluckily, at the moment... Have you got any help for me, sir?'

'Not yet.' After all, this was not his case.

'We ought to keep in touch, don't you agree, sir?'

Of course, Coffin thought crossly. 'How did he die? Anything new there?'

'Blow to the head...then cut up when dead. Freshly dead.' That was the kind of detail that Davenport relished.

'Would it have taken a lot of strength?'

'Well, no, but a frail old lady couldn't have done it. What there would have been was a lot of blood. All over the place, and we are keen to find that place. Haven't yet.'

Like Devlin in the Second City, thought Coffin, a nasty parallelism, but police work could be like that.

'How did the body get to the park, and then to the bandstand?'

'Must have been by car, not something you could carry through the street wrapped in brown paper...it was wrapped, by the way, but in a sheet. The park gates are open all night, in fact, I think it's years since there was a gate. That bandstand is derelict, never used. As for the rest…well, there are urban foxes round there, a real, rough breed down by the river. I heard they had mated with wolves from Russia.' He laughed heartily at his own joke.

'I'll keep in touch.' Coffin did not laugh.

Paul Masters came back with Augustus, both of them refreshed by their walk. Augustus bustled up smelling of dog, and grass and earth.

'Had a good time, did he?'

Augustus answered for himself with a feathery wagging tail, and positioned himself at Coffin's feet ready for another walk.

'Oh Paul, I may be away from the office for about two days, but I will get back sooner if I can. You can always get me on my mobile… And I will phone you as and when.'

Paul Masters was too discreet to ask any questions, but having copied the files for Coffin could make a guess what it was about.

He also had his own private theory: he gets fidgetty when *She* is away.

'I'll see you get to know everything important, sir.'

'And nothing that is not.'

Goes without saying. But he did not say it aloud, contented himself with his polite, enigmatic smile (Go on smiling like that, his wife had said, in that tart voice that occasionally made him feel like straying, and they will think you are hiding the secret of the Third Man, or was it Fourth and Fifth) and went away. He knew his smile, which he had worked upon before perfecting it, was a good, workable professional tool which would see him through many a crisis.

'And you can wipe that smile off your face,' said Coffin, as the door closed behind Masters. 'I'm getting fed up with it.' He too had watched its progress during the last few months.

He gathered up his papers, put Augustus on the leash, then walked homewards at such a pace that Augustus began to lag behind, pointing out that he was a peke with little legs, not a bloody Great Dane.

Back at his home in St Luke's, he fed the dog, and considered making himself a meal. He was a passable cook if the frying pan and the grill were used. Then he stopped, changed into something more casual than his dark working suit (Makes you look like a coroner's favourite pathologist, Stella had said once, which had rankled) and prepared to go to Max's restaurant. Not the one in the theatre, but the bigger and grander one round the corner. Max, as chef and proprietor, had started small and was getting bigger every day.

He went down his winding staircase with Augustus following him at every step. He manoeuvred himself to the door before shutting in a protesting peke face.

'Don't go on like that, Gus, or I will buy you a cat to keep you company.'

IN MAX'S NEWLY redecorated restaurant, the proprietor stood in a welcoming way at the door. Max had got plumper and greyer and more prosperous in the years since he had set up; over these same years, his family had shrunk, then grown again. The daughter they called the Beauty Daughter had married and gone away, then another daughter had departed, leaving numbers seriously low, but now both girls were back without husbands but with several offspring.

Max approached Coffin with a sympathetic smile. He knew that Stella was away, everyone knew, and he let Coffin see that he understood loneliness. Not that he suffered much from it himself, especially at the moment with four grandchildren taking up what felt like unofficial residence, but still…a man could imagine.

He led Coffin to a table nicely placed near the window. 'Miss Pinero not back yet?' he said, as he handed Coffin the menu.

As if you didn't know, Coffin muttered inside, as he took the menu. He pretended to study it, but he always ate the same thing here: that which Max recommended—it was wisest.

'The brill is very good tonight.'

'Right, brill it is.' Coffin closed the menu. 'Salad with it, please, and claret to drink.'

Max looked sad at the choice of claret with brill, an expen-

sive Montrachet would have been better, but he sped away to
serve the fish.

'The chef has poached it with a little basil,' he confided as
he offered it to the Chief Commander.

Coffin ate the brill, thinking wistfully of the days when fish
was fried and served with chips. You could still get such meals
in the right places, but not where the Maxes of this world ruled
the menu. He wondered what Stella was eating in Los Angeles,
or if she was eating at all, since she might now be under the
surgeon's knife. She had refused to let him know when the
operation was to take place because she didn't want him to
worry.

Strange idea of worry she must have, he decided, since I am
worrying about her all the time. Not the nose, Stella, he said
again over a mouthful of salad, nor the mouth: I love both of
them.

As he ate, he mulled over the two big problems on his mind:
the pharmaceutical affair which Ed Saxon had delivered to him,
and the missing boys. Since one had been found dead, he had
to assume the others also were.

What was the list?

Charles Rick, missing since mid-May, the second boy to go
and not yet found.

Dick Neville, a fortnight earlier, he was the first, and he went
the first week in May. May Day, in fact. Was that important?

Archie Chinner, the last week in June, the last to go and the
first to be found.

Matthew Baker, last week in May. A month before the next
boy went. Was that important?

Who knows, he thought to himself, with some anger. You
never know until it is too late.

Across the room he could see a table of the cast of the play
now in rehearsal at the Stella Pinero Theatre in the St Luke's
complex of the theatres. This was the main theatre, created out
of the old church, but in addition there was now the much
smaller Experimental Theatre and the Theatre Workshop. The

last two theatres received grants from the local university in return for allowing its drama department to use both theatres.

He knew from Stella that the play under rehearsal was one of Pinter's: *The Homecoming*. She had had it in mind for a long while, but had handed the production over to a friend, Alec Macgregor, always known as Mac. Mac was at the table too, and waved to Coffin, whom he had got to know well over the years. He was a tall, slim man with a mop of grey hair and bright, dark eyes. A fond parent had left him a pleasant fortune, so it was likely that he was paying for the dinner, and not the cast who probably could not have afforded it, since Max's prices had risen with his success. Coffin knew that Stella was not a lavish payer, although Equity rules did not allow too much stinginess.

As he waved back, he saw that Mac was getting up and coming over to him.

'How are things going? Heard from Stella since you got back?'

'She rang up and I spoke to her yesterday.' He thought it was yesterday, with all the pressures on him events began to run together. He was beginning to worry about his memory. Could you get Alzheimer's through stress? No, it was congenital, wasn't it, and the one thing he knew about his mother was that she was both long-lived and articulate. About his father he knew much less, and that was down to his mother too, since she had never been quite definite about who his father was. Give birth and move on, had been the name of her game. 'Stella's enjoying herself, going to the theatre every night.' That was more or less true. 'How are you and the production?'

'That's what I wanted to say and what you must tell Stella when you next speak with her—she was a bit vague about her movements to me. I think we are going to make a good thing of this production. I had my doubts, I must admit, at first.' He fixed Coffin with an intent brown gaze. 'It's a play that needs a middle-aged cast, it's about the angst of ageing...or that's one of the things it's about; you can't pin things down with Pinter, the play makes itself, don't you agree?'

Coffin bowed his head but said nothing.

'And this is such a very young cast, all under thirty, but they are going great guns.' Mac had had a spell in the navy and on occasion it showed. 'Such a joy.'

'She will be pleased; I expect her back before you get on stage, so she will see for herself.' No doubt wearing dark spectacles.

'Give her my love.'

'I will do.' The love was quite platonic and no threat to Coffin. Mac had a beloved house guest of his own, and although the name and character might change, the sex never did. But he was reputed to have the kindest heart in the business and any lost kitten or stray dog could find a home with him.

'Must get back to my young party, or they will be ordering more champagne, and it's my treat.' But he said it with a cheerful laugh. 'We're celebrating. They don't know it, but I do. See that lad at the end of the table? The one with that crest of yellow hair? He's the love of my life, I never thought to find one, but there he is, trying to act a rough old man of fifty, bless him.'

Coffin could almost hear Stella's reproving voice: 'Another love of your life, Mac, how many does that make?' But he said nothing, just smiled.

'It's to be hoped he loves cats, for I am rather well provided with them at the moment: six, my dear, and a pregnant tabby.'

'Isn't it more important he should love you?'

'No, just to look at a creature like that is enough, or sometimes enough. I don't bully them.' And he gave his wide, generous smile as he turned away.

You really are a nice man, thought Coffin, and he shook his head. Kind, but reckless, Stella had said.

Max was advancing with his coffee, together with a sorbet which he had not ordered and did not want but would be obliged to eat under Max's eyes.

Max planted the coffee pot and the sorbet down in front of Coffin and stood back, watching. 'A lemon sorbet, very refreshing...' He hesitated, then said: 'Sir...?'

Coffin looked up from his sorbet, at once alert. 'Yes, Max?'

'Of course, we are all anxious about the disappearances of the four boys, fearful, I might say, sir, in my case, since my two grandsons are here now. One of them goes to the school, the junior part, he is still a little boy, eight, nearly nine, but a clever boy, with lots of older friends…a good sign, that…we keep an eye on him.'

'I'm sure you do.'

Max hesitated, while Coffin wondered what was coming.

'My grandson, Louie, told his mother that he saw one of the boys, Dick Neville—he knew him, they live near to each other in East Hythe—he saw Dick walking away with a man the day he disappeared.'

'Has he told anyone of this?'

Max shook his head. 'Only his mother, who told me.'

Coffin tried to remember what he had learnt of the sequence of events; Dick Neville had been the first boy to go missing, in early May, two months ago. May Day, with people on holiday.

'When did your grandson tell his mother about this?'

'Only this week.'

Coffin sat considering what he had heard. The boy must be questioned, of course.

'He is not a liar,' said Max heavily. 'He knows to speak the truth. And he is clever.'

'Why has he been so slow?'

Max raised his shoulders in an expressive shrug and waved his hands. 'He is not a liar, but he is only a little boy…nothing was discussed in front of him at home, perhaps he did not think it mattered what he saw.'

I bet there was talk at school, Coffin thought.

'Besides,' said Max slowly. 'He said Dick went off with a policeman.'

In the silence that followed, Coffin found himself thinking what fool would abduct a child when wearing a uniform. Was it a uniform that Max's grandson recognized, or did he know the man and know him to be a policeman?

And yet somehow his nerves told him this was important, crucial evidence, a key which might unlock a dirty door.

'We will have to talk to the boy,' he said.

'Yes, that was expected. I have his address.' And Max pushed a piece of paper across the table. 'He is a nervous child.'

'He will be handled carefully. And, of course, his mother will be there, too, all the time.'

Max gave a dignified bow, then he left. The theatre party with Mac was breaking up. He must present the bill.

Across the room, Coffin saw the restaurant door open. Chief Superintendent Archie Young stood there; he was looking round the room and when he saw Coffin he walked across quickly.

There could be no good news in this visit, Coffin thought, and wait till he hears what I have to tell him.

'Hello, how did you know where to find me?'

Archie Young sat down facing Coffin. 'I asked Paul Masters for a suggestion when I discovered you were not at home. I got him on his mobile... When I banged on your front door, the dog barked, by the way.'

'He always does, thinks he's a watchdog. Have some coffee.'

Archie Young shook his head. 'No, thank you.'

'So what is it? I don't suppose you've come just to keep me company.' He saw the look on the chief superintendent's face. 'No, don't tell me, let me guess: you have found the body of another boy?'

'All three,' said Archie Young. 'Together. You might call it a communal grave.' He added with feeling: 'Trussed up together like turkeys and crammed in together.'

THE KEY

FOUR

CROSS THE RIVER, go through the tunnel, on to the motorway, choose your route. Take the M25 and then on to the M40 because that will give a sight of Oxford where you will be going next, then on the motorway to Warwick and Coventry.

The University of Warwick, one of his calling places, is in Coventry, although they don't dwell on that much.

The mind split two ways: thinking of Coventry and Tim Kelso, who had sounded abrupt and unwelcoming on the telephone, but thinking also of the dead boys cocooned together like dead larvae.

Split three ways, because there was always Stella. With new nose or not. He wished he could drop that rueful, irreverent thought. It wouldn't be a whole new face, after all, would it?

And then: I bet I am the only leading police officer with a wife with a new face. But there must be a lot in the media, probably happened all the time. You went out, shot a film in India, say, or did a long run in a provincial theatre (were you allowed still to talk of the provinces?), came back and your wife had a different face. You still knew her, though.

He felt guilty at going, leaving the investigation behind, but would have felt just as bad if he had not set out.

It was important, hundreds of people, perhaps thousands might suffer, or die, if they took corrupted, diluted, worthless drugs.

Besides, he had left a very competent team behind. Inspector P. Devlin, Sergeant Tittlemouse...no, mustn't call him that, it was Tittleton.

It was borne in on Coffin that he had had very little sleep last night, or the night before, what with setting up the office and organizing a home elsewhere for the dog. He had arranged for Paul Masters to pick him up, left Augustus eating, and got into the car. Didn't want to upset the old boy.

It was a calm, misty early morning.

On either side of the motorway, the countryside was green and damp and empty. Very tidy, not a soul around. When did the farming work get done? Did a great machine creep out at night and sow, and later creep out to crop what it had sown? No need for the peasant to come out and weed as in medieval tapestry because there were no weeds. Slain at birth, before it even, they never came to birth, by the chemicals he would be investigating.

He had managed to talk with Inspector Paddy Devlin yesterday. A nice woman, but toughish. Had to be to have gone so far and ambitious to go further, she was still forty-two and looking for promotion. He had studied her record. A degree from Durham University, she had started on the beat and worked her way up. She was ambitious; he got the impression that although she was something of an expert on crimes concerning children, she would want to move on to more general fields, such as Serious Crime with a view to climbing the ladder.

He had liked her: a tall, solid, youngish woman, not pretty, no, never that, but handsome in an unobtrusive way. Well groomed, he had been around Stella long enough to know a good haircut when he saw one. She was divorced and rumoured to be hard to get close to.

Sensible woman, Coffin thought, knowing some of his colleagues. But she was also said to be a decent sort who did not let you down. In a war, she would have been a good soldier.

Their conversation of yesterday was running through his head as he drove. Inspector Devlin had come to sit in his car to talk while Sergeant Tittleton walked around the burial pit with the Scene-of-the-Crime team. It was at this point he told her about his conversation with Max. She listened carefully.

'It might be well to see the boy and his mother.'

'I certainly will, sir. Thank you.'

They both looked towards the sergeant's slow walk round, staring in at the bodies and photographing them.

The triple grave was on the same patch of woodland and scrub where the first body had been found, but it was deeper into the trees.

'Not found by chance,' said Devlin. 'Once the Chinner boy's body was found we started to take a good hard look round here.'

'Of course.'

'We had help, one of the SOCO's team on the first burial is a keen gardener and he pointed out that there were signs of track marks in the grass—such as it is, hardly a lawn—as if something heavy had been wheeled over it. Only a gardener could read the signs.' She was half laughing. 'Of course, we were looking and would have found this grave, but his sharp eyes helped.'

Coffin was thoughtful. 'They have not been officially identified yet but I suppose there is no doubt these are the three other missing boys?'

'They have to be,' said Devlin confidently. 'They haven't been touched yet, just photographed. The police surgeon gave a quick look just to say they were dead.'

'You could see that,' said Coffin, remembering the discoloured, swollen faces.

There had been a moment of silence then.

'I am guessing,' she said, 'but my guess is that the Chinner boy was the last killed. The pathologist and the forensic teams will set us right.'

'Sure. I suppose you will be using Denis Garden?' Garden was a famous local figure, a professor in the old Docklands University, now upgraded to a superior status if with not much more money, as was the Thames Water District Hospital where he had a pathology department; a man much loved by the media for his careful, slightly flamboyant dressing. He photographed well.

'As usual, he can be very difficult, but he is very good. If not, then I shall go for Dr Bickley from the Lane Grove Hospital, he would probably do it in the old police forensic lab in Swinehouse which would be easy for us.' Devlin was moving on: 'The other boys were killed earlier, and at different times...guessing again, but it seems likely.'

Coffin nodded.

'But we think they were all three buried here at the same time...only the one set of wheel marks and those not so old. Even our sharp-eyed SOCO man would not have noticed them if the grass and weeds had had time to grow over.'

'So only one trip. Possibly not long before the other boy was buried.'

'And separately.'

'No room in the grave,' replied Devlin bluntly. 'But you see what it means, don't you, sir?'

He thought about it: only one trip for the three bodies.

'They were killed and kept somewhere else.'

'Yes, for some time, it looks like in the case of at least one boy...' The most decomposed, she meant, but did not say.

'Professor Garden will help you there, as well as the forensic team.'

'We have to find where that place is.'

'And the vehicle that was used to bring them here...the tyre marks may help to identify the car. If it was a car—a four-wheeled vehicle of some sort.'

'Well, good luck.' He knew how these hunts went: following hopeful leads that turned out to be rubbish, following hints and whispers that got you nowhere. Starting off with energy and enthusiasm (because you always did, however often you had done this sort of thing before) and ending up dogged, and tired but persevering. In the end, perseverance could pay off.

'Thank you, sir, we are going to need it.'

'If you need more officers, let Chief Superintendent Young know...I am sure he will do something about it.' Not only have I told him to be generous, but he has his own interest: the Chinner boy is his godson.

'It's bad for him, sir.'

'He's better in there working. He will keep in touch... I want the details, not just the general picture.' His eyes signalled that he wouldn't nag, but he wanted to know.

'Right, sir.' Devlin had given that little jerk with her head that he was beginning to recognize.

She had one last piece of information to hand on, something for Coffin to chew on as he drove north and west.

'There was a suicide in East Hythe a week ago. Floating in the canal. He was Joe Partoni, a known paedophile—I've been trying to convince myself he was our murderer.'

Coffin looked at her in query. 'But he isn't?'

'Be so easy, wouldn't it, to have solved the case before it's started. You get sick, sometimes, when you don't find out who did the killing, don't even get close. Or worse, when you know and can't get proof.' She shook her head, that little jerk, half bitter, half amused. 'Sometimes, I hate this job, but someone has to do it, and I am good at it…I suppose Joe could have killed those boys, I would like him to have been the killer, and dead, because he was a horrid little man.'

'He is dead,' Coffin reminded her.

'It's just possible he was murdered, there was a bruise on the side of his head that might mean he was beaten and thrown into the river. I hope he was. I cherish the thought. But Big Jim…' Big Jim was Jim Matherson, the Home Office pathologist. 'Big Jim did the autopsy and he is the king of pathologists and he thinks not, it was suicide.'

Down below there was Oxford, he couldn't see it through the mist but it was there.

He wondered why Devlin had fed him that bit of information about Joe Partoni, suicide. She meant something by it and for certain she wanted him to remember Joe.

One thing was sure, Partoni had never been a policeman. Could have got a uniform, though, from a costume-hirer. Or perhaps he had been a postman…they hardly wore uniforms these days, did they? His thoughts were moving fast, and concentrically.

The mist lifted, but still no sight of dreaming spires. Coffin had had an early and successful case in Oxford, he had enjoyed it and had happy memories of the city. Must take Stella there, have a meal, go to that place in the country where they do operas…Garsington…she'd like that. She had played the old Playhouse once, but that was when they were at odds. Dead, dusty years, better not think about them.

Think instead about the job ahead: a traitor, and almost certainly a murderer, in Ed Saxon's team.

There was a stirring and heaving beneath the coats and rugs he had thrown on to the seat beside him. Coffin, startled, turned around to look.

Augustus rose from beneath them, first his head, then the rest of his white, furry body, he gave himself a shake.

'Gus, how did you get there?'

'I got in the car while you were on the telephone…you do go on, you know. I made myself cosy, knew you wouldn't want me to be uncomfortable.'

Thus would Augustus have spoken had he had speech. As he was speechless, he was far too canny to growl, but contented himself with a slight flick of his feathery tail. Nothing too strong, just a gentle indication that he was happy to be here. Sometimes the motion of the car made him sick, he hoped it would not do so this time.

'If you are sick,' said Coffin fondly, 'then I will kill you.'

He drove on, Oxford behind him, forward on to the motorway, passing the Banbury turn, till he came to the Coventry exit. The traffic had been getting heavier all the time, and he meant heavier, with great lorries nudging at him as they passed.

The road into the city itself was quieter. He stopped at a pub for an early lunch. A large notice said NO DOGS PLEASE, but he solved that problem by taking Augustus for a brisk walk down the road first—it was well lined with trees, which suited Augustus who lingered here and there to read the smells which sent out signals of the new land he was venturing into. He seemed well content: new country, old smells.

Coffin ordered a sandwich for himself, then took a hamburger out to Augustus, before going back to drink coffee, a glass of doubtful red wine and to eat his sandwich. Neither his body nor his spirit felt nourished by his meal, and he was not surprised that Augustus had spurned the hamburger and gone to sleep.

From there, on his mobile, he telephoned Tim Kelso once more.

'Oh yes, I know who you are and what you are; Ed had to tell me: you are our secret number. No one else is to know.'

'That's about it, I suppose.' It was a long while since Coffin had been a secret figure.

'You can talk to me whenever you want, but for the others...so few, so few, you are on your own and must scrape an acquaintance how you will.' Kelso sounded very cheerful at the thought.

'I would like to talk to you.' I shall need some addresses for a start, and a quick look at you to sum you up, friend.

'Of course, sir, of course. Want to talk now on the telephone or face to face?'

'Face to face.'

The address and the way there was transmitted clearly and happily.

'City centre, and when you see the City Library look to your left and raise your eyes, and there we are on the third floor of a modest Art-Nouveau building.'

Coffin was already beginning to form a picture of Tim Kelso as thin, tall, with snapping black eyes. A pleasant voice, baritone and lively.

He told Tim Kelso to expect him within the hour, then he drove into a quieter road where he parked, and consulted his documents.

Here, parked under a tree with Augustus snoring by his side, he read again the papers on the pharmaceutical business.

It appeared that there were two ways of getting hold of cheap, fake drugs.

One was called parallel importing. This was when a manufacturer found he could make a drug more cheaply in Taiwan than in Middlesex. The quality of the tablets and their strength would be the same, also the bioavailability...

Must find out what that means, Coffin told himself.

The tablets might not look the same, which would be confusing if it was your regular pill and you were oldish and your sight was not good. The instructions could be in Mandarin or high Japanese.

Coffin could see this was a sharp practice and tiresome but would not kill you.

Counterfeiting, however, could kill. This was a big problem, the cardboard boxes are printed as exact copies of the real thing, but the drug inside could be made in a backyard in Burma or Greece with bioavailability, purity and contamination all different from the genuine article. Unscrupulous pharmacy importers buy them, false serial numbers and all. They then offer them to pharmacists at a very reduced rate. This enables them to make a hearty profit on the NHS prescribing while poisoning the hapless patient.

Sometimes the pharmacist concerned was an innocent party, but sometimes not.

Also, you might not like the idea of drugs from a country with which you or your father had once fought a war.

He absorbed what he could, then drove on to see Tim Kelso in his office near the City Library in Coventry. It was easy to find, but hard to park. When he at length tucked the car away, he had to solve the problem of Augustus who stood up at once, ready to take the air.

Coffin debated whether to take the dog, then decided that although he might be a useful ally when he met the bouncy Tim Kelso, he was better off in the car.

He had expected Kelso to be a tall man wearing bright tweeds, with a golf bag propped up in the corner of the room.

In fact, he was a thin, neat fellow wearing jeans and a sweater; his voice was bigger than he was.

In this voice, which remained friendly and cheerful even as his face grew more and more serious, he managed in a few minutes to get more information over to Coffin about the nature of the TRANSPORT A operation than Ed Saxon, weighed down by his miseries, had achieved in half an hour.

'We don't expect to be a long-term operation...it's like in war, we are a kind of special unit.'

'Commandos,' said Coffin, looking at the feet of Tim Kelso which were encased in muddy white trainers.

'Something like...we are sent in to snuff out the enemy in the shape of the people who are either importing these fake drugs or making them here.'

'They aren't all from abroad?'

'Far from it, the UK has got a bad case of it, and the sources are scattered around. That's why Ed created regional squads... When I say squad, there is only me and one other.'

'Leonie Thrupp?'

'Yes, seconded for the purpose. You understand we are meant to be very quiet about things because, well, it can be dangerous. Not the people actually making the drugs, or I don't think so, nor the poor little pharmacists who buy it, but the man or men who are organizing it. Because it *is* organized and we are meant to find out by whom.'

'You think these men are killers?'

'Not perhaps themselves, but there are contract killers...'

Coffin was silent while he thought about it. No doubt Larry Davenport had contract killers on his list. But contract killers who went to the trouble of depositing the trunk and limbs in a South London park seemed unlikely, he thought. Something more personal there.

'Harry Seton was killed.'

'Tell me something I don't know.'

'Does the name Pennyfeather mean anything to you? Do you know him?'

'Never heard of him.'

Coffin nodded, wondering if this was true. He would go on asking.

Without prompting—perhaps, thought the sceptical Coffin, to move the subject away from Pennyfeather—Tim Kelso explained what they did: when a drug was reported fake or a copy, either by a suspicious doctor or patient, then Tim and Leonie went out to trace the source.

'Like looking for a fish in the sea...but you get to know the signs. It's low-key work, but we are supposed to be invisible more or less. It may sound as if this drug business is a cottage industry but it is not, not now. There is a good brain behind organizing drugs and outlets. It makes money. We are meant to go round and clear up local manufacturing units and carriers, but others spring up.'

He looked at Coffin, his face more serious than ever. 'That's why Harry Seton was sent out: someone knew what we are doing almost as soon as we know ourself.'

'And you think Harry found out who this was?'

'We all think that, and now you have arrived to find out what Harry knew. Well, good luck to you, sir.'

For the first time, like a soldier in battle, but remembering to strike the right note, he acknowledged Coffin's rank.

Coffin felt that he was the beast with two heads: he was to find the traitor in the camp, but, because one thing led to another, it might be that he would be helping to find Harry Seton's killer.

He was studying Tim Kelso for clues, to see if it was him. Coffin did not believe that faces necessarily told you much, he had met too many good liars in his time to believe in frank faces. Even an expressionless one was not a sign of guilt, although it could be irritating.

Tim Kelso's face was serious and tired. But he did not seem anxious, his hands were still, nor did his feet fidget.

'Harry came round here, went through everything, probably checked my bank account and Leonie's too, I expect. I have an overdraft, if that is of interest. I don't know about Leonie, you will have to ask her.'

'I will do.'

'I drive an old car, have been in the red for years and probably always will be. I don't believe I would bother with that if I was coining in dirty money.'

'You could have other accounts.'

'Harry could not find one, I am sure he looked. I never go

to Switzerland, by the way, and I last went to Jersey when I was ten.'

'And the name H. Pennyfeather means nothing to you?'

'You asked that just now, and I answered, never heard it before. Doesn't sound real.'

Coffin had thought the same himself. 'Maybe, maybe not.' But he was suddenly irritated. 'Shut up and listen: I want all the help I can get; if you have any to give let me know, otherwise keep quiet.'

Tim Kelso was silent for a minute, then he said: 'Well, H. Pennyfeather doesn't mean anything to me—Harry asked me the same question. So it did to him... I liked old Harry, I don't like what happened to him.'

'I am not primarily concerned with his death. That's for the Met.'

'I know: Larry Davenport. I know him. I believe he knows the Second City, sir.'

'Yes.' And the Second City might be deeply involved in this drug racket. Harry Seton must have thought so and made a report to that effect, but not to Ed Saxon.

Does that mean I have to put Ed Saxon high on the list of suspects? If so, no wonder he was uneasy.

You could go mad doing this job, he told himself. Perhaps Harry Seton had gone mad.

He showed Tim Kelso his copy of Harry's map of Coventry with the ringed area. 'Mean anything to you?'

'Like Pennyfeather, you mean?' But he bent his head over it. 'I think the circle links up all the chemist shops in Coventry which were selling suspect drugs on the last clear-up we did. They were home-made jobs. Brand name ANTAC, drug was hantidine. They contained substantial impurities. We cleared them all up, and the chemists concerned got into such trouble as we could hand out.'

Tim was quite good and informative when he wanted to be.

'But Leonie knows more about this than I do, she went round the shops locating those that had the drug.'

'Where did they get them from?'

'Ah, that's the question, isn't it? They weren't too keen to answer that; again, Leonie can tell you more, but there seemed to be a stall in Coventry marketplace, if you can believe it. Not there now, of course, moved on. Because no doubt other drugs will pop up. But see Leonie Thrupp.'

'And where is she?'

'Down the corridor. Next door. You're lucky we are both in, and that is because it is what you might call a quiet time. If we get word of another outbreak like the false ANTAC then we are out shopping.'

Coffin got up. 'Who else is there?'

'Just us, and the pharmacist who analyses the suspect drugs...he works in the Hale Road Hospital of St John, you can find him there.'

'Right. Let me have copies of all your records, please.'

Kelso looked thoughtful, like all policemen, he hated handing over his records. But he turned to a shelf behind him and handed over a thick yellow envelope. 'Here you are.' Being a careful man, he had his own copies.

'Thank you.'

At the door, Coffin paused: 'And Margaret Grayle, do you know her?'

'She's Oxford. Know the name. That all?'

'For the moment,' said Coffin.

LEONIE THRUPP had a question mark by her name, remember that fact.

She wasn't in her room. But presently she appeared down the corridor from the staircase direction. She was no beauty, but trim of figure, and well dressed in a neat suit.

'You looking for me? You can't get in, the door's locked. I was just down in the road because I heard a dog whining so I went to see. Shut in a car, poor brute.'

'Did he stop whining when he saw you?'

She nodded. 'Yes, I spoke to him and rapped on the window and he wagged his tail.'

'He's my dog, he likes company.' Coffin felt an explanation

was demanded: Augustus was, after all, not a poor brute. 'I didn't want to bring him, but he stowed away when I wasn't looking.'

'Come in, sir. I imagine you want to talk, to ask questions. We knew you were coming, supposed to be secret but things never are.'

She led the way into her room, which was smaller and less tidy than her boss's. It also smelt of cigarette smoke, although there was a no-smoking notice on the wall. So Coffin guessed it was not only charity to dogs that had taken her to the street but the need for nicotine. Come to think of it, the smell of cigarettes was coming from her rather than the room.

'Funny thing, these operations are usually a cottage-industry business, but not now.' So Tim Kelso had said, thought Coffin, they seemed anxious to make it clear to him. He watched her face as she went on. 'The place can be flooded with cheap, parallel fake drugs, groomed according to season. I won't swear he's got a factory somewhere, but I think he must have... Or she,' Leonie added thoughtfully.

'You think it might be a woman?'

'Women can make things,' she said sharply. 'Pretty good chemists, some of them.'

'I am prepared to accept a woman,' said Coffin gravely.

Leonie looked at him, then laughed. 'I'm a pig, but you get like that in this business. Women are not really popular and certainly not mates. They miss all the locker-room larks, you see. Don't care for them, in fact. Now your wife is an actress, I happen to know.'

'Plenty of people know.'

'Ah-ha, now you're defending her. Yes, I admit I said that just to see how you reacted. She's famous, admired, and I think she's marvellous, but I bet you wish she was at home more cooking your supper. Isn't that what you think?'

The absence at the moment of the much-missed Stella almost silenced Coffin, but not quite.

It's like being in a robbers' stronghold here, he thought—

no, like a commando HQ, they live by their own rules. Probably have to.

'No,' he said, 'I don't think like that. Tell me, why do you think that Harry Seton put a question mark by your name in his notes?'

'Perhaps he didn't see me last time he came,' she suggested.

'He came more than once?'

'Oh, he was trawling round. Didn't Tim tell you?'

Coffin did not take up that gambit. 'So he did not see you last time?'

'Well, now I think back, I believe he did.'

'Did you have a disagreement?'

'Can't remember what we talked about…we had a drink in a pub near the hospital because he was going on to talk to the pharmacist, but there was nothing to it.'

'Go on, you might find you remember more.'

After a pause, Leonie said, 'I can hear your dog whining again.'

'He can wait. So can I, while you think about that question mark.'

'I wouldn't necessarily know, would I?' She moved restlessly in her chair. In a child you would have called it fidgeting.

'Go on thinking.'

She shrugged. 'Just a thought…'

'Let's have it.'

'He seemed worried that I had bought a new car.'

'Oh.' Getting information out of Leonie was like peeling an onion, the effort made you cry. He did not cry. 'What sort of car?'

'Just a second-hand car from my brother.'

An old Ford, a little Metro? 'What sort?'

'An old Porsche, my brother was getting rid of it.'

'How old?'

Reluctantly, she said: 'Couple of years.'

'Are you surprised you earned a question mark?'

'No.'

With genuine interest, Coffin asked: 'What does your brother do?'

'He's an estate agent.'

'He must be a successful one.'

'It's rich country round here, and there are still big estates. Yes, he is successful. And if you are dealing with successful people then you have to look successful yourself.'

'Hence the Porsche. So what did he upgrade to? A Bentley?'

Even through the window, Augustus's wails could be heard. Coffin went to the window and waved. Augustus stopped at once. Company was on the way.

'So being the third owner of a Porsche, because my brother didn't buy it new, it had been in an accident too, so it's a repair job, puts me in as prime suspect, does it?' said Leonie.

'Thanks for helping me.' Coffin made for the door. 'Am I far away from the hospital with the obliging pharmacist?'

'He's a decent sort, so don't go suspecting him, and if it's any comfort to you, he always looks dead broke.'

Looks are deceptive, Coffin thought, you don't look like a Porsche owner. Not even a second-hand Porsche owner.

'Out of the city centre, back towards the motorway and you will see the hospital. There are signs.'

'Thank you. By the way, where is your brother's office?'

'Warwick.' As Coffin got to the door, she added deliberately: 'And he has an office in Oxford too.'

'Not called H. Pennyfeather, is he?'

'No,' she said crisply. 'And before you ask again, I do not know anyone called Pennyfeather... What is this with you and Harry Seton? He asked the same question.'

She closed the door firmly behind him.

COFFIN GOT IN HIS CAR, where Augustus at once climbed on to his lap. 'She's a powerful lady, Gus, and I see why she got a question mark from Harry Seton. She gets one from me.' He put the dog on the seat beside him, then started the car. 'What do you make of her, Gus? And Kelso?'

He didn't know what to make of them himself, but he got the scent of group loyalty.

He sat there thinking and he remembered what Tim Kelso had said, or nearly said: It started as a small operation, we were to go in, clear things up and get out, but it hasn't worked out like that.

It really was like a war: you chose a group of people for a particular task, limited, you hoped. There were difficulties and the group were welded together by loyalty. Before you knew it, you had a private army.

The Hospital of St John was easily located on the main road out towards the motorway, just as Leonie had told him. Nor was it difficult to locate Dr James Rexan in his laboratory. Although as he pointed out, Coffin was lucky to find him there.

'I was just leaving. I have a meeting in London tonight.'

'Just a few questions.'

'Ask away,' he said cheerfully, 'but make it quick because I am late already.' He was a tall, muscular young man with a crop of fair hair.

He answered Coffin's questions easily and even fluently. 'My part is simple. I am just a journeyman doing the analysis of suspect drugs. Samples come in to me and I deliver a report. Sometimes the counterfeit medicines are easily identifiable: if tablets, they look wrong; if powder or liquid, then the powder is too coarse or too fine and the liquid the wrong colour. Mostly though, and increasingly so as the counterfeiters get cleverer, I have to do a complete analysis.'

'Do you have much to do with Tim Kelso and Leonie Thrupp?'

He shook his head. 'No, I deliver the reports but not by hand, if very confidential then I send them by messenger, otherwise I usually fax them together with any great thoughts I might have that seem usefull…that's not often, they are the detectives, it's their job to go out and find where the stuff is coming from. Also who makes it,' he added wryly. 'Must be a good chemist as well as good at business. There's money there, has to be.'

'I think so too.'

'And don't look at me like that, I've never felt tempted. I like to be on the legal side of things.' He grinned at Coffin. 'Answering a question you haven't asked.' He had started shovelling papers into his briefcase, battered, as seemed to be the case with most of his possessions from tweed jacket to brown shoes. 'We all knew what Seton was doing up here: looking for the snake making money.'

Still smiling, he said: 'Sorry to be in a hurry, but I must be off. London calls.'

'I'm going that way myself.'

'You can follow me if you like: you ask me questions on your mobile, and I will answer on mine.'

'Doesn't sound a safe way to drive down the motorway.'

'Who said it was?' He led the way out, his interview finished, whatever Coffin had planned.

Hadn't planned anything, Coffin thought as he followed the tall figure out to the hospital car park. Just trying to see what turned up.

Dr Rexan's car was as well used as the rest of his possessions. 'But it goes,' he said, watching Coffin's eyes. 'Look, I had better explain something: my meeting in London is with a doctor at St Thomas's. My child is in there, she has cancer. My wife was killed in a car accident. I was not driving. And what I want to say is: Yes, I could do with money, everything I have goes to and for Chrissy, but if you have a child as sick as that, somehow you want to stay legal. I can't explain, but I do.' He got in his car. 'And if you want to know if anyone offered me money, then the answer is, No.' He started the car. 'But if I wanted it, I would know how to get it.'

Coffin opened his mouth to speak, but the car was already on the move: 'I shall want to speak to you about that statement.'

'Sure...but not now.' A wave of the hand and he was gone.

Coffin walked over to his own car, and got in beside Augustus. 'I am baffled but not beaten, Gus...he is one on his own, that young man.'

He drove out of the car park and headed south. No sight

anywhere of the red car which might or might not be going to London. You couldn't believe all you were told.

But whatever that young man is, Coffin said to the sleeping dog which he was letting lie, he is not a member of the local commandos.

As he drove, he tried to assess what he got out of this trip to Coventry. Not too much, except the strong conviction that Tim Kelso and Leonie Thrupp might not like each other very much, probably did not, but they fought on the same side. Why did he keep thinking of terms of a war?

He didn't see himself coming in as a crusader.

Then as he drove further south, inevitably the Second City and its problems came to the forefront.

First and most painful were the murdered boys. Nothing could be more important than to find the killer. He wondered how Inspector Devlin was getting on.

It was not the only problem of the Second City force: there was an important fraud case, involving mortgages and borrowed money, just coming to the boil, and, in addition, the Home Secretary had just announced his intention of visiting the Chief Commander, taking lunch with him, and viewing the Second City. That had to bode ill.

His mind summoned up a picture of the Home Secretary's well-known face. They had met once and liked each other, or so Coffin thought. There was humour in those dark-brown eyes...if a politician could afford humour, but he doubted if the man had invited himself to lunch just to share a joke.

Could it have anything to do with this drug scam? Surely not. Pharmaceuticals were important, but not that important.

The face of the politician faded, and instead he found himself remembering the dead boys, and he was once again looking in their grave.

BACK IN THE Second City, Inspector Paddy Devlin was consulting anxiously with Chief Superintendent Archie Young. The chief superintendent had been something of a patron to her as she climbed the professional ladder. She knew also that he was a friend of the Chief Commander.

'We will have to tell him,' she said. 'Shall I telephone now? Get him on his mobile?'

'No.' Archie Young was sombre. 'Wait till he gets back.'

FIVE

TWICE THAT DAY on which the Chief Commander had gone off to Coventry, Inspector Devlin had sat in her car in the school car park to watch the school bus first deliver the pupils who travelled on it, and then at the end of the day to pack in the homegoers and drive off.

Each time Sergeant Tony Tittleton had done his part of following behind the bus.

Earlier that day they had interviewed Louie, grandson of Max, known to them both because of his good food, about this story that he had seen Dick Neville going off with a policeman.

No, he had not recognized the man, he was too far away.

Why did he think it was a policeman?

The boy thought, and, perhaps pushed too hard by Devlin, said after a pause that perhaps it was the uniform, or someone might have told him.

'You mean you knew the man?' Just from a back view, said a sceptical voice inside her head.

The boy just shook his head and smiled, and murmured that he looked like a policeman. Perhaps it was the hat.

'And it was Dick Neville with him?'

A vigorous nodding of the head. Yes, he knew Dick.

'Right, thank you,' Inspector Paddy Devlin had said to him and his mother. 'Good boy.'

'He has been helpful?' asked his pretty, anxious mother. 'My father told me I must tell Mr Coffin...he has been such a friend, and his wife, oh, I admire her. And these poor boys, if we could help...' Her voice trailed off.

'Oh yes, very helpful,' Devlin had answered, admitting to herself that she had pushed too hard. 'Let me know if he says anything else.' Well, the uniform had been a help. Who have we got who wears a uniform? There was something interesting about this child, but she could not identify what her feeling was.

'I don't know if we were wasting our time or not,' she said to Tittleton over a drink that evening. 'I just wanted to see how the school run works out.'

'And the driver does have a uniform.'

'Yes.'

'Well, it works just as you'd think it would.' The sergeant chewed on a ham sandwich. 'He collects the kids at two meeting places, drives to the school, and the same in reverse in the evening. He's careful, I noticed that, checks the kids in both times. They seem to like him and trust him.'

'Peter Perry.' Devlin was thoughtful. 'He was one of us, uniformed, never progressed far, but he was popular and liked. And he does wear a uniform.'

'It's a two-man firm, his brother is the other partner and they have two buses and a run-down backup for when a van breaks down, but the brother is a good mechanic so nothing ever does break down. Or not for long. They are not making a fortune between them, but they do various odd weekend trips with football teams and dancers off to a festival and skaters off to a competition. Oh, and he takes a school party off to the ice rink once a week.'

'What do we know about the two Perrys?'

Tittleton shrugged. 'Not very much, I asked around among some of the people who served with him, he was well liked, as I said. Not a great brain but thought to be a decent sort. Both brothers live quiet lives. Peter is a widower, his wife died just about the time he took early retirement, but he has a much younger girlfriend. His brother George is married, lives in apparent peace with his wife.'

'Children?'

'Peter has none, George has three, all grown up and living away from home. He's been away sick, hip operation, so Peter has been carrying the team. I didn't speak to Peter. He knew I was there, though.'

'He hasn't been questioned about the four boys yet, but he must guess he will be...he certainly knew them, they all four used his bus. But let's leave him for a bit. He'll keep.'

There were plenty of other names on her list: four sets of parents, all manifesting grief and anger in different ways, all of whom had to be questioned with care, delicacy and also with a sharp questioning eye.

Because, alas, you never knew.

She ran over the interviews with the four families:

Dr Chinner, whom she knew, and whom she handled with great care; he was in shock.

Mr and Mrs Baker, Sergeant Eddy Baker, CID, Spinnergate, this hobbled her a bit, he was a colleague, but he was going to take leave. Wisest.

Rosy Neville and her partner Andrew Carmichael...he was the boy's father and it appeared a stable relationship. Rosy worked on the catering of the police kitchen at headquarters in Leathergate. Andrew was not working, but as a young actor this not unusual. He might land a job tomorrow...probably would now, he'd be offered something in the latest crime drama. If he could bear to take it.

Sylvia Rick and Phil Rick. A nice family, two other children, they seemed happy but she thought they might shout at each other a bit when alone. The neighbours said so. Phil was a detective constable in Spinnergate.

One way and another they were all connected with the Second City police. That wasn't to say that they all knew each other, but they might have rubbed shoulders.

Also, Spinnergate seemed to come into the story quite a lot. Four children from families with connections with the police and Spinnergate.

You always start with the family, she told herself, but four families? Still, a first short interview had been inflicted on each set of parents, aunts, uncles and grandparents where available.

But she had also made contact with PETS, the ironically names unit set up to list all known paedophiles, with starred references to those known to be violent. She already knew those living in the Second City, but PETS could tell her if any from outside were coming her way.

But she had the feeling that this killer was a home-grown, Second-City product.

Bad old world.

PETER PERRY WAS AWARE that he was being watched. He was unsurprised. 'Would have done the same myself.' He drove with special care since he was being observed. In any case, he was a careful driver, always conscious of his cargo of young hopefuls whom he had long since learned to control with the threat that if they didn't behave they would never get on his bus again and could walk to school. He allowed himself more latitude when he took the weekly late-afternoon trip to the East Hythe swimming pool and ice rink, but he felt this was legitimate since he made a very small charge to what he called 'the lads and lassies', and felt he was off duty. He liked a swim and a sauna himself, and even the occasional twirl on the ice where the skating coach was an old friend. Oliver Deccon's wife was dead, and Perry had heard he hadn't treated her very well: he'd always been out skating or training skaters or judging skaters. His sister, Edie, had known Maggie Deccon, though, and had said she was happy enough with her husband. Peter was so very much older than Edie, they had never been close and he could not claim to understand her. George, the other driver in this coach business, had been more Edie's pal. But then, he wasn't always that close to George, but what he did know was that George was a good driver and a better mechanic. You needed that in this business. He would be glad when George was back.

It was the afternoon, end of the school day run, he achieved it neatly and on time, not even bothering to put his head out and wave to Tony Tittleton following at a remote but steady distance. He had meant to wave, but hell, why bother, the chap probably knew he knew.

He was not followed to the garage where the two coaches were kept, although without doubt, Sergeant Tittleton knew where it was, and might even have had a look round. Not inside though, because Perry, the ex-copper, kept a tight security lock on the place. It was a run down old tin shed of some size which had once housed a small factory, the bins and cupboards lining the walls remained. Not a place of beauty it was more convenient than it looked. At night he removed an essential part of the engine from both coaches which he took home with him, so they could not be stolen, although they could be vandalized. Hence the expensive lock and alarms.

He parked the coach, got out of his uniform, which he hung in the small cloakroom and lavatory before going home. His brother should have been doing the driving tomorrow, they took turn and turn about. As a rule, although George was always shifting days around and sometimes getting more than his free time. Like now, having extra time off because of his hip. It was rotten being the eldest of the family, you got exploited.

He patted his uniform as he hung it up, he felt at home in it, part of his past. It gave him authority too, and a presence. A good one, he hoped.

SERGEANT TONY TITTLETON thought Perry had a good presence too, and his record in the Second City uniformed force had been checked and found straightforward: not a great brain, but no fool and had been commended for bravery when tackling a killer with a knife. Broke the chap's jaw, although stabbed in the arm himself.

None of this would have ruled Peter Perry out as a suspect, although you could call it a good character reference. No one could connect him, except for this story retailed by a small boy of Dick Neville going off with a man who was a policeman.

Inspector and sergeant sat companionably over their drinks. 'I hate this business sometimes,' Paddy Devlin said. 'But at least we have some guidelines to follow, they give us rails to hold on to. So you run your eye over all our local sex offenders, and see how they measure up. None of them so far have looked like killers, but you can never tell…they could change.'

'I have started thinking about our locals. Arthur Willows has always had a touch of violence.'

'Well, check on him.'

'Could be a woman…not likely, I know, but not impossible. We won't know about body fluids and so on until the autopsies are done.'

'I can get on to Bickley, see what he's got. And Big Jim is on the job too, that pair won't miss anything.'

'I'm glad I haven't got any kids,' said Tony. 'They'd have a terrible life with me, I'd probably keep them chained to me as a security measure.'

Paddy Devlin kept silent; she had a much-loved child, a daughter, but the girl had moved out when she went to university and had not come back. She was not lost, she kept in touch with her mother, but at a distance. Her other parent, an academic, lived in America. She did not like her mother's profession, trade, she called it, but her father lectured on English literature so he was pleasantly out of touch with the world. All the same, relations were strained there too.

'Whatever you do, you get it wrong,' he muttered after a while. 'I don't see myself having any kids. My wife's not keen, and I don't see it as fair to inflict pregnancy and childbirth on a woman just to satisfy your own ego.'

'It's a bit more complicated than that…there are pleasures as well.' She didn't know much about Kate, his wife, or about his marriage, but she wouldn't mind betting that sooner or later they would part and then there would be a second Mrs Tittleton.

'She's very ambitious. Good at her job, clever.' Kate was a teacher. 'She teaches history at Queen's Acre.' This was the big, expensive, private school across the river in Blackheath. 'I never took much interest in the past before, but I am learning quite a lot about medieval England. I like the old Anglo-Saxons better though. I think I come from the Anglo-Saxon side. Kate says there weren't many Normans really, most of the country was still full of the English, and that's why we talk English, and not a kind of bastard Norman-French.'

'You went to university yourself.'

'Yes, sure. But I was science and maths...not all that good at either.'

'Have you found them useful in the police?'

'Yeah, I have. A bit, anyway. I can add up, that helps, and I usually know when people are lying. I suppose that's a legacy from being a questioning scientist, putting things to the test...you are supposed to do that.'

'I didn't want to go to the university myself...wanted to go straight into the police. My father was a copper. ''Go in and best them, girl,'' he said to me. ''But get a degree first. It carries weight these days, especially for a woman. Go for the top.'' So I did.'

Tony looked a bit daunted at her words, so she gave him her best smile, one that was, she hoped, friendly and not too alarming.

'My father is a surgeon, and he said, ''Keep away from medicine, you haven't got the mind for it.'' I thought it was cheek, but I guess he was right.'

'You're not too old to try if you want to, Tony.'

'Heaven forbid...here, you're not telling me to hand in my resignation?'

'Of course not. You are doing well.'

'Am I?' A smile lightened his face. 'Good-oh... That's made me feel thirsty.'

Tony got up to get them each another drink, although both were drinking fruit juice, not his favourite tipple, but on the job, especially this job, you kept sober. You couldn't go breathing gin over desperate parents. Or frightened kids to whom something horrible had happened.

As he came back with the drinks, bringing a packet of crisps and some nuts as well, he said: 'What do you make of this kid's story that he saw the Neville lad going off with a policeman?'

'Not a lot at the moment. Louie seemed bright enough, but the person with him at the time...he has a sort of walker, a nice fat woman called Rose, to take him out, they were going shopping, and she didn't see anything, so there's no back-up.'

'You think he's making it up?'

Paddy frowned. 'No, no, I don't think that. But I shall want to talk to him again.' She finished her drink and stood up. 'Well, I'm going back, I have some work to finish. Thanks for the lemonade.'

'It was orange juice.'

'I never had any taste,' she said sadly.

THEY WALKED SLOWLY, side by side, to the police centre in East Hythe where their incident room was placed. Two men, detective constables of equal rank and more or less the same age, were working at computers. At intervals a telephone would ring and be answered tersely. It seemed to make no difference to the world ticking on all around them. Perhaps they were just getting a time-check or the latest football score.

Paddy Devlin stood there looking at them in silence. There they were, her team, and she wasn't sure how well they were going to do with this case.

The sergeant began a quiet conversation with one of the other detectives.

The fax beeped, announcing that it was about to utter. Paddy walked across to read what was coming.

'Oh, hell.'

Sergeant Tittleton saw her reading and grimacing and came across to see. 'What is it?'

'The postmortem report. A joint effort from Bickley and Big Jim. The Neville boy was killed first, Archie Chinner'—she paused—'as we guessed, he was the last killed. The other two, Charles Rick and Matthew Baker, seemed to have been killed soon after they went missing.'

'And whose leg was it?'

Inspector Devlin took a deep breath: 'It wasn't their bloody leg.' She was angry. 'It's a stranger's leg. It did not come from any of the boys.' She looked him in the eyes, still angry. 'It was the leg of an adult female...I suppose we should have been sharp-eyed enough to notice. I didn't, for which I don't praise myself.'

'I don't know about you, but I took a quick look at the first boy's body, just enough to see what it was, and the same with the leg. I knew that pathologists and the forensic boys would do the close work.'

'Thanks for the support.' Paddy Devlin turned aside. 'It wasn't a pretty sight, but it was my job. And I didn't do it.'

Fatigue was making her drive the knife into herself. 'Damn.'

Then she laughed at herself: 'Shut up, Devlin, and stop taking yourself so seriously.' And she turned to the report again.

'The boys were all killed in the same way: strangled. Abused in the same way.'

'Blood?' queried the sergeant, recalling the two blood types on Archie Chinner, the boy's own and one other.

'One set of stains matches the blood on the Chinner boy's clothes.'

'Not that they were his clothes,' put in the sergeant. Thank God, she's got her mind back and working, he thought.

'No, not his clothes. None of the clothes seem to be a match with the dead boy.'

'Stripped and then dressed in anything to hand.'

'Looks like it. And the blood on Chinner, a rare type, does not match any of the boys.'

'From the killer?'

She shrugged. 'Who knows? There may have been more than one person involved.'

'A sort of paedophiles killing party.' He was not joking.

'Do you think invitations were sent out? Yes, I think so: Drop in for a drink and a little light killing. I wonder how the invitations go out: by the post or word of mouth? And how many accept?'

Tittleton was relieved, he liked his boss to be bubbly, energetic and cracking jokes. Not that they were good jokes, still you could get a laugh. But she was given to great dips into gloom. It's the Irish in her, he told himself.

'Got a queue waiting, I expect.'

'Yes, and it's for us to locate that queue and nail the party host.' She spoke the word nail with force as if she was hammering nails into hands, wrists and ankles. She shuffled the file of papers together. 'I think there is a copy of this for you over there on the desk—I asked for two, it's probably come through. Start reading it and see what ideas you get. Then go out on the streets and see the locals. Try Arthur Willows; even if he is in the clear himself, he may have ideas. Get him to utter. And go to the swimming pool, that and the skating rink interest me, people go there for other things than swimming...I fancied Joe Partoni myself, I've put him away once and suggested castration, but he seems to have drowned himself. Maybe it was guilt. He had plenty to feel guilty about, even if not murder. He used to swim a bit. He called it that, anyway. So try the games and leisure centre on Drake Street. See what you can find out. He may have some pals there. You never know.'

'I go there myself,' said Tittleton, hurt.

'Go there for another swim, put on your best bathing trunks and an innocent boyish smile and see what happens to you.'

'I don't think the Chief Commander would like that. Isn't there something called entrapment?'

'I wish I knew where he was, I'd like to speak to him. He can be really helpful on a bad case like this if you catch him at the right moment.'

'He's got some great enquiry on, that's the word.'

'I'd like him here.'

'There's the chief super.'

'Oh, poor Archie is all wound up at the moment, judgement gone.' She did not call him Archie to his face.

'Brings it close,' said Tony.

'It *is* close if the killer is one of us,' the inspector reminded him sharply.

'Yes.' Tony tried to read her face. Did she, didn't she? 'What do you make of that story?'

'I haven't made up my mind. It is one of the things I would like to talk to the Chief Commander about.'

'You never know where you are with children.'

'Children never know where they are with adults,' she said sharply.

Sergeant Tittleton could see his chances of promotion disappearing rapidly. 'I only meant you have to take care with a child's statement,' he blundered on. He could see by his inspector's face that he was not out of trouble, and might even be deeper in. 'Oh damn,' he ended.

To his relief, Paddy Devlin laughed. 'Stop talking and take a deep breath.'

The fax machine spoke again, then began sending out a silent message. The officer working on the computer next to it let his eyes fall on the message coming out.

'Bloody hell.'

Inspector Devlin walked across the room. 'What's this? What's going on?' She could swear herself when she had to; in the macho world in which she lived and had to make her way, it was almost a rite of passage, but otherwise she was a careful speaker. She had discovered that to be prim of speech, with an infrequent and even outrageous obscenity when the occasion demanded, worked well with her masculine colleagues. 'I can do it,' she was saying to them, 'so watch your step.'

She picked up the fax. 'Oh God.' She stared at it, then passed it over to Tony Tittleton, who read it silently, frowned and handed it back.

'There's always a price to pay, isn't there?'

'What does that mean?' she asked with irritation.

'I just meant there is a price to pay for being coppers. And no one knows that more than the Chief Commander, I guess.' It was generally agreed that John Coffin had paid more than once for being what he was: incorruptible but occasionally fallible, but always a survivor. You have to be a great man to make mistakes and come through to success like Coffin's, Tittleton, a natural admirer, proclaimed to anyone who would listen. Tittleton didn't see himself emulating that career, but in spite of his modest words to the inspector, he was young and had hopes. 'I suppose what I mean is that I know Jeff Diver and I can't believe...'

The door opened to let in the tall figure of Archie Young.

His normally cheerful face now looked drawn and harassed. 'I guess you know why I am here, we've both heard the same news.'

'Just this minute, sir,' said Paddy Devlin. 'Just taking it in, trying to assess it.'

'What I came to say'—Archie Young sounded quiet and despondent—'is that we must take this quietly: not jump to conclusions until we know exactly what happened to this officer. Remember, we do not know where he is, and until we find him, in whatever state, we can't make a judgement. In particular, great discretion to the media. I think the local Second-City press and radio and TV stations will handle it that way, can't say about the nationals.'

He paused. 'The Chief Commander is driving home and I have spoken to him on his mobile and asked him to get in touch as soon as he gets back. I will tell him myself.' He had not told Coffin much, just the bare news that a detective constable was missing.

He paused again.

'Mrs Diver had the good sense to come straight to headquarters in Spinnergate, and the officer on duty saw the importance and brought her straight to me.' Another pause. 'She gave me this letter that her husband had left behind when he went.'

He held it out to Paddy. She saw it was a photocopy. All it said was: *I am sorry, so sorry. I could not help myself. I must atone.*

When she had read it, she looked at Archie, who gave a small nod of assent, then she handed it on to her sergeant.

'How long has he been gone?'

'Since yesterday morning. She saw him at breakfast. Found this note in the bedroom, she waited all day, and when she realized he was not coming back, she came to me.'

'Brave of her.'

'A woman with a conscience. She may know more of her husband's life than she is saying yet. It's clear that she thinks the worst.' He had got the impression that she was anxious to keep herself and her daughter well out of trouble. She had been a touch hysterical, to tell the truth, and he hadn't handled her well. 'One daughter,' he said to himself, thoughtfully, wondering if he could think the unthinkable...a daughter could be vulnerable to a lusting father.

He took a deep breath. 'Do either of you know Mrs Diver?'

'No,' said Inspector Devlin at once.

'Yes, I do,' said Tony Tittleton. 'A bit.' He had known Belle Diver before she married Jeff, and had admired her as a natural beauty with good legs.

'Go and see her. She needs someone to talk to. Let it be you.'

To himself, he said: I want the lid kept on until John Coffin gets back. Mrs Diver may be wrong, we may all be wrong, the man may just be having a perfectly straightforward nervous breakdown. I might have one myself any minute.

So what had the Chief Commander said to him on his mobile? 'Archie, don't tell me any more now. I am passing Maidenhead and I will be back with you soon. Tell me then.'

TO HIMSELF, John Coffin thought: My mind is full of Coventry and the people there, from Leonie Thrupp to the young pharmaceutical researcher, and all the time there is the thought of Harry Seton dead.

So I am coming home to the Second City where, so I am informed, the chief suspect in the phoney pharmaceuticals lives, the city which may indeed be the centre for the whole lousy enterprise. It's an old city which has known smuggling, fraud, rape and murder, so why should it not have this honour too?

And there are the dead children for me to think about. Oh, Stella, how could you stay away?

Augustus rose in his seat and looked around, and, as they approached where he lived, he gave small excited barks.

SO SERGEANT TITTLETON set off on his dreaded interview with Mrs Diver, while Inspector Devlin applied herself to the list of

names and pictures and records that had just come through on
the fax from PETS, while morosely running over in her mind
the list of locals. Arthur Willows, the offender that Tittleton
had suggested? She must tell him he had her orders to interview
Arthur Willows after Mrs Diver. From what she remembered
of Arthur, he never went to bed, which, as he lived in an old
tunnel, was understandable, so he and Tony could have a late-
night meeting. Or should she interview Willows herself?

And John Coffin drove home knowing that one of his detective constables had gone missing, leaving a letter that sounded
like a confession.

On one of the quieter stretches of the Spinngergate bypass
system (it circled round a pleasant, for Spinnergate, residential
area), he passed a gang of some half a dozen young boys and
a couple of girls, who were even younger, skateboarding, eyes
down, feet and legs moving smartly.

Dangerous, he thought, they haven't seen me, and tooted his
horn. Augustus joined in and gave a peremptory bark.

But they had seen him.

The country of children has many tribes, but communication
between them all is swift. News, useful information and even
jokes, pass between groups with speed as by osmosis. They
seem absorbed with the air that is breathed in, words are hardly
necessary.

It was a long time since Coffin had been a boy, possibly
owing to the vicissitudes of his childhood he had never been
such as these, and had forgotten that they did not need mobile
phones to be instantly informed about what went on. And
where.

'Back then, he is.' It was a comment from the eldest skater
and not a question.

'Knew he was coming. My mum cleans his office. He's got
the dog with him.'

The group stopped and drew into the kerb, then mounted the
pavement for a silent consultation. The girls were kept on the
edge, but joined in the communion anyway.

After a while, they resumed skating.

The burden of their silent agreement was that They Knew what He did not Know. Or seemed not to know, you always had to remember that sometimes the grown-up world knew more than you thought. This time though, they thought he was in trouble.

There was no agreement to tell him more yet. They valued their own security and it might be dangerous to talk until they saw what would happen.

They had done all they could for the moment. They knew the limitations on the power of their tribe.

Skate on.

COFFIN TOO THOUGHT he was in trouble. Or knew he had troubles.

Oh yes, and when he got into his office to read all the reports, he learnt for the first time that the Second City had the left leg of an unknown young female.

Another body to be found, another identity to be established, another death to investigate. His cup of joy was full.

Archie Young was there in his office, waiting for him, anxious to talk it over. So there was no getting away from it all.

His telephone rang while they were still looking at each other.

'Hello, there you are at last.' It was Inspector Larry Davenport, from London where he was busy with the death of Harry Seton; he was alert and cheerful. 'Been trying to get you all day.'

'I've been out of the office.'

'Gathered that. Any progress on your side of things?' His tone implied that he knew all about Coffin's task of enquiry.

Coffin was vague. 'Coming on.'

'I just thought you would like to know that we now know that Harry was over your side of the Thames twice in the last week of his life. Visiting, we know not where as yet. If and when we flush up a name or street where he was visiting we will be asking you for help.'

'Thanks for telling me,' said Coffin, not sure whether to be pleased or not. But he had known from the beginning that the Second City came into it somewhere. It was why he had been pressed into service.

Pressed was the word, he thought. Wasn't there a medieval technique for wringing the truth out of a suspect. Ordeal peine forte et dure…

'I suppose you don't happen to have a dead female, not too old, with a missing leg, where you are? We seem to have one to spare.'

He met Archie Young's disapproving stare, he did not want this news discussed with Davenport.

'We do, as a matter of fact. Don't think it would do much good to you, though.'

'Try me.' How splendid if they could tie two cases together.

'She's old, very old. Dug up out of the Thames mud. She's kind of mummified, and the general view is she might have been there for a thousand years.'

Coffin put the telephone down and returned to Archie Young. 'Sorry, Archie. I think I am what Stella calls overwrought.'

Doing too much, decided the chief superintendent, he always does. He admired Coffin for being hard-working, overworking.

'Well, come on, Archie, tell me. Fill me in, as they say. All I know at the moment is that Max's grandson, little Louie, fingered a policeman as the pederast and killer. And that a detective constable, stationed in Spinnergate, has disappeared. You did say Spinnergate?'

'That's about it, sir.' It pleased Archie to remind Coffin of rank occasionally. 'He left a note, a very short one. Here is a copy.'

Coffin read it.

I am sorry, so sorry. I could not help myself. I must atone.

'We are looking for him, of course,' said the chief superintendent. 'No traces so far.'

'What is known about Diver?'

'His inspector at Merrywell Substation says he was a decent sort and is surprised. Can't believe he is the killer of the boys.

Sergeant Tittleton, who knows the man, has called on Mrs
Diver.'

'I will want to talk to him…'

'He is waiting. I asked him to hang around.' He was probably
drinking tea in the canteen. 'Inspector Devlin is carrying on
checking other suspects. One Arthur Willows.'

Coffin nodded. The name of Willows had got through to him.
'I'll leave her to tackle Willows and Co. She's a capable
woman. Anything else I ought to know, Archie? You look as
though there is.'

With some reluctance, Archie Young said: 'I looked at his
record. Diver only transferred to CID about a year ago, before
that he was in uniform. One of his jobs was to go round the
schools in Spinngergate… So Louie may have seen him.'

Coffin looked towards the window where the light was fad-
ing from the sky. Distantly, he thought he heard the roll of
drums, the rattle of the tumbrils, the fall of the guillotine and
then the footsteps of a headless Diver staggering towards him.

No one knew better than he did that there is more than one
way of lopping off a policeman's head. He had had his chopped
off more than once, the trick was to learn to grow it again.

Then he had another look at the head and saw it was not
Diver, whose face he did not know anyway, but Harry Seton's.

Hell and hell again.

SIX

'YES, SIR,' said Sergeant Tittleton, meeting Coffin's eye with his practised innocent gaze which came in so useful when encountering his superiors of high rank. (Not such as Paddy Devlin, who would have sharply ordered him to smarten up.) 'I have been to talk to the boy Louie again. I had been there with Inspector Devlin earlier, then I remembered Diver had been on the school visits. I did a bit of that myself early on, and we had a talk about it one day.'

They were in Coffin's own office; the outer one, where Paul Masters held sway, was now empty as night came on. Tittleton, who had made an arrangement with a friend while sitting in the canteen that they would go out together for a drink, was relaxed about talking to the Chief Commander himself, but uneasily aware that DC Amanda Harden would not wait around. Also, his wife was at home, cooking the evening meal, so he could not be too late. He hoped the Big Man would get this over fast, but work and promotion prospects had to come first, and Amanda would have to lump it. And if she waited, then it would show she was keen, and that in itself was worthy of a thought.

'He was a friend was he? Close?'

'Not close, sir, but we got on.' Tittleton was quietly observing the room; he had never been here before and might never be again. It was tidy enough but there were papers heaped everywhere on the desk. No flowers, but a photograph of a beautiful woman with a cat: he recognized Stella Pinero. A computer and several telephones.

'Common interests?' Coffin was not sure why he asked that question, but he noticed it got a reaction.

'No, not really, sir, it's as I said: we just got on.'

Coffin nodded, wondering exactly what that meant, picking up a note of caution, but he didn't press it. Other things were more important.

'And when I remembered, I thought that Louie might have seen Diver at school and recognized him. And it was partly something Mrs Diver said that sent me round.' He looked at Coffin questioningly.

'Tell me that later. Get on with Louie.'

'So I went along to talk to him.' It seemed necessary to say something else. 'Inspector Devlin was going after Arthur Willows, sir, but she fancied Joe Partoni more. You remember him, sir? A monster, really, although he has been quiet lately, so she was going after Joe too. Just his style she says, but I don't know, he's never killed before. Might have fancied to, think he has, but never done it, might have acted it out in front of a mirror, enjoyed himself that way.'

'I thought he was dead, drowned.'

'Oh yes, but she thought he might have done the killings then drowned himself. Conscience, fear of getting caught. She's been working on it... Anyway, when this news about Diver burst in on us, and it did burst, sir...'

'I can imagine,' said Coffin dryly.

'The chief superintendent told me to go to see Mrs Diver, and then I went to see the boy Louie. I wanted to get clear in my mind what he might have seen.'

'Right. So you went to see Louie Damant—that's his name?'

'Yes, sir. I know Mrs Damant a bit...used to see her in the café.' He gave Coffin a cautious look.

He got around, Coffin thought, realizing that he was a good-looking, lively youngster. Married, but that might not control the hormones. And Louie's mother was the one they called the Beauty daughter.

'She was there, of course, when I spoke to Louie and I took PC Harden with me as well.'

'That was wise.'

'I thought so, sir. In the circumstances.' And, of course, he had a fancy for Mandy Harden, and rather hoped he was inspiring one in her. There had been one encounter already.

He met Coffin's ironic blue eyes, which decided him to forget hopes of his love life in case it got across to the Chief Commander. He'd only be guessing, of course, but one had heard he was phenomenally well informed.

The sergeant was remembering his visit to the Diver house. One of a row of six, each small, well-kept residences, which lay within easy walking distance of a few shops: a baker's, a butcher's and an old-fashioned chemist's shop, gleaming with great red, green and yellow bottles which he thought charming. Unusual too, not so many about in the Second City. In fact, it was probably the only one, a survivor from the past. Except that he noted it was trim, newly painted and looked prosperous.

'I wanted to find out if Louie knew Diver from a school visit.'

'It would have been some time ago, wouldn't it?'

'Yes. But he would remember, I thought. Or anyway, if he had said so clearly that would have been something... But I didn't want to push. So all I said was had he seen the man before? Perhaps at school.'

Coffin waited.

'Inspector Devlin had spoken to him before, and she felt she had taken him seriously, but with caution. Knowing that Jeff Diver had gone missing, she felt perhaps I could get more. I am not sure if I did, sir. Louie hung on to what he had said. As far as I could tell, he repeated it word for word... I can remember hanging on to a story as a kid, and when I did, the more unsure of what I was saying, the more I clung to the word-for-word technique.'

'You mean he was lying?'

'No, I am not saying that, but I don't think he's as sure as he sounded. He's still young, very young, I reckon he is anxious to oblige, to say what is expected of him. But that doesn't mean it is not true. DC Harden had the same feeling, sir.' He gave Coffin what was almost a pleading look. 'I may just have muddied the waters.'

'So now tell me about Mrs Diver, and in particular, what she said to you that sent you off to churn up the water.'

This prolonged interview with the admired, much-feared Chief Commander was proving a strain to Tony Tittleton. He felt that if at this point he could quote something wise and strong from a poet or a philosopher, as had sometimes happened to a policeman in some of the detective stories he read when staying with his mother, if he could have done this then he would have been strengthened. But alas, as a schoolboy he had liked football (never rugger), swimming and pop. Reading of any sort had come well down the line. As indeed had education of any sort. You might say he had been educated in spite of himself.

He hesitated.

'Think for a minute,' said Coffin kindly. That is, he meant it kindly, but a suggestion like that is always unnerving.

The sergeant thought: Mrs Diver had met him at the door without surprise.

'Thought you'd be round. I'm glad it's you, Tony. You know him.'

He had nodded, no comment.

'We haven't seen you for some time.' She had looked towards the window, he noticed her eyes were puffy and red, with crying, he had thought. 'I'm glad you didn't come in a car, flashing with lights, I don't want the neighbours wondering too much... It'll come, of course.' Her tone had been savage. 'You're looking for him, I hope.' It wasn't a question.

'No news yet, I'm afraid.' He had sought for her name and ended lamely, 'Belle.'

'I've been out looking myself...places he went to like the library and the sports centre...no sign, no news.'

'I'm sure he'll be back,' Tony had said, admitting to himself that he was far from sure.

'Yes, that's what your Chief Superintendent Young said, and he didn't sound as if he meant it, either. And before you ask, I'll tell you what I told him: my husband should never have written that letter, he never would have done if he had thought what it would mean to me—he was having a nervous break-down.'

'What makes you say that?'

'Not sleeping, talking in his sleep, going off like that.'

'Had he asked for help?'

'This is asking for help,' Belle Diver said fiercely.

'Yes,' said Tony. 'I reckon it is.' One way and another it was, probably. 'But what was he asking for help about?'

'He may have heard what that little liar said about seeing a policeman with the Neville boy.'

Tony Tittleton looked at John Coffin. 'I didn't answer her there, but she looked at me and said everyone knew what was being said and did I think Louie's mother was keeping quiet even if we were... Inspector Devlin had said to keep quiet till we knew more.'

'So then you went to see Louie?'

'Yes, sir, and really got nowhere much.' Then he said: 'Belle Diver had just come in from somewhere, just walking around looking for her husband, I guess. Her coat was thrown over a chair, it had been raining a bit and the coat was wet and so was her hair. She said she'd been to talk to his friend Martin at the swimming pool... I don't know why, but I didn't believe her. There was something...' He shook his head. 'She knows something, sir, that she isn't telling us. Or not me. Inspector Devlin will be seeing her, of course, but Mrs Diver wants to see top brass. She said she went to headquarters to report her husband missing and show his letter, and she wants someone who will understand.'

'What does she mean by that?'

'I don't know, sir. She wasn't going to say more to me, that was clear.'

Coffin remembered what Archie Young had said when he telephoned: I saw the wife, and I didn't handle her well, she started to cry.

'Maybe she would tell you.'

Or perhaps you could get it out of her, you're well known for being able to do that.

'She was beginning to cry.' Then he added slowly: 'I think she was putting it on, sir. I've got a sister, and I've seen her do it, and I recognized it.'

'What about DC Harden, what did she make of it?'

'She didn't get much chance, sir. Mrs Diver wouldn't let her stay in the room...she had to watch from the hall through an open door.' Amanda Harden hadn't liked that very much. As they left, Belle had called out: 'I don't want to see another one of you today. And if you see any of those kids skateboarding outside here, tell them to go away too.'

There were none, as it happened, but Amanda picked up a woollen glove that she said might have been worn by one. She put it on the garden wall before giving as her opinion that Belle Diver was on the edge of a breakdown, or perhaps break-up might be a better word, as it was going to be explosive, and she for one did not blame her. But they got out before the storm burst.

'You are beginning to give me a very clear picture of Belle Diver. Thank you.'

Tony Tittleton considered and then said: 'I shouldn't like to leave her alone with Louie.'

Coffin was startled. 'I hope I don't understand what you are saying. She knows that Louie told the story about seeing one of the missing boys with a policeman? Do you see her as a threat to him?'

'She's bitter, sir. There's been a lot of gossip, I think she minds that a lot. Word gets around...after all...' He paused again. 'Diver himself knew what was being said.' As did almost everyone, he thought to himself. Who doesn't know by now? Spinnergate could be a village. For instance, I know that your madam, the lovely Stella, has gone to Los Angeles to have her face lifted. And how do I know that? Because Mimsie Marker selling newspapers outside Spinnergate tube station told my wife when she was having her hair washed. And dyed. There is something about a darker shade of red that loosens the tongue. He looked at Coffin and smiled: Of course, the Chief doesn't know what I am thinking.

Coffin saw the smile: What's that young devil laughing at?

'I'll go and see Mrs Diver.'

Tony hesitated. 'I don't think she wants to see anyone else tonight.'

'She may have to.'

Better you than me, sir, Tittleton said to himself, because if Amanda is right you will come in for the explosion. The tears I saw might have been phoney, but that doesn't mean the emotion isn't there.

'Does this mean we give up on the bus driver and the others, sir?'

'No.' Coffin was decided. 'Keep after the lot.'

'Right, sir.'

SOONER THAN HE EXPECTED, he was on the corridor walking into the canteen where Mandy still sat. 'I'm not sure I handled that too well,' he told her. 'I talked too much…too wordy.'

'Stop talking about yourself, and start thinking about me. The Crown tonight? It does a good chicken in a basket, or we could go to the Boozy Arms.' The Boozy Arms was called after Charles Dickens who had had the pseudonym Boz. The Boozy part was a Cockney corruption of Boz.

'Everyone'll be there,' complained Tittleton with some truth, for the Boozy Arms was popular with CID and Uniformed alike. 'I can eat chicken at home.' His wife was cooking it.

'You can ignore them and concentrate on me.'

'I heard there was always a dog,' Tony said absently. 'I didn't see a dog.'

Augustus, dog in chief, and, if the arrangement was left with him, only and forever sole dog, was at home in the tower of the old and now secularized St Luke's Church. Coffin with Stella lived in the tower, which was now a pleasant if unusual home, while the rest of the church was subsumed into the theatre. There were now three theatres on the site: on the old church, and two smaller ones, Max also had a restaurant there.

WHEN COFFIN GOT BACK, his mind still divided between Harry Seton dead in London and the dead boys in Spinnergate, he heard Augustus barking.

His excited bark, a crescendo of little yelps with a high whine at intervals.

Coffin's first thought was burglars, but no, Gus was happy, not frightened or aggressive. Then he noticed a smart leather travelling bag from Vuitton and got a whiff of l'Heure Bleu. Then he was leaping up the stairs.

'Stella, you're back.'

She came forward, tall, beautifully dressed in something pale and suede (new, too, he was rational enough to notice, almost certainly expensive in New York). She kissed him, with delicate precision, on the cheek.

'You came up those stairs like a rocket.'

'Didn't know I had it in me,' he said, panting. He put his arms round her and kissed her back with more energy. 'Come on, no more stage kisses.'

Stella laughed. 'You noticed?'

''Course I bloody noticed. Just let me get my breath back.'

A bottle of rye whisky, Southern Comfort, her usual transatlantic present, was on the table, together with a small gilt packet.

'I'm only home for a few days, break in the schedule, and I am utterly broke.'

Augustus was leaping up and down with pleasure, in his mouth was his present: a chocolate-covered bone.

'It's called Chocobone,' Stella said. 'I don't know whether they eat it or bury it.'

Coffin was unobtrusively studying her face. It looked the same. So had she not been 'fixed'? And if she had, would it be wrong to ask.

'You look lovely, dearest,' he said, taking the easy option.

'I'm still swithering about having the face job—it is expensive.'

'So it is,' he said happily.

'But I could claim it on expenses for the tax man, that is the best of being an actress, he'd accept that, and there's no denying you photograph better with a less decided nose than mine.' She was studying her face in the big looking glass on the wall. 'Do you think I have an aggressive nose?'

'No, dearest Stella, occasionally your tongue is sharp and your temper can flare, but your nose gives me no trouble at all: a very good nose.'

'Thank you for that vote of confidence in my nose.'

'And now, Stella, tell me why you really came home?'

The phone rang; Coffin considered not answering it while he looked at Stella.

'I was missing you terribly. I just wanted to see you.' Her voice was soft.

'That's a lovely answer, Stella, and almost makes me leave that phone ringing. But I can't, there's too much going on here at the moment.'

He began to move towards the telephone.

'No, let me,' said Stella. She stretched out an arm. 'Hello... Oh, of course...' She offered the telephone to Coffin. 'It's a woman, she wouldn't give her name, but she wants to talk to you, must do, she said.'

Her voice was husky and controlled, my best drawing-room-comedy voice, she called it.

Coffin gave her a cautious look—Somerset Maugham and Noel Coward, with a touch of Lady Macbeth, he thought as he took the telephone from her. Or wasn't there some Greek queen who specialized in killing husbands? Skinning them first, probably.

'This is Margaret Grayle,' announced a voice, not as soft or carefully produced as Stella's, but just as clear and well modulated. A woman of education. But with just a hint of something rougher behind. It was interesting how certain tones always came through. Even darling Stella, who was always reserved about where she came from, sometimes let a hint of her native Dundee slip through. The past was always with you.

'I've heard you were looking for me?'

'Who told you that?'

'These things get around.'

'I do want to see you, Ms Grayle. I am planning to come to Oxford.'

'That's good, because I want to see you. There's something you ought to know.'

'What is it?' Out of the corner of his eye he could see Stella was watching him. She was stroking Augustus and listening to him.

'Not now, not on the telephone. Tomorrow I shall be in the Station Hotel in Oxford at one o'clock. Join me there.'

'How shall I know you?'

'I will know you.'

The telephone was put down. He knew he could get the number, but it was probably a public call box. Or in the hotel she had named. The Station Hotel? He ought to find that easily enough.

Stella watched him gravely but said nothing.

He returned to her side. 'A case.'

'You didn't look too pleased.'

He shrugged, not wanting to talk about it.

'I know I can't help,' said Stella.

'You don't usually want to,' he said, surprised.

'Well, that's true.'

'There is something you could do. If you really mean it.'

'I do, I do.'

'I have to see the wife of a man who is missing, who may be a suspect in a murder case.'

'You are talking about the dead boys?'

'You know about it?'

'I was across the Atlantic, John, not on the moon… Anyway, I read the London papers on the flight back.'

'If you would, I'd be glad if you came with me.'

'You think she will faint or something?'

'Or something.' He looked at Stella, a pale suede suit made in Italy, bought, possibly, in Bergdorf Goodman's, was not the best thing to wear when encountering a woman whose husband might be a pederast and multiple murderer.

Stella read his mind with her usual skill. 'I will just change into jeans and a sweater. And when I come back, I'd like a few more details about this case and that one…' There was a delicate emphasis on the last reference. Coffin guessed she meant the woman caller. 'Nothing confidential, of course, I wouldn't expect that'—a touch of heavier irony than Stella usually allowed herself here—'but enough so that I know where not to put my foot.'

'Right. Glad to, it'll give me a chance to think things through.'

Stella gave him a loving, sceptical look as she sped up the stairs to her dressing room. Coffin called it the bedroom, but as Stella's clothes filled a wall cupboard whereas his were exiled to an attic room, Stella was not without justification. But it was good for him, he accepted, working in his macho world, to find himself and his clothes skyed.

Stella reappeared in jeans that did her legs justice, but were still suede, and with a heavy cashmere sweater—Italian again, he guessed.

'I'll talk as I drive… You know this because you've read your newspapers on Concorde.' He gave her a sideways look.

'It wasn't Concorde.'

'From your reading,' he went on, only half believing her. If the film company was paying, then it was Concorde. 'You will know that four boys, much of an age, have disappeared over the last two months. The last boy to disappear was found first…or his body was: Archie Chinner, son of a police surgeon. Also the godson of Archie Young.'

'I wondered about that…the name.'

'Yes. Archie is very, very cut up, so he is keeping his distance on this one. Inspector Paddy Devlin and a lively young spark, Tony Tittleton, are handling it. Paddy is experienced in pederasts and similar cases…she's handled plenty over the past few years, unhappily.'

'I have met her, I think. Tall, handsome rather than pretty. Very strong minded…needs to be in your lot.'

'Thanks,' he said dryly. 'Devlin manages very well, she's

going up the ladder fast, but this case is important for her. For all of us: we have to catch this killer. I saw the first grave, and a few days later I saw the three other bodies crammed together. Monstrous, I want that monster.'

They stopped at the traffic lights.

'Seems funny to be in the car without the dog. What have you done with him?'

'I shut him in the kitchen.'

'He'll hate that.'

'He couldn't come on this visit. What you don't know, because we kept it quiet, was that Max's grandson, Louie, claims he saw the first boy to go missing walking off with a policeman.'

'Ah.'

'And today, a woman, Belle Diver, reported her husband, DC Diver, was missing. He had left behind a note, apparently, claiming guilt for something nameless... She went straight to Archie Young because she wanted top brass...her phrase. That's me.'

He had turned the corner into the quiet street, still peaceful, he was glad to see, although he knew the discreet white van parked down the road was a police van, keeping surveillance on the Diver house.

'And I wanted a woman with me.'

'You think I will cheer her up?'

'You'll cheer me up,' said her husband. 'Also, if I don't go in with a policewoman she won't think I'm going to take her in for a thorough questioning.'

'And you won't be doing that?'

'Later, yes. Have to. Devlin will. But not tonight.'

'Belle Diver,' said Stella with a frown. 'I think I remember her, she had a job in the theatre... No, not the theatre, for Max, helped in the restaurant. Pretty woman.'

'Is she?' said Coffin absently.

He parked the car under a tree. A cat was sitting under it too, looking at them as if they were of some remote interest.

'Wait a minute,' said Stella. 'What's this other case, the one that is taking you to Oxford tomorrow? Oh, don't worry, I just heard that word.'

'Oh, that's something completely different.' Or so he hoped. The most ill-disposed of deities surely could not make the two cases run together. 'London-based. You won't remember Ed Saxon, but it's a do of his.' And Harry Seton, but he was dead.

'I think I'll come to Oxford with you. After all, I did come home to see you.'

The peace of the street was broken by a posse of skateboarders and rollerbladers skimming fast along the pavement, some six of them.

'That's a dangerous sport,' said Stella, 'and shouldn't they be home and in bed?'

'It's not that late.' Coffin was getting out of the car. A couple of the skaters looked bigger and older than the others. There was even one girl. 'And kids never go to bed these days, hadn't you noticed?'

He led the way up the garden path, observing that someone did some gardening here, weeding and planting out. 'There's a kid here, a daughter, I don't know if she'll be here or in bed, as you advise.'

THE SKATEBOARDERS had paused for a rest round the bend in the road. It would soon be dispersal time, because in spite of what the Chief Commander had said, rules were laid down by parents, some of which were obeyed. Skateboarding was an expensive business if you did it right with the best equipment: for this expenditure willing parents were required.

They circled the white van, twice, wordlessly, then sped away.

COFFIN RAPPED on the door while pressing the bell with his other hand. 'Just making sure,' he said to Stella.

'I think she'll have heard that. Of course, you could shout as well.'

He rang the bell again.

'She may not be there,' said Stella, hopefully. She had had enough of this jaunt already.

But presently they both heard the soft slur of footsteps.

'Wearing slippers,' said Coffin.

'Barefoot,' corrected Stella. Long years on the stage had taught her something about the sound of footsteps.

The door opened and there was Belle Diver, wrapped in a towelling robe, her eyes unfocused.

Drunk or drugs, Coffin thought, possibly both.

'Sorry,' Belle said. 'Sorry, had a bath, took a moggy.'

And she doesn't mean a cat, Coffin told himself. 'I'd like to talk; I was told you wanted to talk to me.'

'Know who you are,' said Belle, squinting at him as she tried to focus her eyes. She turned to Stella. 'You too, Miss Pinero. Saw you on the telly the other day.'

She stood aside to let them in. 'Think the papers are on to me...phone call from a strange voice...asked to speak to Jeff. I said he was out. I think it was a journalist.' She had difficulty getting the word journalist out.

'Is there anywhere you can go?' Coffin asked gently.

'My mother...already taken my daughter there.'

She had led them into a brightly painted sitting room with red poppies on the walls and poppies on the curtains and chairs. Oddly enough, the room did not look unpleasing, it was cheerful and homely. Not much had been spent, but it had been used with love. Coffin noticed a photograph of a young girl sitting on the grass holding a puppy.

Belle saw him looking. 'That's my daughter...the dog's gone with her.'

Stella saw that something was needed from her. 'A pretty girl.' But then her mother was a pretty woman, even flushed and untidy.

'Thank God it's been boys he's been after and not girls,' said Belle.

'You don't know yet.' Coffin was careful. 'Can't be sure.'

'I've known something was wrong for a long while, wondered, worried…well, I know now…' She took a deep breath, seeming to steady down. 'I've got something to show you.'

She went to the small table in the window, opened a drawer and drew out a couple of photographs. 'Here.'

Coffin looked at them. Two largish photographs, taken, he judged, with a camera with remote control.

Two men, naked, on a bed, arms around each other. One man had his back to the camera while the other faced it. In the second photograph, the positions were reversed. Coffin had no difficulty recognizing Jeff Diver.

'Where did you find these?'

'He left 'em around. In the kitchen. Reckon he wanted me to find them…at least he's not with one of those lads.'

'No. Do you know the man?'

After a pause, she shook her head.

'I'll have to keep these.'

'I don't want them back. And if I do miss them, I daresay I might find others about the place. Could be videos too, for all I know.'

Suddenly, she was crying and shaking. 'Don't let her see them.'

Coffin heard Stella move from where she had been standing by the window. She put her arms round the woman. 'Come and sit down. Belle, I am not here as a witness, just as a woman to help you. I remember you from the days when you worked for Max.'

Belle said through her tears, 'I enjoyed it, but I gave it up when the child came.'

'Well, you can go back when you want to. But what you need now is sleep. Those moggies you took need sleeping off. Come on, I'll help you to bed.' She started to walk Belle upstairs. Over her shoulder she gave Coffin a long look. 'Keep quiet and stay where you are.'

With Belle leaning on Stella, the two went upstairs, Belle muzzily uttering words that sounded like 'thank you' and 'ever so kind'.

Coffin heard footsteps above, a short period of silence, then true to her word, Stella was back.

'Bed's the best place for her,' she said. 'She'll sleep it off. I think she'd had some vodka as well as the sleeping tablets. I don't know what she'll be like in the morning.'

'As long as she wakes up,' said Coffin, somewhat alarmed.

'Oh, she will.' Stella was experienced in helping drunken and drugged young performers, distraught because the performance had gone badly, off to bed.

'Thanks, Stella.'

'I didn't think you wanted me just to make her a cup of tea.'

'No, you did what was right.'

'Someone ought to come and see her in the morning.'

'Oh, they will,' Coffin promised. 'Devlin will have to go over the house, search everything. If he did kill the boys...'

'What did you make of those photographs? I did see them, of course, I could see what they were as she handed them across.'

'What they are is obvious, much less obvious is if Jeff Diver had any connection with the boys. But I think he may have known something.'

'Lock the door carefully. Belle was anxious about that.'

Coffin closed the door and tested it. 'Best I can do.' Then he led the way to the car.

In the car, he sat looking up at the house. Tomorrow, the whole place would be gone over; for Belle Diver it would never be the same again. Let her have this night of rest.

'You did the right thing,' he said again to Stella.

He looked at her fondly. 'And why did you come back?'

'I told you, darling. I wanted to see you. I missed you.'

He drove on, turning into the road that led home. 'Stella, you are an actress, but always remember, I am a detective.'

'Well, the truth is, I wanted to see what my old nose looked like in my own environment before I had it altered. Check, you know. You lose perspective away from home.'

Thoughtfully, Coffin said: 'That's a better excuse than the first one, I give you that, my love. But still not quite good enough.'

SEVEN

IN THE MORNING, while Stella took the dog for a walk, Coffin had a talk with the investigating team, Inspector Devlin, Sergeant Tittleton, and DC Amanda Harden, who was looking as attractive, well turned out and well bred as her name suggested. A woman Chief Commander in the making, Coffin told himself, and saw that Paddy Devlin felt the same. Was there a hint of rivalry brewing there?

Chief Superintendent Archie Young joined them, as one having a watching brief.

Coffin nodded at Inspector Devlin. 'Go ahead.' He knew he could get to Oxford in just over an hour, even if Stella and Augustus insisted on joining him.

'First of all, there have been no sightings so far of Jeff Diver. We do not know where he is. I had another session with his wife earlier today.' Devlin paused. It had been very early and Belle Diver had come to the door in her dressing gown. Sober and controlled, though. 'She says she has no idea where he is and I believe her. We are looking, of course.'

'He'll turn up in the end.'

'Dead or alive... Sounded like a suicide note to me...'

'He could be in the river,' said Archie Young.

'One of my suspects was there,' said Devlin. 'Joe Partoni drowned. I am still thinking of him as the killer... Big Jim Matherson, from the Royal Infirmary, says suicide is almost certain. Partoni could just have done the killings but it depends on the estimate of the deaths of the boys. When they died. All a bit iffy at the moment.'

'Let's rule him out for the time being, unless something turns up that ties him in.'

'One problem is resolved: the boys' clothes. You remember

the Chinner lad was wearing clothes not his own, this was the case with all four. It seemed likely'—Devlin took a deep breath—'all the boys had been stripped and then dressed later, when dead, in any pair of jeans and shirt that came to hand. Either the killer didn't know or more likely didn't care which clothes the body got. After forensics had finished with them, and they were quick and thorough, sir, we asked the parents to view them and all could identify a couple of garments. There seem to be a couple of sweaters and a shirt that no one owns to.'

'Does that mean another dead boy we don't know about?' asked Coffin.

Paddy Devlin shrugged. 'I hope not. And I don't think so. There is always a problem left unanswered. The killer provided himself with spare clothes, no doubt.'

'Might be a boy that got away,' said Sergeant Tittleton.

Devlin shrugged again. 'Nothing has been reported.'

'Not always reported.' This was Archie Young's sharp contribution to the discussion. 'We know that.'

'True, sir.' Devlin turned towards him. 'I am bearing it in mind.'

'Seems odd,' said DC Harden, 'that the boys should be dressed when dead.'

Devlin said that there was no accounting for everything that a bloody pervert would do.

'Forensics any good on where the clothes had been kept... they had to have been stored somewhere?' Coffin asked.

'Somewhere very clean was all they offered, hardly any traces. They think they might have been washed, sir, just given a bit of a tumble dry as well.'

'Nearly everyone has a washing machine.'

'It's something for us to think about further, sir. Of course, there was blood on the Chinner lad's clothes.' She was careful not to look at Archie Young. 'His clothes had not been washed. Might not have been convenient.'

Nasty housekeeping evoked here, thought Coffin.

'And the blood?'

'Some from the boy himself, some from one other person. I am guessing the other set of bloody traces was from the killer.'

'And the leg? Anything there?'

'Nothing, I am afraid. The truth is, I don't know where to look. I made investigations at the hospitals, thought it might be a medical specimen, but no one admits to losing it.'

'Would they admit?'

'I think the days of medical students playing that sort of joke are over,' said Paddy Devlin. 'If they ever existed. Everyone is so serious now.'

'Think urban foxes,' said Coffin, remembering what had been said about the limbs of the dead Harry Seton.

He looked around him: he had silenced the room.

IN THE CAR, some time later, there was silence too, even though Stella was sitting beside him and Gus was lolling on the back window ledge enjoying the view. Both were experienced, quiet travellers and although both had a tendency to say that they simply must get out of the car for a minute—the one to admire the view, and the other for more practical doggy purposes— today both sat still.

As he drove, Coffin ran through a list of names: Tim Kelso he had seen and reserved judgement on; he was off to Wessex to see Peter Chard (who did not, as yet, know it) and Margaret Grayle, who did; ahead of him in the days to come were interviews with Joe Weir in Newcastle, and Felicity Fox in Cambridge. There was also Susy Miller who 'floated around', she would be obliged to float his way. All of these were almost certainly already alerted and waiting for him. Harry Seton passed their way, now it was Coffin's turn.

Down Headington Hill, over Magdalen Bridge, and through the High.

If these spires are dreaming, thought Coffin, they must find their sleep disturbed by the roar of traffic and the smell of diesel. A quiet university set now in an industrial belt, Oxford had nothing on Warwick, both were inheritors of the motor car, one in Cowley and the other in Coventry.

'We have just passed the park-and-drive car park,' said Coffin, 'but I have made arrangements to put the car in the official police car park just beyond Christ Church, then I will walk to my appointment. You and Augustus can amuse yourselves in the city. I don't think the colleges let dogs in.'

'You seem to know your way around,' said Stella, getting out of the car with Augustus in her arms.

'I had a case here once, a long while ago, but I have never forgotten it.'

'I was in a Shakespeare at the old Playhouse in Beaumont Street,' said Stella. 'Loved it. I had lodgings up the Iffley Road and I used to go for breakfast at Ma Brown's in the market... I expect that's gone, it was a long time ago.'

'Still be somewhere to eat in the market, I expect. I don't know about Gus, though.'

'Oh, the two of us will manage. We might go to look up old friends.'

'Have you got any?' said Coffin in surprise.

'Oh, I expect so, they were all students in those days, but I should think they will be fellows or even heads of colleges now. You may have to come looking for me.'

'You had better tell me which colleges to try first.'

'Oh, I will leave a message on your mobile... you have got it with you?'

'Yes.' He was not sure how to handle Stella when she was in this mood. 'If I don't hear I will look for you in the University Parks on one of those benches near the gate.'

Stella considered. 'Or we could come down to the Station Hotel and sit while you interview your lady.'

'I would rather you did not.'

'Only teasing,' she said coolly.

THE STATION HOTEL was within walking distance and Coffin wanted the walk. He needed to think, to reorient his mind away from the murders in the Second City to finding out who was the traitor for pay in the pharmaceutical unit. Another murder there too, sitting like a stone at the back of his mind: Harry Seton had been killed.

The lounge of the hotel was empty except for an old man sitting in one corner drinking sherry and reading *The Times*. Coffin ordered a drink for himself while he waited.

'I am not doing very well with this pharmaceutical business,' he told himself. 'Nothing as yet is clear. Well, let's see how it goes today.'

He was looking at the door as a tall, curly-haired woman in a very short, dark-blue skirt and a bright tweed jacket walked in. Coffin had lived with Stella long enough to know expensive clothes when he saw them. Could Grayle afford such clothes? And if so, then how? In his mind, suspicions were totting up. If a woman liked couture clothes enough, she would want to earn them, somehow.

She came straight up to him and held out her hand. 'Margaret Grayle...I said I would recognize you.' She looked at him appraisingly. 'You haven't changed all that much.'

'No?'

'Older, of course, but so am I. You have quite a distinctive appearance, you know. I saw you on television once doing an interview and that refreshed my memory, but I remember you from a time you had a case in Oxford... I was a schoolkid. I used to think I would like you, or someone like you, to be my uncle.'

'Great-uncle now, I should think.'

'No, it doesn't work like that...as I get older, you get younger, the gap lessens.'

Coffin, who was not often silenced, was silenced now. He was wondering exactly what was on offer and why. He began to have some idea why Stella had been firm on coming to Oxford with him. Did she have precognition or some such?

'You wanted to see me?'

'I heard you were looking for me. I know why you are here and what you are looking for. No secrets here, really.'

Except one big one, Coffin thought: Who is the secret traitor in the machine and why was Harry Seton killed? Did he know who the betrayer was and why was it so dangerous?

Come to think of it, that was more than one question.

No, just one question: Why was Harry Seton killed?

'Is that what you had to say? If so, I have come a long way to learn nothing.' He stood up. 'Let me get you a drink while you think out what you really want to say. While you are doing that, you might try to remember if the name Pennyfeather means anything... What would you like to drink?'

'Vodka and tonic, please. And no, Pennyfeather is not known to me.'

When he returned with the drink, she was smiling. 'They said you were clever and you are. Well, I'll be honest.'

'It would be wiser.'

'I suppose I wanted to warn you.'

Coffin was silent. He had been warned before, several times, in fact, and never been stopped from doing what seemed the thing to do. Not necessarily the right thing, often he had doubts about that, but what seemed his destiny at the time.

'You know what happened to Harry Seton, we all know.'

'Everyone knows.' Coffin did not believe his destiny was to be killed on the job. Margaret Grayle was easily the best suspect so far. Warning him off, indeed...he wondered who had put her up to it. 'Are you saying it might happen to me?'

'Harry is dead. There has to be a connection with what he was doing here... Asking questions.'

Coffin sat back in his armchair, which gave beneath him as if it had had a long and wearing life. The old gentleman who had been reading *The Times* seemed now to be tearing it up. Here and there with his teeth. Coffin shifted again in his chair, which poked him in the back, while across the room the reader had torn out one piece from the newspaper and was now engaged with a second.

'Haven't got a pair of scissors on you, sir, have you?' he called across. 'Desperate to cut this article out. No? Bad luck.' And he went to work with his incisors, which even at this

distance Coffin could see were too blunt for the job and probably false.

Coffin reflected that he could think of more comfortable con-
ditions in which to be suborned by a handsome young woman.
If that was what she was doing.

According to Saxon, Harry Seton had his doubts about Margaret Grayle, and she certainly seemed questionable. Anyway,
her behaviour did.

'Harry must have got some right answers to those questions,'
said Coffin.

'It was the questions that killed him, not the answers,' she
said fiercely. 'If you can't see that, you are nowhere and will
be the next to go.'

Well, she had offered him her own answer to the four-horned
question he had put to himself.

'Would you mind amplifying that?' he said.

'No, it's a statement.'

'And there was me thinking it was a threat.'

They were not getting anywhere. 'I'm sorry,' Coffin said. 'I
shouldn't have said that. Of course you weren't threatening
me.'

Across the room, the man, having finished destroying *The
Times,* had gone to get another drink and another paper to de-
vour. He was massaging his front teeth with his tongue as if
they ached.

'I liked Harry, he had the will to win and a lot of good that
did him. A lot of women find that quality attractive. I did. But
he looked at my clothes, and because they looked good and I
had some nice pearls, he thought I was suspicious. I might be
making money out of trading information, as and when I got
it, mark you.'

'And are you?' Nothing like a direct question on occasion.

'No. I've got a rich uncle.'

Ask a direct question, get a direct lie.

She leaned forward. 'That chap across the room keeps looking at you.'

'Yes, he wants some scissors.'

'But you told him you hadn't got any.'

'I don't think that's going to stop him.'

And indeed, the man had risen and was coming toward them.

'He's mad.'

'No.' Coffin had recognized him now, no one he knew, but someone who was famous enough to have a face you knew. 'He's a distinguished scholar on the loose.' A Nobel-prize winner, a philosopher, he thought, this was Oxford after all.

But it was Margaret Grayle he wanted. 'Have you got a safety pin to spare, my dear? Ladies often have.'

Silently, Margaret produced a small golden safety pin. The man's face fell. 'Oh, nothing bigger? I have all these pieces of paper to pin together.' He had indeed a handful of newsprint, a little damp, but legible. 'I am afraid I may lose them if I don't bind them fast.'

He spoke in beautiful, lucid tones, and thus explained, his behaviour seemed explained. Unusual, but understandable.

Coffin had no scissors and no safety pin, but he produced a small paperclip from his pocket. 'Any good to you?'

'Oh, thank you.' He retreated, binding up his papers as he went straight out. The room seemed the lesser for him somehow, Coffin thought. It was almost as if the great Sphinx had been there with them.

He expressed his feeling: 'I think philosophers are often maddish.'

'Not a philosopher, a chemist,' Margaret said quickly. And then, 'Oh damn.'

Many things which seem mysterious have a rational explanation, Coffin thought.

'You knew him,' said Coffin. 'And he knew you.'

'How could I possibly know a Nobel-prize winner?' she said coldly. 'I worked where he worked at one time, but in a very humble capacity.'

Coffin said nothing, just waited to see what she said next. Let her fall into her own hole.

'You can't suspect a Nobel-prize winner,' she said.

'I can suspect anyone.' He added slowly: 'Everyone needs money.'

Margaret stood up. 'I've done what I can. I have told you, now it's up to you.' She draped her coat over her shoulders. 'Goodbye. Remember to watch out for the knife between your shoulders.'

She swept out. It was a fair description of her exit as her coat moved the air. Coffin knew about clothes through Stella, and that coat was couture.

Coffin ordered himself another drink, while reflecting that she had meant it literally. Not a bad hand with a knife herself. He gave a sigh. The barman looked at him with interest. 'Here for the day?'

'More or less.'

'A lot to see in Oxford.'

'Who was the old gentleman in the corner?' Coffin asked. 'I know his face.'

The barman was pleased to be asked. 'Sir Jessimond Fraser? We call him Sir Jess. Comes in here every day. Did you see his hands? Crippled. Arthritis. Small stroke as well, poor chap.'

There is often a rational explanation for many things which seem extraordinary, Coffin reminded himself once more.

'Marvellous son. His hands, as you might say. Sir Jess's got a lab around the corner, in Canal Road, doesn't do much now—retired.'

'It's a university lab, is it?'

'UnivLab? I am sure they'd let him have one. But he's got a private one. Don't think he does much, to tell you the truth, but it keeps him in touch with his world. I think the son has a job elsewhere now.'

Coffin finished his drink, and went in search of Peter Chard, who was said to be in charge of the Wessex group, whatever that meant in this strange organization. 'Ed Saxon,' he said to himself, 'you have always been a devious bloke, and now I need to read you aright.' He was not sure he had done this yet.

He ran over the names he had been given: Peter Chard in Wessex; Anglia, Felicity Fox; in Deira or Newcastle, Joe Weir.

He had been given addresses in Oxford, Cambridge and Newcastle for the names on this list.

No address for Susy Miller who 'shot around'.

He recited the names in a sad litany as he walked towards the Banbury Road, where Peter Chard had his office.

Narrowly escaping death at the junction of Beaumont Street and St Giles as he stepped out into the traffic to move towards the Banbury Road, he walked briskly northward. Coffin enjoyed the walk up the road, looking at the prosperous Edwardian houses, now mostly divided into flats, he marvelled once again that the row of shops called North Parade should be so far south of South Parade. No wonder Lewis Carroll was a product of this city.

Chard's office was above a shop. Nothing marked it out as his, anonymity had been preserved, so Coffin rang the bell and waited.

A tall, lean figure appeared, and nodded at him unsurprised. 'Found your way here, then? I thought you'd be here. I expected you. Expected you before this, as a matter of fact. Come on up.'

He was led up a neat carpeted staircase to a room at the top. 'I don't have all the rooms.' Chard nodded towards the room opposite. 'That one is a milliner...private customers, a lot of dons' wives wear hats, it seems—College functions, university big days, that kind of thing, he makes them. He thinks I am a typing bureau. And I wonder if it is really just hats he is doing there, but that's my suspicious nature.'

'What else could be going on?' Coffin had long sight and could read the name: Elysium.

'Oh, I don't know, something where lots of pretty young things are needed. Ladies by the hour, drugs...he's probably equally suspicious of me.' Chard pushed open the door. 'Come in, come in. That's what brings you here, isn't it, suspicion? We are honoured to have such a high-ranking inquisitor.'

Coffin reflected that Ed Saxon had certainly chosen articulate characters.

Chard pushed a chair forward, then sat down himself. There

were only two chairs, but the desk was provided with all the electronic equipment to be wished for: computer, modem, fax and answerphone.

Chard saw him looking. 'I prefer a notebook, but we have to impress.'

Coffin found himself liking this tall, talkative fellow. His conversational style was wry with a hint of mockery behind it.

'To tell you the truth, when we were set up, under Ed Saxon, whom you may know better than I do.'

Coffin shook his head.

'You refuse the honour? Well, in spite of what he said about how important this investigation was, our mission, he may even have called it, I thought we were just a bunch of has-beens farmed out before culling... I couldn't see it as that important, but as things went on and we never succeeded in eliminating the source of the counterfeit drugs...that is, we did, often, but then a mushroom growth would spring up elsewhere, drugs on wheels, it was. Then I began to take it more seriously, where there's big money, you do.' He looked in appeal.

'You do,' agreed Coffin.

'Then Harry Seton arrived trying to search out which of us was in the game there, taking our profit in return for information. I found that hard to accept too... I'm just a sceptic, I guess.'

'And then Harry was killed, so you took it seriously?'

'Right.'

'Did you know Harry well?'

'Better than I know Ed Saxon. Bit of a paper man, that one, I think.' Peter Chard got up and began to move around the room. 'Sorry, I have to keep moving, my leg stiffens up.'

Coffin saw then that he limped with his right leg.

'We don't use ranks here, but I'm Sergeant Chard and I was on special duties till I got myself shot in the leg.'

'You caught the chap?' He was beginning to remember Chard's distinguished career.

'Chapess, actually. A bitch of a woman, but fortunately not

a good shot. She'll be out soon and I will still be limping around.' There was no bitterness in his voice.

'We had our little successes all right, at the beginning, but gradually we were losing the war. It may be our fault, we may not have a traitor in our midst as Ed thought; I thought that way at first, now I don't know what to think.' He looked at Coffin. 'I suppose Harry could have been killed for some other reason, or just chance, he got in the way or walked where he shouldn't have done. It happens.'

'Inspector Davenport is investigating Harry Seton's death,' said Coffin cautiously.

'I know that. Davy's had his men down here poking round. Didn't come himself. I was a suspect myself when it was found out that my daughter is a chemist and worked with Sir Jess for a bit... Ah, you've had a meet with our Ms Grayle, of course, she was in here yesterday saying she was going to get at you. I expect she showed you where Sir Jess hangs out?'

'Yes,' said Coffin simply. 'She said she doesn't know him.'

'Not to say know, you couldn't call it knowing, but she was secretary in his department once, which was more or less what she was here, just helping out one way and another, but these great scientists don't remember secretaries.'

'I'd call her pretty memorable.'

'Oh, she is, she is, and several people have good cause to remember her. Not me, I hasten to add. I don't know what is on her mind but she is one anxious lady.'

'I got that impression. She advised me to stop asking questions.'

'Ah, she would do. She thinks she is a suspect, you see. In spite of what I am saying we are all pretty twitchy. Harry gave me a going-over just because I own a small farm in Devon, as well as the daughter I told you about who once worked with Sir Jess. Mercifully for me, the farm was inherited and is very small and a bit of a black hole as far as money is concerned.'

'And your daughter?'

'She has been working in Australia for the last two years.'

Well, thought Coffin, you have got out all you want to get across to me. Was it rehearsed?

He then took Peter Chard through the same list of questions on career, money, and contacts as he had done in Coventry with the two there and had notably failed to do with Margaret Grayle. He included Pennyfeather and got the denial he was coming to expect.

At the end, Chard sad: 'I went through all this with Harry.'

'Just trawling,' said Coffin peaceably. 'No doubt I would find all this in Harry's computer records.' Only most have been deleted from the word processor or burnt. John Armstrong's silence must mean he'd had no luck in retrieving the deleted files.

'Let me have a copy of all your relevant addresses… chemist's shops, centres from which the drugs were being sent out, and which you located and broke up. Even manufacturing sites.'

Chard shook his head. 'We never found those.'

Don't look, won't find, Coffin thought. He was beginning to be deeply sceptical of the whole operation. He held out his hand. 'What you've got then.'

Chard hesitated, then reluctantly opened a drawer, took out what was in it, and handed over a pile of blue folders.

'Thank you. What about computer records?'

'All printed out and in what you've got there.'

Coffin nodded. 'Good.'

'I hope you are getting somewhere.'

'Do you know, I think I am,' said Coffin.

COFFIN WALKED BACK down the Banbury Road to his appointed rendezvous with Stella in the University Parks.

'They were gun parks once,' he told Stella when he found her sitting on a bench near one of the gates. 'In the Civil War the cannons, royal cannons they must have been as Oxford was for the king, were parked there. That is why the area is called Parks and not Park.'

'What's that parcel you are clutching?'

'Information.'

'Useful information?'

'Probably not.' He turned to face her. 'So what did you do? Find any old admirers?'

Stella laughed. 'Didn't even try. Found a lovely dress in Annabelinda... Fancy, she's still here, such a delight, and it has to be altered round the waist. I am too thin,' she ended smugly. 'Then Gus and I went for a walk round the market, and then we came here. I think Gus is tired.'

Coffin remembered that a stall in Coventry market had sold doubtful pharmaceuticals. Someone else, was it Kelso or the woman, had mentioned a market. 'I'd like to look at the market. If you haven't eaten yet, why don't we have a late lunch there?'

'You will have to carry Gus.'

Gus and Coffin eyed each other warily. 'Make yourself light, Gus,' advised Coffin. 'You know you can do it, turn into a dead weight and you can walk.'

THE COVERED MARKET was crowded, but there was a pleasant mixed smell of fresh vegetables, fish and flowers. Coffin walked round it with Gus lolling in his arms, enjoying the view. Man and dog could tell at once that this was not the sort of market where you sold drugs or counterfeit pharmaceuticals.

You might meet people there, who did, of course.

There was an eating place on one corner. 'Was this where Ma Brown's was?' asked Stella. 'I can't remember. Looks the same. The same but a bit different. Let's go in, have some coffee and a sandwich.'

'Will they let the dog in?'

'Just carry him in and see.'

Stella stood in the doorway and looked around. 'We used to come in here for coffee in between rehearsals...John, Peter, Alex and Susy... I kept in touch for a long while but I haven't seen them for an age. Read about them in *The Stage* sometimes.'

That was the way of the theatre, while you were playing

together you were friends, lovers, but when the run ended you drifted apart. Still friends, but you just didn't meet.

And Stella had been much the most successful. She was a Name. That separated you from old friends.

Also, she was married to a high-ranking policeman and that made for a division too.

'Let's take it away, coffee and sandwiches, and something for the dog, and drive away. Into the country.'

He had in his mind to drive to one of the country addresses, say Bicester or Banbury or Aylesbury, where drugs had been sold to a clutch of chemist's, and see what he could make of it. Pick up the spoor of the so-called traitor.

Stella was amenable, she could already sense that she had grown away from the girl who had drunk coffee with friends in a place like this, perhaps even this very place, and that there was no going back.

'Yes, let's. I'll choose the sandwiches.' She accepted the death of the past; Stella was good about putting things behind her and getting on with the present. Even the future.

'Are there any more markets in Oxford?' He heard his own voice doing the asking, so it was clear he was not giving up on markets.

'You're the one who's supposed to know that sort of thing. Yes, I remember one up the Cowley Road. Don't think it was there every day.'

THERE WAS NO LONGER a market where Stella had remembered it up the Cowley Road, instead a large supermarket stood there. They ate their sandwiches in the car; Gus had his share—then took a stroll up and down the road, stopping at several trees, each of which bore a sign asking him not to use it for his convenience.

Then they drove home, Coffin still thinking of markets. Nothing obvious in Banbury, but as they went through Aylesbury there was a yellow notice pointing to 'The Market: 8 a.m. to 5 p.m.'.

Stella was incredulous: 'I don't believe it, it's a fantasy, just for you.'

'In time too,' said Coffin.

He found a parking slot and raised an eyebrow at Stella. 'Coming, or will you sit in the car?'

'Gus and I are coming, we are going to inspect the market.'

'Don't let Gus get into a fight, there are powerful looking dogs around here and I daresay they don't like white Pekingese.'

'Snobs, that's colour prejudice.' They both knew that it was Gus that started the fights, he found Alsatians, particularly if in couples, and Dalmatians, especially riling.

Coffin wandered off on his own.

The market was arranged in three aisles with no cover from the weather. Fish and meat shared one aisle, with fruit and vegetables on a second. The third aisle was a glorious jumble of clothes, china, fake jewellery and pretend antiques which deceived no one and were never intended to. One stall was piled high with shoes and handbags hanging pendant from the side. Next to this stall was one with sweaters and shirts, fake Italian, he speculated. At the end was a stall of scent and make-up with a substation of medicines and health foods.

Coffin approached this stall with circumspection. Out of the corner of his eye he could see that Stella had reached the fake jewellery stall and was bargaining energetically for a necklace which looked like amber.

As was fitting, a woman was in charge of the make-up stall. He came up close and the smell of scents and powders drifted towards him. Nothing expensive here, he told himself, having learnt much in marriage with Stella.

The name above the stall said Flora Love, make-up that is good for you, take her advice.

He saw that Flora was observing him with sharp black eyes which twinkled at him, but there was amusement without friendliness in their glint.

Also a hard observation; he would not be able to pretend

with this woman who had weighted him up for what he was as soon as he came within her vision. No pretending with this one.

She didn't speak but gave a long look and waited. Canny woman, Coffin thought. He was silent because he did not know how to begin.

At last he found his voice: 'I see you sell a range of natural-cure medicines, if I can call them that.'

'You can.' Her voice was clear and yet soft with a slight accent. West Country, he thought.

'What have you got that is soothing, relaxing?' He could do with some of that himself.

'Lavender oil, rubbed in, is very good.'

She was laughing at him. Almost certainly.

'I don't know about rubbing it in, anything by the mouth?'

'Valerian is said to be good.' She held out a packet. 'Quiet Time sells well.'

He pretended to consider. 'Give me a packet, worth a try.'

He noticed a stack of aspirin on an upper shelf.

She barely turned her head to look. 'Oh, just samples. I'm not selling them.'

He held out his hand. 'I won't offer to pay then.'

She sighed as she handed over a packet. 'I guessed what you were as soon as I clapped eyes on you, but I thought I'd chance it...if I'd moved those packets when you came along that would have been a dead giveaway. You're one of those inspectors, aren't you? And not from round here.'

'That's right. Tell me how you get these drugs—you do realize they are fake?'

'No, not fake, genuine drugs. I wouldn't sell anything that could harm a customer, no, they are real, but source a bit iffy.' She turned her head to the shelf behind. 'Some lovely scents too, not quite what they pretend to be but not bad at the price.'

'So how do you come by them?'

'I buy them, of course, nothing's free in this world.'

'From whom?' She was willing to talk, but not ready with information; she would give as little as possible, any time, any question.

She sighed. 'I've answered these questions before, at least twice. Feels like more but my memory gets worse and worse.'

'Try it. Where do you get them?'

'They are good value...a lot of my customers need drugs they can't afford...for asthma, arthritis, gut trouble, painkillers...'

'You sell all those?'

She shrugged. 'I bought what came in. It varied, sometimes one drug, sometimes another. Nothing hard, you understand, that wasn't the business at all.'

Coffin was rolling the packet of aspirin in his hands: it was a neat job of packing and labelling, but done on the cheap. Like the drugs.

'I wasn't the only buyer, plenty were at it round here, not just chemist's but your friendly corner shop.'

'Good profits.'

'Well, of course, that's what it's all about. I don't stand around here in all weathers for my health.'

'So where did the stuff come from?'

She sighed. 'You do stick at it. I'll tell you what I told the others and much good may it do you: a white van would come in, and the customers would follow. I got a telephone call and I guess they did.'

'Simple.'

'It shifted around, you'd get used to one selling point and then it would disappear; not safe, I suppose, although it wasn't illegal.'

'Deception can be illegal.'

'Seen from where I stand it was no fraud, just good value.'

'Go back to the white van...it disappeared, did it?'

'Yes, supplies dried up. But they came back. I have several stalls, several different places, and after a bit, I noticed a van, not the white one, doing the same business...'

'No telephone calls?'

'I didn't need it, I knew the way of it: see what was there, cash and buy.' She nodded. 'Yes, they moved on, saturate one area then go to another. Safer too.'

'Was it?'

'Yeah, because there were people like you nosing around, checking up, drug inspectors, or from the big pharmaceutical companies, but they were always on the late side, white van or dark blue, it had moved on and not come back. It had its own information service, I reckon.'

'Could be.'

She was pretending to be uneducated, but she wasn't, might even know about pharmaceuticals herself.

'Is Flora Love your real name?'

'Flora is, not the Love part, not too much of that in my life.'

'Have you got scientific training yourself, Flora?'

She laughed. 'You need it, you learn it.'

'I shall need to talk to you again, Flora.'

'How will you do that? I'm not handing out my telephone number.'

'I won't have any trouble finding you; if you come here regularly then you have a name registered with the local police. Hard to disappear, Flora.'

She looked at him silently, then said in a low voice: 'Not while I am alive, easier when I'm dead.'

'What does that mean?'

'The last chap that came talking...he's dead.'

'How do you know that?'

'I recognized his face on the TV...I would recognize you, and know your name. I know it now.'

She laughed. 'When you took the packet of aspirin, your coat opened...' She waved a card in front of him, it was one he carried in his pocket when he wanted quick identification. 'I used to work in the circus, doing tricks...you were easy, not thinking, you see... Here, you can have it back, Mr Coffin.' She tossed his card back across the counter. 'You better watch out for yourself, you know.'

It was at this moment that he realized how important Oxford was in this case; he should have understood this before. You've been slow, Coffin.

Even as this thought came, another burned into his mind: Margaret Grayle's clothes were too bloody good.

She could be on the tape.

Watch your back, he had been told in Oxford. Here the warning came again, and from another woman.

He walked back towards the car where Stella and Gus were sitting on a bench. Stella was nursing a brightly coloured paper bag.

'What did you find to buy?' Although he knew Stella well enough to know she would find something to buy on the North Pole.

'An amber necklace and a nice old Worcester bowl.' She produced it, dark blue and white in a fluted china.

'Old? How old? Is it genuine?'

'No, probably not, but it's pretty and I shall keep potpourri in it. I bought some of that too.' She produced a small bag from inside the larger one. 'Mostly lavender and dried roses, but I like the smell... And I bought a drink for Gus, he was thirsty.'

Gus was asleep, worn out by his day.

'What did he drink?'

'Tea, he likes it with milk and sugar.' She patted the dog's head. 'Are we going home now?'

They got into the car, put the sleepy dog in the back and drove off.

'Did you get anywhere? Any ideas?'

Coffin drove for a moment in silence. 'Yes, I got an idea.'

Stella looked at him in silent query, waiting.

'It's a chimera.'

'A chimera?'

'Yes, and now I am going to drive fast.'

Back to Never Never Land.

THE DOOR OPENS

EIGHT

NEVER NEVER CITY LOOKED much as always as they drove home through Spinnergate, perhaps an extra layer of litter on the pavements. And it was raining.

Even in the rain there was a little clump of skateboarders and rollerbladers on several street corners. The skaters were riding up and down on metal poles, grinding. Dangerous work. You had to wonder what the casualty rate was.

'I enjoyed my day in the country.' Stella sounded cheerful. 'And so did Gus, he's worn out with the day's excitements, poor fellow. But I suppose for you,' she studied her husband's profile, 'it was a waste of time.'

'Not a waste at all.' Coffin was abstracted, watching the road where the traffic was heavy, usual at that time of day. He was driving in past Spinnergate tube station where Mimsie Marker sold papers from a stall. There she was, arms waving a paper, talking away to a group of people: she was the greatest disseminator of gossip in the Second City.

'Mind if we don't go straight home? I'd like to take a tour of the city.'

'Why?'

'Just fancy a look round. Revive my memories of it.'

'It won't have changed since this morning.'

'The Second City changes every hour, it's never the same.' He sounded serious.

He was making a circuit of the inner city. 'That's the new Central Library going up over there.' It was a biggish, white building. 'There's going to be a whole room devoted to drama. I expect they will call it the Pinero Room if you ask nicely.'

'Culture City,' said Stella.

'Now, now.' He grinned at her.

'Let's move out of the tower, Buy a place in the country. Gus would like it.'

'There's no real country within miles of here.' But he was following a road that ran up a hill, towards what open, rough ground the Second City possessed. Stella sometimes drove up here to walk old Gus, who, if lame and worldly, had never wanted to be walked, preferring his solitary roams.

Shadly Woods, the small, ravaged remnant of what had been the old hunting forest of the Norman kings. Known in certain circles as Shady Wood, where you could find a sheltered recess in the trees to make love, or get high, or hang yourself if that was the way it took you. It was across the road from where the old factory had stood, but not far away from where the boys had been buried.

'I've just got a feeling…' He turned to look at her.

'I hate your feelings.' He had the look in his eye, distant, intent, that she had seen in the eyes of their old cat when she set out on a hunting expedition, a look that saw the future and not the present.

But he had found what he was looking for. On the slope of the hill he could see two police cars parked and another just drawing up.

He turned to Stella. 'I shall get out, then you can take the car and drive home with Gus.'

Stella nodded. 'Yes, all right, but phone me, please. Don't leave me too long without a word.' She might be a well-loved actress with her own theatre but on occasion she still got the same treatment as all police wives: silence, absence. She was used to it and accepted it, but she did not like it.

Coffin did not even say: I promise, but kissed her cheek and got out of the car. Stella would have liked him to look back as he strode up the hill, but he did not, and she knew that she was not exactly forgotten, but put aside to be considered later. No use fretting, it was work, and, after he went off, she smiled at the thought of her new nose.

From out of the bushes emerged Inspector Devlin. Some leaves and twigs had got stuck in her hair, disarranging her usually carefully immaculate appearance. She looked distressed. Behind her came Sergeant Tittleton. And behind him one of the police surgeons whom Coffin knew by sight only.

A man called Kilpatrick, he thought. Kilpatrick was shaking his head.

Coffin felt as if he had blundered into a scene that was not on his programme, an extra act in an unpredictable play. He felt a new pain down in the guts—first sign of some mortal illness? First pain of the season.

He stopped himself muttering such rubbish; he had noticed before he had a tendency to ramble to himself when his thoughts were really elsewhere.

Now he was saying to himself: Something bad there, don't cover it up.

He quickened his pace, marching up the slope until Devlin turned round and saw him. Tittleton and Dr Kilpatrick caught up with Devlin, all three stood waiting.

'I don't know how you knew, sir,' said Devlin, 'but I am glad you did.' She walked towards him, leaving the other two behind.

Another body? A fifth boy? Or a young policeman called Diver?

Devlin answered the question before he asked it. 'Not a boy this time, but a young woman…or what's left of her.'

'How was she found?'

'Oh, we've had a search going on over all this ground. Just looking. And there she was.'

Coffin followed Paddy Devlin towards the group, where Sergeant Tittleton stood silently by Dr Kilpatrick, who was murmuring that he had to be off soon.

'She's been dead some time, we don't know how long yet, of course. Dr Kilpatrick could only make a guess at this stage…decomposition and so on…he thinks six to eight weeks.'

Devlin led the way into a thicket of brambles fringed by young self-seeded trees.

'Not a nice sight.' Devlin sounded apologetic. 'Some animals have got at her.'

'It happens,' said Coffin tersely, thinking of Harry Seton. He pushed his way through to the middle of the tangle of greenery.

At the centre, the ground fell away into a small hollow and this was where she lay.

'I'm thinking that it may be her leg that got buried with Archie Chinner, it was quite a small leg.'

'She's small,' said Coffin. Small, young and chewed up.

The head was there and the face battered and decomposing but still somehow young and innocent. A traveller in life who had got lost. By the head was a leather bag.

'It may be suicide,' said Kilpatrick, who was ill at ease. 'Can't tell yet. Whoever does the postmortem will find out.'

'Nothing has been touched as yet, sir.' Devlin liked to have procedures exact and right. 'But the photographers and the SOCO team is on the way.' She looked: 'In fact, I see them arriving now.'

'She doesn't wear a wedding ring.'

'That doesn't mean anything.'

'No.' Coffin nodded. 'No rings of any sort, but a watch and the remains of one earring on the left ear.' None of them were expensive but the hands of the watch still told the time. 'She wasn't killed for her jewellery.'

'There's that handbag by her side, with any luck it will help with her identity. If there is any money in it, it will rule out robbery, which I pretty well do anyway, sir. Doesn't have the look. Murder or suicide.' She added doubtfully: 'It could be natural death.'

'You mean she came up here and sat down and died?' said Tittleton.

'No, not likely, I agree.'

Coffin withdrew through the bushes. 'It's not so far away from where the boys were buried…explains the leg, I suppose…if anything can. We don't know how it got there, though.'

'It may have been carried that way by a fox or a dog…' Or a human, but she didn't like to think that, but it was heavy for a dog. A fox might do it.

'Well, she's missing from somewhere. Someone will know she's gone.'

'She might be on the missing persons list,' said the inspector doubtfully.

'The bag looks interesting.'

'I thought that, sir.' A girl, and perhaps she was no more than that, often carried half her life around in her bag.

'If she's got her name or an address in her handbag that will be a start...a credit card, a bill.'

Coffin started to walk away.

'Do you want me to carry on with this too, sir?' asked the inspector.

Coffin stopped. 'No, you've got your hands full, I'll speak to Chief Superintendent Young, he'll sort it out. But keep in touch just in case it touches on the death of the boys.'

'It is connected in a way.'

'Yes,' said Coffin, 'but I don't know how.'

'We will find out who she is and it might become clear.'

'I can see you are an optimist, Inspector,' said Coffin, as he trudged away. 'Oh, and any news of Jeff Diver?'

'No, sir.'

Coffin stopped. 'You don't want to let go of this, do you?'

Paddy Devlin walked up until she was level with him. 'No, sir. I feel that somehow there is a link between this poor girl and the boys.'

'And what about Jeff Diver?'

'I don't know about him, sir. No firm opinion yet.'

Coffin moved on again. 'Right. Good. Carry on then, but you will need a bit more help. Ask for what you want.'

Inspector Devlin watched him walk away down the hill. A nice man, she thought, perhaps too nice. If he said she could ask for what help she wanted, it meant she would get it, something not universally true. She already had DC Amanda Harden. She was aware of Tony Tittleton's interest in Amanda, and she was a friend of both the Tittletons, but people had to look after themselves in that respect, she thought. Amanda was good and clever, Amanda was the one she wanted. Her own sex life was peaceful, being nonexistent, at the moment. Not that you could count on that going on; in her experience, things hit you when you least expected them.

Absently, her eyes traced Coffin's descent down the hill. Nice shoulders, a pity he was so thoroughly spoken for.

Push such thoughts aside. 'Tony,' she called. 'Over here.'

The sergeant approached with his own slow, loping stride that yet covered the ground quickly.

'The forensic team are here, and the photographer is doing his bit.'

'I noticed.'

'Kilpatrick has cleared off. He looked a bit sick. I think he likes his bodies freshly killed. Which she wasn't, poor girl. Still, she's not our problem.'

'She is for the time being. And to help us I am going to put DC Harden on it, and she can establish identity as the first thing.'

'Right, well, Harden is a bright girl.'

'Yes, and don't make too much of a play for her, I don't want her mind taken off the job.'

'As if I would.'

One of the white-uniformed forensic team walked towards Devlin. 'The handbag has been photographed in situ, no hope of fingerprints because of exposure, but you can open it now if you want to look in. Or wait till we get it back to the lab, but I thought you might like a quick look.'

'You think right.' She followed the scientist back to where the body lay, now protected by a small tent.

'Looks as though it's got plenty of stuff in it…one of those big satchel bags, but loaded.'

'I noticed.' The bag had rested on the ground by the girl's head like a pushed-aside pillow. It was brown leather, or had been before staining, and shaped like a knapsack to hang from the shoulders. Now the bag was on a sheet by itself with Sergeant Tittleton staring down at it. He looked up and shrugged.

'I don't see how this is going to help us with nailing the killer of the boys,' said Tittleton.

'I don't either, but it's connected, it connected itself.'

'The leg, you mean? But if it's hers an animal could have carried it here.'

'And buried it?' Devlin was crouching by the bag, gloves on

her hands, preparing to open it. 'I might need some photographs here.'

The clasp of the bag was gummed up with earth and dead leaves but Devlin forced it open. A wodge of stained tissues lay on top, stained with lipstick and coffee and something darker and stickier… It might have been blood.

'Could be vomit,' said Devlin. She picked out a small bottle. 'Aspirin, empty. Might be what she took.'

Also in the bag was a small bottle that had contained brandy.

'And she took it with this…meant to do the job, and do it here.'

'We can't know for sure before the PM,' Tittleton reminded her.

'Likely, though. She took the aspirin, washed it down with brandy and then was sick…but she'd taken enough to become comatose and then die. That's why she was here, so that no one would find her and bring her round.'

'Do you think she'd tried before?'

'I do.'

A small diary was tucked into one corner of the bag; Devlin drew it out carefully to flip the pages over.

'No name, no address and no telephone number. Not a girl who confides much in her diary.'

'It's a university diary, though,' pointed out Tittleton. 'There's the university coat of arms on the cover. That ought to be a help.'

'You're right. Aren't we lucky to be educated? She's a student.'

'Or college lecturer.'

'No, I guess she's too young.' But once again, they could not be sure until the postmortem. She was ageless as well as nameless at the moment, this young woman.

There was a handkerchief, and a spare pair of tights as well as the diary inside the bag. There was even a paperback book, a copy of *Jane Eyre*.

'She covered some eventualities,' said the sergeant. 'No contraceptives, though.'

'You've been mixing in the wrong circles,' said Devlin.

'Since I joined this job.'

A leather wallet with some money, but no credit cards, was at the bottom of the bag.

Tittleton sorted through the wallet. 'No driving licence, no cheque book, no identification… I reckon she cleared such things out before she came here…she wanted to make things hard for us.'

'I don't think it was anything personal, she just wanted to die anonymous.'

Behind the wallet was yet another division in the bag, it seemed empty except for a tissue stained with lipstick. The lipstick was at the bottom of the bag. Devlin fished in to draw it out. Her fingers felt paper.

'Aha. A letter.'

She straightened it out. 'No address here either.'

Dear Ally,

Cheer up, don't go down that dark tunnel as you called it last time. And don't do anything silly, you know what I mean, I don't want to hear someone found you in bed, doped out, and had to rush you to hospital. It won't be me this time because I am off on the field trip and won't be back till Christmas. So there.

But seriously, Al darling, and when am I ever anything else, there is no need to be this way. You will pass your finals, get a good degree and go out into the world. If you let yourself, that is.

And don't fall in love with your professor, that's a cliché, dear, a classic mistake, especially with that one, he has a new girl every intake. New boy too, I've heard.

Totty

Devlin read the letter once, then read it again more slowly before handing it over to the sergeant. He handed it back quickly.

'With friends like that, who needs enemies?'

Paddy put the letter back in the bag. 'Have to get this fingerprinted... It is a bit tough, but I reckon Totty, sex obscure, had had enough.'

'Also didn't believe "Ally" was really serious in heading for death.'

'That too... Well, you were right about one thing: she's at university, probably in the Second City, and I was right in saying she was a student.'

Devlin peeled off the protective gloves, wishing she could peel away the uncomfortable feeling this death gave her. 'The letter has helped us with the girl: suicide of an unknown student, and pretty soon we will know who she is. Universities keep records, but I don't see we are any further forward in finding the abuser and killer of the boys.'

She rubbed her hands together as if cleaning them. 'Better get hold of DC Harden and send her out to both the universities in the Second City to find out if they have a student called Ally who hasn't been turning up for lectures.'

'We don't know it's a Second City university.'

'Well, we will start here. I don't fancy going nationwide just yet. She must have some connection with the Second City. She may already have been reported missing.'

COFFIN WAS DRIVEN BACK to St Luke's in a patrol car. He heard Augustus barking a welcome as he put his key in the door, and Stella running down the stairs.

'So? What was it?'

'A dead girl, probably a suicide.'

'Not Jeff Diver? That was what you feared?'

Coffin nodded. 'This body has one connection with the dead boys—it was her left leg, poor girl, that was buried with the Chinner lad. I don't know why, perhaps there isn't a reason, or not one I can understand, at all. I daresay I will find out when it all winds to a conclusion, if it ever does.' He bent down to pat Gus's head. 'Have you fed him? Good. Let's go to Max's to eat. I haven't booked a table, but he will take us in.' He hesitated, then said, 'Would you mind if I asked Phoebe Astley to join us?'

Stella shook her head. 'No, in fact, I will ring her myself.

You look as if you need a hot shower, a change of clothes...
I hate that shirt you are wearing...and a strong drink. I'll get
you the drink.'

Stella had to use her powers of persuasion. 'Oh come on,
Phoebe.'

'I don't know, I've got to do a mass of work...' Although
she admired Stella, she wasn't sure if she liked her. A touch
jealous, perhaps?

'Oh do, Phoebe, think of it: Max's food and some good wine.
Put something delicious on and come.'

Phoebe ground her teeth, she would wear old jeans and a
shirt. 'I suppose it's work,' she said grudgingly.

'I don't know, truly not, but come.'

Phoebe made the sort of noise that meant yes, then felt
ashamed of herself because a meal at Max's was a treat, so she
said: 'I'll look forward to it, thank you for the call, Stella.'

Stella knew that Phoebe was not one of her true admirers,
she had long ago accepted it. After all, you couldn't get good
reviews all the time.

'She's coming,' she called from her bedside phone.

'Oh, I knew she would, you can rely on Phoebe,' called a
confident masculine voice from the shower.

Stella shook her head.

MAX WAS PLEASED to see them both since they were important
customers. He advised them firmly on what he recommended
tonight: the lamb was good, as was the salmon, the chef had
done something very good with potatoes and salad, of course.
The wine he would leave to them, but he would always be
ready with advice; a little bow followed while he waited for
the order.

Phoebe stood at the door, studying them: Coffin looked tired,
Stella cheerful and well groomed, you couldn't beat an actress
for putting on the public face, she might be wretched inside,
but it would not show.

Phoebe herself had put aside the pleasure of wearing old
jeans and baggy sweater, and had put on a plain, dark-blue
dress that had been chosen for her by her friend Eden, who had

once kept a dress shop and knew about clothes but had never learned about men or money. Consequently, she now worked in the wardrobe room at the Pinero Theatre and was a great admirer of Stella. Phoebe was never sure if this pleased her or annoyed her.

She had dropped into the murder room on her way to dinner to hear if there had been any developments. It was always as well when seeing the Chief Commander to be up to date with the latest.

She had found Devlin and Tittleton drinking coffee while the rest of the team studied files or sat at computer screens. At intervals, a telephone would ring, and be answered, apparently to no great moment, and then to ring again. Phoebe had worked in such incident rooms herself and knew it was how things went. Hard, monotonous work requiring concentration and persistence. Perhaps persistence, just keeping on till a pattern emerged from the welter of details was the most important quality of all.

'I heard about a body. No good?'

'Yes and no… It wasn't Jeff Diver.'

'I heard.' News such as that travelled fast. 'I'm glad about that, though.'

'Yes, he's probably dead, though. Topped himself. Or in the river.'

'I agree. You think he is the killer of the boys?'

Devlin hesitated. 'The general opinion is that he confessed and that's that. I believe his wife thinks he is the killer. I don't know. People do confess to crimes they have not committed. I want hard, solid evidence. We've been all over his house, nothing, no sign of anything connected with any one of the boys…'

'Garage? Car?'

'I agree he would have needed transport, but he didn't use his own car because he didn't have one… He had a motorbike and his wife can't drive. Nothing in the garage, which was used as a general dump for things not needed in the house… Of course, he may have had a lock-up or a shed somewhere else, we are working on that, but so far nothing.'

'If he did have one, then he could be hiding out in it.'

'True. Or be dead in it.'

There was a moment of silence, then Devlin went on: 'You can understand why we turned out in force to see the body.'

'But it's the wrong body.'

Devlin nodded. 'What we've got is the body of a young woman...probably suicide, but nothing is for sure yet.'

'Not one for you, then.' But Devlin sounded interested, so there was something.

'Except that it was probably her leg that was buried with Archie Chinner.'

'Ah,' said Phoebe thoughtfully.

'We don't know why or how yet, but the Chief Commander thinks it is important...connects the girl with the dead boys, and I suppose it does.' Devlin sounded tired. 'And is important. Just an idea he had, one of his ideas.'

Coffin was famous for them in the Second City detective force. Some people cursed him for them, others were grateful, no one laughed at them.

'He is often right.'

'Don't I know it? Anyway, we have to establish identity, and I have put Amanda Harden to work on it.'

'She's good.'

'Don't I know that, too? Do you ever get the feeling that the hungry generations are pressing on you hard?'

Don't we all? Thought Phoebe as she departed.

COFFIN AND STELLA were sharing a bottle of the red Sancerre which Max, ever shrewd about a good sale, had assured them was an 'interesting wine'.

'I didn't know it came red,' said Stella. 'I thought just white.'

'Rosé, as well, I think. Or so Max said. He's a wily old salesman. Still, I like the wine.'

'Red, white or golden, it's all the same to me,' said Stella, happy to see her husband relaxing. Across the room, she saw Phoebe come through the door. She waved a hand. 'Walk across the room and greet her,' she said to her husband. 'She came because you asked her. Perhaps I actually issued the invitation, but you wanted her.' Phoebe looked straight at her, their eyes met, and then both women smiled.

It was a moment of friendship, unexpected to both of them and the more to be appreciated. 'I like her,' Stella thought, just as Phoebe was acknowledging to herself that she admired this woman, Stella Pinero. 'Life's interesting,' she said to herself, 'you never know what's coming up.'

Oblivious to this sweep of emotion, the man in the middle made welcoming noises and explained he had chosen the meal and the wine.

'Max chose it, in fact,' said Stella.

'As he always does.'

Stella laughed. 'I wonder what he eats himself?'

'I happen to know.' Phoebe took her seat and accepted some wine. 'I know his daughter, the Beauty One, and he likes a good hamburger when off duty. He shares this taste with his grandson, Louie.'

Coffin took a swig of wine. 'Ah, Louie, what do you make of him?'

Phoebe did not speak until the waiter had laid plates of Parma ham with slices of some bright-orange fruit in front of them. 'He's a clever child, cleverer than his mother. Not so pretty, though, but she has put on fat this last year or two.' She ate a mouthful of ham, since no one had laughed at her little joke. 'I know what you are getting at though, he's a kind of witness, isn't he?'

'Could be, could be. He might be inventing it.'

'No, he doesn't strike me as that sort. Not much imagination in that family. No, if he said that was what he saw and that was what he thought, then it was how it was. There has been plenty of discussion of it.'

Coffin drank some wine without answering what Phoebe had said. Stella smiled at Phoebe and shrugged. That's the way he is at the moment, the shrug said.

'You're taking a personal interest in this?' It was more a comment than a question from Phoebe.

'I always take a person interest,' said Coffin.

Phoebe and Stella looked at each other. Stella gave another

small shrug. 'I've had cause in the past to be grateful for your personal interest,' she said.

'It's the way he is,' said Phoebe.

'I wish you two wouldn't talk about me as if I wasn't here,' said Coffin.

'You're snappy this evening.'

'I feel snappy.' He poured some more wine for the two women, although they had drunk little. 'I expect you want to know, Phoebe, why I asked you to meet us here tonight.'

'What, not just for the pleasure of my company... No, I had been wondering.'

'I want you to take some leave...'

Phoebe opened her eyes wider.

'No, don't worry, I shall see you get that leave made up to you in some way, because you will be working for me. In a way, you will *be* me.'

Phoebe opened her mouth to speak, then closed it again. She was silenced. 'Thanks,' she said after a bit. It was all she could manage.

'I will see you get leave in recompense. You can say you are sent out to set up meetings for me.'

Thanks again, thought Phoebe, but this time she did not say it aloud. She did not feel particularly grateful.

'I don't understand.' Stella looked from one to the other. 'But I suppose I am not meant to. Professional secrets. I hate dark talk.'

'Is it dark?' asked Coffin.

'Yes, and you know it. Phoebe knows it too. But then it's her trade as well.' Stella drank some wine, nodded her head appraisingly. 'That's not a bad bit of dialogue. Not quite Pinter, more Graham Greene.' She pursed her lips. 'Perhaps sub-Graham Greene.'

But Phoebe and Coffin looked straight at each other and their gaze said the same thing: She's playing games and you and I are doing it for real.

COFFIN WALKED Phoebe to her car which was parked in the dark behind the restaurant. 'Come into my office tomorrow and

I will give you names and addresses in Newcastle and Cambridge... Check them, you are looking for evidence of more money than there should be. In fact, keep your eyes, ears and nose out for corruption. Pharmaceuticals,' he said quickly. 'Fake drugs.'

He peered into the darkness. Was there movement in that dark corner? No, probably not. 'Where's your car?'

'Over there.' Phoebe pointed. 'In that dark bit—I always go there, the kids seem to give it a miss when they fancy a bit of vandalism.'

They walked across together. 'Are you driving up?'

'Thought I would do.' Phoebe had a new car, a red Rover, of which she was proud.

'Don't always park in the darkest spots.'

'Is that a warning?' Phoebe was unlocking the car door.

Before she could do more than get into the driving seat, there was a swishing noise and a shout, and a trio of helmeted figures swooped into the car park, round the car, and out again.

Startled, Coffin said, as he jumped away, 'Do those rollerbladers never go to bed?'

Phoebe, more up to date in the ways of the youth of the Second City than the Chief Commander, laughed. 'They prefer it at night, less competition from the traffic. Those weren't the littlest boys.'

'One of them was a girl,' said Coffin.

'Yes, I noticed. We ought to recruit them, they get about and know everything. It's a kind of junior Mafia.' She drove off at her usual speed.

Stella was waiting for him, talking to Max.

'He's worried about his grandson, Louie,' she said, walking forward. 'The boy is having nightmares.'

'I hope it's not because he was lying.'

Stella shook her head. 'No, Max thinks it's because he knows something else, but he won't tell.'

'I'll tell Devlin, she can go and talk to him, he may tell her.'

Stella said diffidently: 'I think he'd like it to be you.'

Coffin looked into the darkness behind Max's restaurant. He

had no car parked there, the two of them could walk home from here.

'It's the inquest on the boys tomorrow,' he said. He took her arm. 'And you, what about you? Are you still here tomorrow?'

'I'm staying a bit longer,' said Stella.

NINE

THE INQUEST WAS HELD in the early-nineteenth-century building which had once housed Dr Arnold's Charity School for Boys. It was a long, plain building in whose hall the whole school had once sat, perched on benches, learning by rote from one teacher. It had undergone various vicissitudes in its long career, being turned into a set of slum tenements, then becoming an ARP centre for bombed-out families in the war against Hitler. Reduced to penury after this period, the building was in great danger of being knocked down, but then found itself raised in status by being taken over by the Second City Arts Committee and turned into a cultural centre, so that the walls were now lined with pictures done by local artists, some good and some not so good. The river figured prominently, as was natural, since the Thames had run through the Second City, providing work and occasional floods throughout the centuries. Apart from the river with its barges, animals were well represented: there was one whole wall of dogs, and a lesser array of cats.

Now, seats had been brought in and a low platform rolled in for the coroner and his clerk.

A small bus was parked outside when Coffin arrived in time to see the parents, grandparents, aunts and uncles, friends and neighbours disembarking from it. Last out of the bus was Dr Chinner, who had organized the whole party.

The driver, Peter Perry, he who drove the school bus, and his friend Ollie Deccon from the sports centre where the boys had gone swimming and skating, were both dressed in dark clothes, with black ties. Peter wore his cap, and Oliver Deccon an old bowler hat which he had borrowed.

'You look like nothing on earth in that hat,' said Peter, who was nervous and tetchy and in pain. 'It's the wrong size, so big it's sitting on your ears.'

'I know.' Ollie was humble. 'I borrowed it from a man with a big head.' His own was on the small side and had always been a worry to him. He was afraid his head was growing smaller. Impossible, he told himself, but was never quite sure.

They filed in behind the families, seating themselves on a bench at the back of the room so as not to be noticeable. Peter knew that some suspicion still hung over him.

Dr Chinner passed down the aisle to take a seat near the front. Inspector Devlin and Sergeant Tittleton had already arrived and were seated unobtrusively in the middle of the hall, which was crowded.

Coffin hung back to let the parents and friends of the dead boys settle into their seats, then he sat down at the back. Peter Perry shifted uncomfortably, edging away from the Chief Commander, whom he recognized. They can't hang a man until he's proved guilty, he told himself. Didn't hang you anyway. No capital punishment, but from the look on Dr Chinner's face, he thought that the doctor might find a way to see you got it.

The coroner, Dr Sam Edginton, who was both a doctor and a lawyer, one of the best coroners in the Second City, strode down the centre aisle, a tall burly man in a dark suit that was unbrushed and shoes that were unpolished. He bowed towards Dr Chinner, whom he knew, then swept on.

'I always want to stand up and sing "God Save the King", when he comes in,' murmured Devlin. 'He gets to look more like George III by the day. Do you think he's descended?'

'Could be. Plenty of royal bastards around; I'm a republican myself. He's a good man, though.'

'The best,' agreed Paddy Devlin. 'He'll get through this as quickly as possible with no fuss and the least pain.'

She was very aware of the four sets of parents sitting behind her. She had got to know them, just a little, in her visits to them over the last few weeks. Dr Chinner did not have the monopoly of pain. Mat Baker's parents, looking old and drawn, Dick Neville, his parents, were younger than the others, the mother in the canteen at Leathergate, a pretty woman with bright-red curls. The Rick parents were sitting close and holding hands, he was a detective constable in Spinnergate, didn't make it easier being on the job, harder, probably, because he knew more of what was going on. Could see more clearly what had happened to his son.

You had to ask, and Paddy Devlin had asked herself, did this killer have a grudge against the police? Or did he just find the sons especially attractive? Her colleagues on the force had asked the same question, and a search was being made of all likely suspects. So far to no avail. All the most virulent police-haters seemed straight about sex. But they were going on looking, but without much belief that they would turn up the killer that way.

What they needed was a straight bit of forensic evidence, a weapon, a shoe, a personal memento of the killer, preferably one with his name on, and they had none.

Perhaps the killer chose them because they went on the bus.

For a moment, her mind dwelt on Peter Perry. There was no evidence against him: he did his work, then stayed home and tended his garden. Or watched television. His girlfriend said so and his neighbours agreed.

Then, after all, there were thirty other or so boys that used the bus and they were still alive and well.

Or, you took the straightforward view that the killer was the missing Jeff Diver and concentrated your energies on looking for him, as it now seemed that Arthur Willows was out of it.

She made unobtrusive notes of the thoughts while the coroner got down to business, meaning to pass them to the Chief Commander. She knew he was there in the hall somewhere, and wondered if he was sitting under the portrait of his dog Augustus, which she had heard he had commissioned from a local artist and which was hung on the wall in this very hall.

Coffin was indeed aware of the portrait of Gus, he had noticed this at once, but he was listening to Dr Sam who was conducting proceedings with his usual measured dignity and discretion.

He took the evidence of the young couple who discovered Archie Chinner's body, as well as that of the police team who found the multiple grave. He was tactful with the medical evidence of the two pathologists.

'He's not mentioning that there was sexual invasion before and after death,' muttered Devlin to Tittleton.

'Bad enough for the parents, anyway,' was his response. He was sitting hunched beside her, his usual good cheer missing. The investigation was getting nowhere and he knew it.

Coffin, who had read the pathologists' reports and knew what Dr Sam was passing over, which included any mention of the dead young woman and her leg, was thoughtful; he wondered what Paddy Devlin was making of it. Did she have any necrophiliacs on her wanted list? Had Jeff Diver's tastes gone that way?

Dr Sam concluded the short inquest and adjourned it to a date to be decided later. Then he rose and swept out, bowing once again to Dr Chinner and bending his head to the rows of parents and friends of the dead boys.

Coffin let them walk in front of him, to meet the photographers and the television crews, to whom Dr Sam was gracious, while diverting them away from the stricken families. A nice man, Coffin decided.

Marshalled by Dr Chinner, all the families got into the coaches where Peter Perry and Oliver Deccon followed them, heads bent down in sympathy and mourning.

The Chief Commander waited for Inspector Devlin and the sergeant to catch him up.

'The funerals next,' he said to her.

'Yes, they are arranged for tomorrow.'

'All of them, all four?'

She nodded. 'All four. I will be there.'

'So will I.'

The young couple who had found the first body and who had given evidence walked out together, hand in hand.

'They got married last week,' said Paddy Devlin. 'Their meeting in the bushes was meant to be a last, open-air loving, before they were hitched. Romantic, really.'

'You're in touch?'

'I go in to see them almost daily in case I can dredge up anything else they might remember. I think they were fright-

ened I would turn up to the wedding, and I felt tempted, but I
didn't.'

COFFIN TRIED AVOIDING Archie Young, who was looking
gloomy and tired, then repented and offered him a lift back to
headquarters and his office.

'Thanks, but I've got my car.' The gloom did not lift. 'And
I've got to drive through the tunnel for the committee on security for the royal visit.' 'Through the tunnel' was police talk
for a visit to the other London. This partly accounted for his
gloom, since meeting with officers from the larger, richer city
was often the occasion for ribald jokes.

'Of course, you'll have come into it at a later date, sir,' he
said with sombre satisfaction. 'You'll be there with the Royals.'

Acknowledging the truth, Coffin took himself back to his
office where Phoebe Astley was waiting for him. Paul Masters
had given her some coffee and Gus was sitting at her feet.

'First cheerful face I've seen today.' Coffin ushered her into
his inner office.

He sat down at his handsome new desk as Paul Masters
brought in a tray of coffee for the Chief Commander, together
with a sheaf of the latest messages. He then bowed himself out
of the door.

'I expect you know something about why I am sending you
on this errand.'

Although it was meant to be highly secret, Coffin was under
no illusions about the power of his Second City colleagues, and
Phoebe Astley in particular, to find out what was going on.

'I have heard something,' she admitted. 'It's code-named
TRAINSPOTTING, isn't it?'

Coffin ignored the joke, he had heard better, but it alerted
him to what the gossips knew and what they didn't: knew the
name began with a T, knew it was regional, did not know its
purpose.

'TRANSPORT A, and keep that to yourself.' Briefly, he told
her about the pharmaceutical counterfeiting, the organization
set up to combat it with a London central control and various
regional centres.

'Heard it had something to do with drugs...didn't know more.'

He gave her the names: Felicity Fox in Cambridge; in Newcastle, there was Joe Weir. And Susy Miller, who 'shot around'.

'Check them all out, see if you can find evidence of unexpected prosperity.'

Phoebe raised an eyebrow. 'Is it serious?'

Coffin phrased his answer carefully: 'It has its serious side.' He passed a file of papers across to her. 'Not a lot of use, but take them for what they are worth. I have nothing else to give you.'

Phoebe took them; she stood up. 'Right, I'll be off then.'

'Expenses to me.' As she got to the door, he said: 'Take care.'

Phoebe turned her head. 'No parking in dark corners? Count on me.'

COFFIN WORKED ON HIS usual routine duties that day, which included going to a lunch given by the vice chancellor of the Second City Inner University——a new university upgraded from a college of further education which had fused with a polytechnic going back to prewar days. The vice chancellor was a charming woman, a scientist of distinction, whom he liked.

The food was uninspired but the company, which included one of the local politicians——a man of some ugliness and great charm who explained what he intended to do when he became Chancellor of the Exchequer——and a famous divine who was interested in miracles, made for interesting conversation. Coffin found himself enjoying it.

But he made his excuses and left early; Dr Madison, the vice chancellor, walked with him to his car.

'You're doing well here,' said Coffin.

She nodded. 'We are, but we are on the cusp between middling good and first class. I think we will get there because we are attracting good teachers and researchers who in turn pull in good students.' She smiled cheerfully. 'No Nobel prizes yet, but who knows? I have about ten years before I retire, maybe we will have one by then. Although I reckon it takes about half a century to create the right seedbed for that sort of plant to flower…that and a lot of luck. One of my successors might see it happen.'

'What about you yourself?' He knew that she was a person of enormous intellectual ability.

'No, I am just an administrator now. You can't do both, I made my decision when I took it on here. And anyway, there's a lot of chance involved in making an important scientific discovery, and someone might always get there before you. We compete, you know.'

'I met a Nobel-prize winner in Oxford recently: Sir Jessimond Fraser.'

Her face lit up. 'Sir Jess?' Then she said sadly: 'He's one of the casualties of success…that stroke.'

'He carries on, I was told his son helps him.'

'He does, indeed. He lectures here, you know, one of our new bright boys, I asked him to lunch but he couldn't make it, he was watching some vital experiment. I think he just prefers to be alone when he isn't teaching or with his father. Social life does not appeal.'

Coffin, who had dropped Sir Jess's name into the conversation pudding deliberately, felt he had been rewarded with a plum. A bit of the luck which Dr Madison had said was so vital.

He drove back to his office, removed Gus from his chair, where he was comfortably bedded down, and got back to the day's routine of telephone calls, faxes, and letters.

If you are an administrator then that is what you are, nothing else. Coffin did not want to be nothing else. He liked active policing, he liked being a detective.

That was enough facing truth for the day, he thought, as he packed his briefcase, spoke to Paul Masters, who was working on, put Gus on a leash, and started for home.

He met Paddy Devlin in the car park. 'A small piece of news: the blood found on the Chinner boy's clothing, you remember there were two types—one type, not the boy's, has evidence of a drug, a painkiller.'

'What is it?'

'A slow release morphine solution. Sometimes shows as the drug, sometimes as metatasis, but is identifiable. Could be just the bit of hard forensic evidence that we need; if we even find the killer, it should be a help.'

When we find him, she thought. She added: 'Nothing about Jeff Diver yet, sir, in case you were wondering. No sightings. Nothing to grab hold of anywhere.'

Nothing was how he felt, the temporary euphoria of lunch-time quite dried up. 'Interesting about the drug,' was all he found to say.

There were no messages from Phoebe Astley, too soon, of course, but one from Stella saying she was going to the National Theatre on business and would be back.

He ate a cold meal, alone.

He fell asleep in the chair, to be awoken by Gus barking and scrabbling at his leg.

'What is it, boy?' He realized he had been asleep for some time.

Gus growled, then ran to the door. Coffin rose to follow him. He stood on the stairs, listening. He heard movement below, someone had stumbled, fallen down a stair.

'Stella? Is that you?'

The choking, gasping noise he heard made him rush down the stairs; Gus leapt past and was there before him.

She was sitting on the bottom step, shaking. He dragged her to her feet and put his arms round her. 'Stella, what is it? What's happened?' She tried to say something but could not get the words out. 'Hold your breath, then breathe in deeply… Right…' As her breathing steadied, and the shaking stopped, he said: 'Now tell me.'

'There was…' She took a breath. 'A man outside…'

'Go on, dearest. When you can.' He was walking her upstairs with the dog jumping ahead of them, giving small excited barks. 'Let's get you some brandy.' This was so unlike the cool, self-possessed Stella. 'I could do with some myself.'

He settled her on a chair in the kitchen, the nearest room, got the brandy, which he poured into two glasses. 'Come on, love.' She was quieter but still shivering. The dog was giving a series of little barks. 'Shut up, Gus.'

The dog, still barking, ran down the stairs to growl and snuffle at the front door.

'Fool dog.'

'No,' said Stella, with a shudder, 'I don't know what's out there but let him bark on.'

Coffin waited while she drank some brandy. 'Tell me when you can.'

'I parked the car...there's not much lighting out there, not enough...no moon and there's a bit of a drizzle...he came at me out of the darkness. His hands came out at me.'

'Did he touch you? What did he do?' Coffin asked swiftly.

'No, I screamed and ran, I had my key in my hand so I got in quickly.'

Coffin stood up. 'I'll go down to look.'

'No, wait...I think he has been there before... I have thought I saw someone before...in the dark.'

'You should have told me.'

'I don't think it was me he wanted... I'm not sure what or whom he did want...'

'He frightened you, that's enough for me.'

'It wasn't what he did, but what he was.' Stella began to shiver again. 'I had this feeling that he was, or had been, dead.'

Coffin looked his wife with doubt, but he tried not to show it. He put his hand on her shoulder, gave it a loving press. 'Sit here, try to calm down. I'll go for a look around.'

He walked up the stairs to the sitting room, where he telephoned police headquarters in Spinnergate to order a search of the area around the theatre.

No point in questioning Stella further at the moment. He couldn't work out what she meant about the man being dead. He doubted if she knew herself.

Gus met him at the front door, speeding out into the courtyard beyond. He at least seemed to know where he was going.

Coffin stood outside, not sure whether to follow the dog or not. 'Can't see anyone,' he muttered to himself.

Beyond lay the bulk of the theatre complex, all in darkness.

Anyone could hide there. The dog had gone the other way, towards the car park, beyond which lay the old churchyard over the road, now a small public garden.

But Gus had stopped and was sniffing at the wall of the grey stone tower.

As Coffin walked that way he was walking into a smell and recoiled. A smell can be like a person, strong and repellent. Coffin walked into this one, then took a step backwards.

The smell was ammonic, richly refulgent of human excreta and vomit, thick and only too grossly human.

Someone had stood here, rested against that wall where Augustus was still sniffing.

And there was something else too, the smell was so strong and complex that you could believe that it came from death. It was the smell of someone whose innards had gone into crisis state; it might be the smell of death.

I have to hand it to you, Stella, he thought, perhaps you weren't so wrong.

But a dead person walking round and reaching out a hand to touch? A little rationality, here, please, he told himself.

The closer he got to the spot on the wall that so engaged the dog, the stronger the smell; when you moved away, it weakened. Still there but not so strong.

A man's body had rested against that wall. Waiting for Stella? Or for anyone?

He walked through the smell and out the other side in the direction of the churchyard, following the scent on the air of ammonia and decaying body fluids.

By this time, a patrol car had arrived, lighting up the darkness. A uniformed officer came up and saluted. He told the Chief Commander that a search party was on the way.

Coffin nodded. 'Good. It might be something or nothing, but my wife was frightened by a man coming at her where she parked her car... There is someone around and I want him found.'

He crossed the road into the old churchyard, with the dog at his heels. The dog followed him, but only for a few feet, then he sat down by the gate.

Coffin wandered up one path, flashing his torch, then he turned.

'Yes, you are right, Gus, we will leave it to those better equipped to do the searching. He's been here, I can smell him, but I doubt he is here now.'

Gus wagged his tail, he was well pleased to leave, feeling that he had extracted all the information he could from various smells. He could have given his master a body picture of the man, but words were not his medium.

Stella had taken a shower and washed her hair; she was drying it when they came back.

'Hello, I thought I needed to wash everything away…I could smell that smell. I didn't imagine it, did I?'

'You did not,' said Coffin with emphasis.

'I'm glad I didn't imagine it. I was afraid I might have done. Did you catch him?'

'Not so far. We will.'

Stella nodded. She was experienced enough to interpret that as hope more than solid expectation.

'Stella, did you see his face?'

She shook her head. 'Not to know him again. I looked and looked away, it's a blur… All I can say, the face was dirty…' She gave a shudder. 'I know his smell, though.'

Coffin nodded. 'That may help.'

Hope again, she thought, no more.

Coffin said suddenly: 'Where were you all the time?'

'Yes, I was late home, I stayed to talk over various plans.' She hesitated. Should she tell him when all that was held out to her was still just up for an offer and might be cancelled? 'They have put something up to me, a threefold contract to produce, act too, if I want.'

'But that's marvellous…congratulations, darling.'

'It's not absolutely solid yet, things could go wrong.'

'Is that why you came back? To negotiate with the National?'

Stella hesitated. Then she said: 'No. No, it wasn't. I told you: I came home to see you.' Then she added, honestly: 'I knew about it, though, knew it might come up.'

Coffin laughed. 'For an actress you are a very poor prevaricator.'

'What's that mean?' said Stella suspiciously.

'A liar... Come on, come to bed. Your hair is dry.'

'Wait a minute. Will we be told if they have found someone?'

'In the morning.'

'Yes, that's reasonable. Tell me, is the man tonight anything to do with the business that you sent Phoebe Astley off to deal with?'

Coffin was silent. 'Yes, I think it might have.'

'Does that mean she is in danger?'

'She could be. And before you ask: Yes, she knew it.'

Stella took it in. Her hair was dry as she shook it out. So well had it been cut that it fell decoratively into place. 'When you are so cool like that, I could almost hate you.'

'It's the job.'

'I only said almost... I was frightened tonight.'

'I know.'

'Will I have to make a statement about the man?'

'You can do it later; I will see to it.'

Stella made a move towards the stairs. 'Thank you. Tomorrow then, what about you? Bad day?'

'I have to go to a funeral.'

Four funerals, he thought, as he stayed behind. He went to the window to look out over the scene below. From this window, he could see the churchyard. Pinpoints of lights flashed in it; so it was being searched.

Pointless really, he thought, as he drew back, you'd need searchlights to see through the bushes and trees, especially where the ground sloped sharply towards the canal.

Anyway, the man, whoever he was, would have gone long since. A walking funeral himself. Perhaps he hadn't gone but had slid back into his grave.

He looked at the brandy bottle, and considered for a moment taking a strong, long drink, but decided against it, and went upstairs to bed with his affectionate but enigmatic wife.

But that was Stella for you. On the whole she kept her secrets. He had lived through a few of them with her, as she had with him, but there were still reserves. The interesting thing was that as the years went on his secrets grew less and hers more.

Damn it, he thought, being a detective made you suspicious.

'Any ghosts?' she said to him from the pillows as he came in.

'No ghosts,' he said. 'Not for me or you.'

Some ghosts out there for someone, though.

TEN

THE FUNERAL was a repeat of the inquest, except that there were two coaches organized by Dr Chinner with the same two drivers. The extra bus was necessary because all the neighbours and friends wished to come. There were schoolfriends present as well, tidied up for the occasion, rollerblades left at home. Coffin observed the bus driver limping in with a friend, the other driver.

There was a short service in St Gabriel's Church in Palmer Street which was crowded with mourners and onlookers. Then they filed out to where the coffins were being placed, two-by-two, in the hearses.

One great wreath placed above the first hearse which bore two small coffins was in the shape of a pair of rollerblades, white and red carnations did the job. The inscription, which Coffin read, said: *From all your mates at school.*

The second hearse had more wreaths on the other two coffins, including one from the police and one from the local newspaper. Mimsie Marker who sold the newspapers down by Spinnergate tube station had sent a simple cross.

The closest schoolfriends of the boys had sent a special wreath, paid for with their own money, shaped like a pair of skates. The boys themselves were present, standing together at their own request, a tight little group. Louie was one of them, the youngest but the best skater, with highest grinds to his credit. They were a well-dressed, muscular group, determined and, at the moment, polite, although they knew how to be rude when it suited them.

Not many words passed between them, because parents were hovering, and one of the things that united them was a distrust of adults. 'We've done what we can,' said Mick Minch, who was as much of a leader as they recognized. 'For now.' The implication was that more might be necessary.

The Chief Commander and Inspector Devlin stood together, both looked sombre.

'Makes your heart break, doesn't it?' said Paddy Devlin from his side, her voice half cynical. 'The coffins match, have you noticed? I don't know if that makes me feel better or worse. Worse, I think. I hate this bit,' she confided to Coffin. 'The inquests, you can call that business, but the funerals, the graves, the burying, that I can't bear. They are all going in one grave, you know.'

'I did know,' said Coffin.

'Dr Chinner fixed it all up. One grave but four small tombstones above. They will come later, of course, you have to wait for the earth to settle or the tombstones will start sinking.'

She really does mind, Coffin thought. He had lost a child himself once, long ago, but he remembered the pain.

'I know what you are thinking, sir, you are thinking that I ought not to continue too long in this pederast job. I think it myself sometimes, but I know it's wrong. I go through this down bit and after it I go on as before.'

'I think it's right to grieve,' said Coffin.

'Is that what it is? It feels more like anger.'

Sergeant Tittleton, who had been circling the whole area around the open grave, came back to them.

'The young couple over there are the pair that found the Chinner boy's body. Mr and Mrs Foster.'

'I saw them at the inquest.' Coffin looked across to where the hearses were drawn up, beyond them on a patch of grass the man and the girl stood. He had his arm round her. 'She's crying.'

He turned to Inspector Devlin. 'Did they come up with any possible extra details? Anything that could help.'

'Not really, no. They were shocked out of their minds, I think. And anything that had gone before was wiped out.'

'Have you spoken to them again?'

She nodded. 'Yes, and all they could say was that they were wandering along, hand in hand, talking about themselves and their wedding—apparently her mother was being a nuisance—

when they saw the man staring in the trees, and they saw the tip of a foot protruding.'

'I'd like to speak to them.'

Devlin nodded. 'They've seen us, so they won't be surprised. A nice little couple.'

'Decent of them to come,' said Tony Tittleton.

'I think they need to do a bit of mourning themselves, they went to that part of the trees quite a lot. They didn't say so but I guessed. And if they were making love while the kid was rotting underground...' She shrugged. 'I think I'd want to do something myself.'

If they were there often, Coffin found himself thinking, they might have some detail, something half forgotten. He kept coming back to that thought as the four coffins were deposited, one by one.

He held right back in the crowd, while the simple, dignified service was gone through. All the time, he kept his eyes on the young couple. When they moved, he moved. He gave Devlin a nod: 'I'm going to talk to them.'

They were walking fast, close together, the man with his arm round his wife. Even in the crowd they were easy to pick out, because she was wearing a bright pink coat, not usual funeral wear, but perhaps it had been part of her wedding clothes.

Tony Tittleton had circled rapidly round the crowd, clockwise, and was already talking to the two when Coffin and Devlin caught up with them.

'There you are, sir,' he said cheerfully. 'This is Mr and Mrs Foster... Mrs Foster thinks she has met you.'

Trust Tittleton to come up with that sort of information.

'We didn't meet exactly. It was a party your wife gave for the helpers in the St Luke's Theatre Charity...I was there.' Mrs Foster smiled, she had a nice smile. 'You shook my hand.'

'Glad I did that.' Coffin reflected as he smiled back that he could probably be her grandfather; she looked about seventeen and her husband not much older, but she had big eyes, a mane of blonde hair and long legs which the little pink skirt just topped like a frill. He noticed that Sergeant Tittleton was eyeing her with appreciation.

'Did you see anyone or anything that night or any other night, Mrs Foster?' he prompted her.

'Sorry, haven't got used to being Mrs Foster yet.' She looked up at her tall, thin husband.

'You better had... I'll have to teach you.'

Paddy Devlin broke up this scene of young love: 'So you didn't remark anything, Mrs Foster?'

Her husband answered for her: 'It was, is, very quiet up there...that's why we went there. You can work that out, can't you?'

Mrs Foster smiled and looked around her as if searching for something, and gave a little shake of her head.

Coffin and Paddy Devlin waited, but nothing more came.

'See you to your car,' said Sergeant Tittleton gallantly. Coffin and Inspector Devlin watched as the pair got into a smart little sports car with the sergeant helping them back away from the close-packed parking and off.

'Thought I might get something more out of her,' he said as he strolled back to them. 'But she's too much into love's young dream.'

Coffin turned to the inspector. 'I thought there was something there too. You might have another go at her later.'

'Will do. We need to find the man with the dog. We're getting publicity on all the media, nationwide, they have been very helpful. There is a lot of emotion swinging around.'

In this country, Coffin thought, dogs can get more notice than people. 'Try mentioning the dog,' he said.

Chief Superintendent Archie Young appeared at his side. 'Saw you here. I was with Chinner, came in the coach with him. He's gone back with the rest of the families. I've left him to it.'

'How is he?'

Archie Young considered. 'Ferocious, I think that's the word.' He nodded to himself. 'Yes, be no trouble to him to tear the abuser limb from limb. He wouldn't need a wolf or a dog, do it himself.'

'I know how he feels.' The more so after the episode with

Stella and the walking dead last night. 'Come for a drink, Archie. Funerals have that effect on me.'

'On everyone.' Archie Young was sombre. 'Walk or ride, sir?'

'Walk. I need the movement.'

Archie Young agreed, said a walk would be good, but was thoughtful. What was the Big Man up to?

He had known John Coffin long enough now to know he rarely acted without some reason, not always apparent. The funeral had taken place at a cemetery on the edge of a built-up area, just beyond Leathergate. It would be a good long walk back to any of the usual drinking spots.

'If we go out of the side gate here, take a right turn and then go left down the hill, we will come to the place where the kids and the girl were found,' said Coffin, who seemed to carry a map of the area in his head. 'Near enough.'

Inspector Devlin and Sergeant Tittleton watched the two men walk away and the Chief Commander's official car drive off. 'Security won't like that,' said Devlin.

'I reckon those two can look after each other.'

'I hope so.'

'I hear there was an intruder outside St Luke's last night.'

'Can you be an intruder if you are outside,' mused Devlin as they went to their own car.

'Dunno. Funny business, though.'

ARCHIE YOUNG was unsurprised when their walk took them to the scrubby, roughly wooded slope where the bodies had been found: at the higher end the roped-off site of the girl's body, and then further down the site of the boys' first burial, where the police forensic team was still quietly at work, sifting the soil, examining each leaf and twig, just in case anything had been missed.

'Do you get any feeling about this place?' asked Coffin.

Archie Young denied it. 'No.'

'No.' Coffin nodded. 'I don't either. There is nothing here which says This is Death Place, Bury Me Here. And yet, down there the boys and up here a body. Why is that?'

'Coincidence?'

'I don't think so,' said Coffin obstinately. 'There's a connection, but I don't know what it is.'

'You aren't suggesting she was killed by the murderer of the boys?'

'No, the pathologists agree it was suicide.'

'She may have known the killer and been shocked into suicide?' It was a hopeless suggestion and Archie Young knew it, but with Coffin you kept on trying.

'No, the dates are shifty but she was dead first.' He added, in a quiet voice: 'Alice Jessimond, second-year student, living out in Alexander Road, her parents didn't even know she was missing, let alone dead. The university doesn't have much of a checking system, and no one noticed she was not at lectures and classes. Or if they did notice they put it down to idleness. Or the love affair.'

For there had been a love affair, they knew now, having been told it by a horrified, unhappy friend. Not a happy love affair, either.

'I know,' said Archie Young gently. It had, in fact, fallen to him to talk to the stricken parents, and later to the young lecturer and tutor who, white-faced, had denied any relationship with the girl except friendliness. 'Slept with her,' Archie Young said to himself, 'but is never going to admit it. Bad career move.'

'Sex and death,' said Coffin. He looked at Archie for an answer.

'There's a lot of it about.'

They walked on in silence. Soon they were in sight of the Marquis of Granby, a quiet, almost country-style pub, where they were sure of not seeing any drinking colleagues.

'Who was the Marquis of Granby?' asked Archie Young. 'Must have been a great drinker, you see his name on pubs all over the south of England.'

'A conquering general, I expect,' said Coffin. 'It's always a general or horse. Perhaps he won the Derby.'

But no, said the landlord as he served them, the chap was a general who lost his wig in the battle and went it bald-headed.

They settled in a dark corner with their drinks. Coffin was abstemious now, and Archie Young had always been a modest drinker.

'I hear you had a bit of trouble last night.'

Coffin had long since accepted that any news about the Chief Commander was passed around with speed.

'Stella got the brunt of it. She was terrified, he didn't touch, I'm not sure if he meant to, I have a feeling it was me he was after… I can't even be sure if he was real…all I got was a smell. What do you make of smells as proof of identity?'

'Smells are real enough,' said Archie Young with feeling. 'I've known one or two ripe villains.'

'I'd certainly know that one again if I smelt him.'

They went on talking about the everyday problems of policing the Second City. Eventually, Coffin said it was time to get off. 'I'll give you a lift back.'

Archie Young looked surprised.

'I told the car to meet me here.'

Everything arranged for, thought Archie Young, admiring the administrative skills of the Chief Commander as he followed him out.

'I want to drive round to the school all the lads went to,' Coffin said, 'not to talk to anyone unless we have to, just to look round.'

'You'll be lucky if you get away without the Head catching you.'

'I ought to speak to the Head first, by rights, but I don't want to. I just want to make a silent tour of the cloakrooms.'

'For what?' Archie Young asked himself silently but knew better than to ask aloud. 'He's on one of his psychic kicks,' he said to himself. He knew Coffin in this mood, sometimes it got results, which he laid at the door of telepathy, or precognition, or just plain luck.

If there was luck this time, Coffin did not acknowledge it. He walked slowly through the ground-floor cloakrooms and lavatories.

Groups of rollerblades, neatly labelled with the owner's name, stood beneath the pegs with jackets and thick sweaters.

Archie saw him looking. 'It's a way of life now, even if they go in the school bus they still have these round their necks. Sometimes clump in on their feet. The Head forbids the use in school or in the playground.'

'Glad to hear it.'

His luck deserted him there, because a tall, pretty woman wearing a smart trouser suit met him at the door. She held out her hand.

'Jennifer Rhodes, Deputy Head. I saw you come in, the Headmaster is away today. Can I do anything?'

Coffin introduced himself.

'Oh, I know who you are. I recognized you at once. I was at the funeral too. I saw you there.'

'I didn't want to disturb you…just wanted to look around. One is always looking for ideas.'

A profoundly sceptical look came over her face. Archie Young sympathized with her, but kept his own expression bland.

'Inspector Devlin has been here several times.'

'I know, Miss Rhodes.' Coffin prepared for retreat.

'Ms Rhodes.'

'Ms Rhodes. I apologize and I won't waste any more of your time.'

Ms Rhodes looked as if she could have wasted it willingly in a sharp reproof, but she contented herself with a dignified bow and an offer to see them out.

Back in the car, watching her well-tailored back, Coffin laughed. 'She put me in my place.'

'Did you get what you wanted?'

'I don't know. I'm thinking about it.'

You've picked up something, Archie Young decided; he had his own touch of telepathy, and it had to do with those roller-blades.

Good luck was offered to Coffin in the next few minutes. They passed the chemist's shop with a window full of great antique jars and beakers, full of nameless liquids of shining colours, sapphire-blue, emerald-green and strong yellow.

Coffin read the name: H. Pennyfeather.

'So that's H. Pennyfeather.'

'Oh, he isn't called that. I believe Pennyfeather lived there about the turn of the century. Tom Barley just liked the name and restored it. His son works in the Second City University, he is a chemist too but more academic. Oxford, you know, degrees and research. Someone told me he was working on something with Sir Jessimond Fraser...or might be with Sir Jess's son.'

'They could be working together.'

'Fraser is a professor there, runs the department of pharmacy. Not been there long, but stirred things up.'

'I believe you,' said Coffin thoughtfully. 'How do you know all this?'

'My wife's nephew, he is doing a degree there.'

COFFIN AND ARCHIE YOUNG were not the only pair having a quiet drink.

Peter Perry and his fellow driver at the funeral were having a post-funeral drink in the long dusty shed where the two buses were housed, as well as several old cars and vans which looked as though they were refugees from a war.

'Thought your brother would be back,' said Ollie.

'Had a few days extra. Can't blame him.'

'You're too soft with him.'

They were drinking tea from a big brown pot, brewed up by means of a kettle on a gas ring. There was a small refrigerator as well. You could live there for a time and on occasion, Peter had done.

He poured them both another cup of tea and popped a white tablet in his mouth. 'Screws are bad today.'

'Saw you limping.' Ollie looked at him with sympathy. 'Pain comes and goes, doesn't it?'

'Comes more often than it goes,' grumbled Peter. 'Drugs rot your brain, but I was born stupid.'

'Never. Not you.' Ollie pushed his cup forward. 'I understand.'

'You would. Another cuppa? You'll have tannin poisoning.' Peter limped over to the kettle, felt it. Still hot.

'I'm poisoned already.'

'Dr Chinner asked us round to his place, but I couldn't do it, couldn't face it, so I said no for us both.'

'I heard. Glad you did.' Ollie finished his third cup of tea, and rose. 'What are you doing for the rest of the day?'

'Schools closed, sympathy and all that. So I shall go home and watch telly.'

'I've got to go to the centre. I've got a swimming class and then a skating group.'

He got into his battered white van, another relic from the war zone, and departed.

Peter tidied up, checked and cleaned the coaches, then he went off too.

BACK IN HIS OFFICE, John Coffin found there was a call on tape from Phoebe. It was one of her fluent monologues.

'I like Cambridge,' she said. 'A handsome town, and the Backs are beautiful. More beautiful than Oxford, perhaps.'

'You aren't there to admire the scenery,' muttered Coffin with impatience.

'Absolutely no sign of unearned riches on anyone, and Harry Seton had already done a thorough check on bank accounts, putting up the backs of several bank managers as he did so. I did a check again and was even more unwelcome. No rich clothes, no valuable cars, all concerned pleading poverty. They knew why I was here, of course.

'Counterfeit drugs still on sale, sometimes from a market stall, sometimes in an outlying village. The team regarded themselves as efficient, and are annoyed that as soon as they clear up one set of outlets there is a rash of others. Never any shortage of supplies…all good stuff, it seems, but copies and dirt cheap. They can understand the attraction for those who buy and those who sell. They had expected to be on the job for a short time and are surprised to see it looks like life work.

'HM Customs bearing down on everyone heavily, no evidence that counterfeit drugs are smuggled in.'

'They are not,' said Coffin to himself, before going back to Phoebe's voice.

'Ed Saxon set the outfit up, as you know. No love lost between Ed and Harry Seton. But I guess you know that too.

'Off to Newcastle.'

Phoebe signed off at this point, with a sigh. She knew the taste of a waste of time when she got one into her mouth.

Coffin listened to what she had to say, rewound the tape, then listened again.

Good old Phoebe, she was getting to the heart of the mission. He considered telephoning, but instead tried for Inspector Davenport of the Met.

The man was not easily brought to the telephone, but this time he came on almost at once.

'Fancy you calling,' he said breezily. 'I was thinking of calling you.'

'You were?' This year, next year, sometime never, more like it. 'So how are you getting on with Harry Seton's killing?'

'I'd like to say we were nearly there'—silence for a second—'but it wouldn't be true. Harry's body was nicely trimmed of all possible clues...'

Coffin winced.

'Done by an expert. You can see what that suggests.'

'A contract killing?'

'Sure. But who bought the contract and who carried it out, we don't yet know...the wife is high on the list. Always look at the family, eh? They were on bad terms, and she's in and out badgering us. I always reckon that's a sign, don't you.'

'Could be,' said Coffin cautiously.

'But I have some good news: we caught the man who torched Seton's office. He's a man we know, a low-grade local villain, Len Macellan; he says he got the job through the post. A letter, no less, and payment half before the job, half on completion. Believe that if you can.' Davenport's tone suggested he didn't. 'I do not see him doing the killing, though, so we are checking his friends and associates.'

'How was he actually paid?' questioned Coffin.

'Pushed through the door...that part I do believe.' A pause during which Davenport thought about what to say. 'I think he knows who paid him but won't say. I put Mrs Seton in the frame here.'

'What's the evidence for that?'

'Money, the place was well insured by Harry. And, as I say, they were on bad terms; I reckon she hated him. And she knew he was on to some work he thought important, some women might be spiteful about that.'

'Arson and killing is a bit more than spite.'

'Isn't it?' agreed Davenport cheerfully. 'She's a remarkable woman. Her shop's on the rocks, you know, rent owing, rates not paid, but you'd never know it from the colour of her hair.' A sigh came over the line. 'Still, there you are, she might have hired a killer, but she's a lovely lady. This is all confidential, of course.'

'I shan't broadcast it. Does Ed Saxon know what you think?'

'Ah now, that's a bit different, sir. Have to keep old Ed in touch, but I don't tell him all that's in my mind.' He added meaningly: 'And I think he's got a bit of a soft spot for Mrs Seton.'

'And you feel pretty sure the arsonist is not also the murderer of Harry Seton?'

'No,' said Inspector Davenport regretfully. 'Not got the brains, couldn't organize it. No, I shall get the man in the end. We are working through the names of likely characters.'

'I hope you pick up the killer.' Coffin remembered the sight of Harry's dead body with some pain.

'Oh, I will,' the inspector said with confidence. 'And when I do I will screw the name of the hirer out of him.'

I think you might be surprised at it when you get it, thought Coffin, who had his own ideas on the subject.

Coffin sat back when the conversation ended, to consider what he believed of all that: he found he could believe that Mrs Seton had hired an arsonist, but it was harder to believe she had hired a killer.

He was interrupted by the entrance of Paul Masters.

'Sorry to break in, sir, but I have had a phone call from Miss Pinero.'

Just for a moment, Coffin felt that irritable scratch that

Stella's obstinate clinging to her own name could arouse. He scratched his arm to relieve it, then reproached himself. Stupid. 'Yes, what does she want?'

'She didn't want to ring you herself for fear of disturbing, but would you bring a special wine home for dinner. She told me what to ask for.' He consulted a bit of paper. 'A Gerwurtztraminer, it's an Alsatian wine.'

'I know that.' The irritation returned and demanded another scratch.

'Two bottles, in fact, sir.'

'Did she say why she wanted it?'

'A dinner party, I think, sir.'

The irritation returned, full force, and he resisted the temptation to kick Gus, who was resting, confidingly, on his feet.

Then his usual good humour reasserted itself. Stella, I love you, he thought, and at least it shows you are yourself again, but you can be a bloody nuisance.

THERE WAS A solitary constable patrolling the area around St Luke's when he parked the car; he saluted Coffin. 'Nothing, sir.'

'Good. Not even across the road?' And the Chief Commander nodded towards the old churchyard.

'No, sir, not even there. Not unless he's tucked up in a tomb.' As a joke, it failed for Coffin who walked on home, just saying: 'Check.'

Stella greeted him with open arms. 'Kiss me, I have a triumph.'

He waited.

'I have a firm contract to produce at the National. Aren't I lucky?'

'What about St Luke's?' Coffin embraced his rejoicing wife.

'Oh, I will do that too.'

'And the film?'

'Naturally, I will do that first. There is a contract,' she said reprovingly.

'And you will keep the same nose?'

She sighed. 'Now that I do regret, but I really can't fit it in. Later perhaps.'

'So what's the party? Here's the wine,' he said, producing the bottles and fending off Gus, who was sitting on his feet.

'We are the party.' She threw her arms wide. 'We are it. Don't you love me?'

'I do, Stella, I do.'

She looked at him. 'It's been a long day, hasn't it? You look beat.'

The bell sounded below. Twice.

'I'll go,' he said quickly, remembering last night.

'It'll be Max, our dinner. I said two rings or I wouldn't open the door.'

So she did remember last night.

'It's fish, sole and lobster and prawns...that's why I chose that wine. The head waiter at the Ritz said that's what you drink with fish.'

'And when did he tell you that?' said Coffin from the door.

'Some day I might tell you.'

'And who was with you?'

'Tell you that too.'

He came back with the great silver tray loaded with heated dishes. 'Where do I put this?'

Stella led the way. 'In the dining room, of course.' She had laid the table out with silver, glass goblets and candles, alight and flickering.

'Did you do this yourself?' Stella was not famed for domesticity. 'Or did Mrs James?'

Mrs James was the small but robust lady who cleaned the tower dwelling from top to bottom, grumbling at the inconvenience of so many stairs while glorying in her illustrious employers.

'I did, as you know. Jean has been away with a bad back.'

'I had noticed,' agreed Coffin lamely. 'There did seem to be a bit of dust around, but she always avoids me when you aren't here. I don't know if she thinks I am some sort of domestic rapist. You've done it beautifully.'

Stella agreed with a pleased smile, without admitting that the table had been laid by one of Max's helpers. Services rendered and duly paid for.

'Put the dishes on the hot plate. Not this one, though.' She was investigating what was on the tray. 'Oysters in a creamy sauce. We eat that first. Have a good helping, oysters are an aphrodisiac. For a happy ending to the evening, you know.'

It was never easy to be sure with Stella when she was speaking for herself or acting in some play.

'I shall look forward to it,' said Coffin politely. 'Now I know what you have in mind.'

'Best ending to a celebration.'

He decided she meant it, for herself and him. That bit of dialogue was certainly not out of Pinter or Tennessee Williams or Shepard. Might be Ayckbourn. He laughed.

'Funny, is it?' demanded Stella.

'No, I am laughing at myself.'

The oysters were delicious.

There was no talk of murders or of intruders at the meal, but Stella told theatrical anecdotes to make him laugh.

'You made that one up,' he said at one point. 'That one about George the Fifth and Queen Mary and John Gielgud can't be true.'

'Well, I doctored it a bit.'

At the end of the meal, Stella stood up. 'It's supposed to be a bad thing to go to bed after a large meal, but a little exercise might change that.' She put her arms round his neck. 'Do you still wonder why I came home?'

'Not at this moment,' said Coffin huskily. 'You are a beauty, Stella.'

'And a good wife?'

'A very good wife.'

They were standing there when the telephone rang. 'Ignore it,' said Stella.

It went on ringing. And ringing.

She took a step away. 'No, I can tell that you can't.' She watched his back as he walked towards the telephone; she knew the call was not for her just as she knew it was bad news.

She listened, trying to assess what was being said.

'Yes, yes, that's right.' Then a pause. 'Yes, she was. On my instructions. Yes, it must be her.' Another pause. 'Thank you for telling me. Let me know when you have confirmation, please.'

He put the telephone down, then stood there looking at it for a while.

Stella came over to him.

'Tell me.'

Slowly, he said: 'A report has come through of an explosion in a hotel room in Newcastle... A woman has been killed, she seems to have been identified as Phoebe Astley.'

ELEVEN

'MY DEAR,' said Stella. She came up and took his hand, holding it gently. 'Dearest, I am so sorry.'

Coffin said awkwardly, as if the very words hurt him, 'They will tell me more when they know it.'

Stella patted his hand. 'I'll get you a drink. Come on, Gus.'

The dog reluctantly moved from across Coffin's feet, where he had planted himself as a gesture of support for he knew not what crisis. He followed Stella while she poured out a strong whisky and soda, then followed her back as she handed the goblet over. The smell from it was repugnant to his nose, but he understood it was enjoyed by his master.

'Thank you.' Coffin took the glass.

'This killing…was it meant for you?'

'I think so, yes.'

'Did Phoebe know there was danger?'

'She knew.' Phoebe had certainly known. He drained his glass.

Stella was silent. She walked up and down the room; it was hard news to take in. She had never been sure if she liked Phoebe Astley until recently when she had realized Phoebe was a woman to like and respect. 'Killed? Are they sure that she's dead?'

Coffin said briefly: 'It was an explosion, tore the room inside out. She's dead all right.'

It could have been him, Stella thought, it could have been my husband. Phoebe died in his place.

'What have you been doing that makes someone hate you so?'

'I've never been sure that it was personal,' Coffin said. 'I think I am just a nuisance.'

'Pretty rough way of dealing with a nuisance.'

'You'd think so, wouldn't you? But then the people who

arranged it are not very nice people.' The memory of Harry Seton flashed into his mind.

'It can't be easy to arrange, an explosion like that,' said Stella.

'Ah, you see, there is money involved. Money can do a lot.' He went to sit on the sofa, he put his head on his hands. Stella came to sit beside him. She too looked at the floor, there seemed nothing else to do.

The carpet needed cleaning, probably beyond Mrs James, better to get in a professional cleaning firm. That was the worst of having a dog, they did bring in the dirt. She gave Augustus a critical look at which he wagged his tail. He was an optimist, never distrustful and appreciated any attention.

'They'll let me know when they know anything more,' said Coffin, to no one at all.

Phoebe Astley went a long way back in his life, into that period when he and Stella had drifted far apart. Phoebe was part of his life in an interesting way: they had never been in love with each other, but had a long, affectionate (and just occasionally something warmer than that) relationship which was now a steady friendship. He trusted Phoebe and there were not many people in his world that he did trust.

She had been working in Birmingham; he had persuaded her to come into the Second City.

Someone would have to tell Eden, her friend with whom she shared a flat. But that could come later. There were parents too.

'Is Eden in the theatre tonight?' he asked Stella. Eden worked in the wardrobe, caring for the clothes of the performers, sometimes designing them and even making them.

'I expect so. Leave her tonight. I'll tell her myself tomorrow.'

'Yes, that would be best. If you don't mind doing it.'

'She had to be off anyway, as I now remember: she was driving to Chichester to talk to a friend in the wardrobe there about borrowing some costumes for *Macbeth*. She won't be back till the small hours. Or she may even stay the night.'

'I booked the room in that hotel,' said Coffin. 'In my name; Phoebe just walked into it.'

'I'm surprised the hotel let her.'

'I don't know what she said; I suppose she explained it somehow.'

Gus stood up, giving a series of little yaps.

'That's the doorbell.' Coffin stood up. 'I'll go down.'

'Do be careful. Just in case.'

She stood at the top of the winding staircase as Coffin went to open the door. Listening, she could hear voices. A man. There was a little rumble of conversation, she heard a couple of words: 'planted under the bed,' came through to her, another short even quieter few words, then the two men came upstairs.

'Oh, Archie,' she said with relief. 'Thank goodness it's you.'

The chief superintendent came across to kiss her cheek and give her a consoling hug.

'I happened to be in my office when the news came through... I don't know any more yet, I'm afraid.'

Coffin had followed him in. 'What *did* happen?'

'She went into the room, was near the bed, and the bomb went off. In her face. It must have been triggered by some tremble device. Probably under or in the bed...they don't know yet, although the explosive people are there.'

'When did this happen?'

'Just about an hour ago.'

So it was hot news, Coffin thought.

'She had checked into this room, booked in your name, said you had booked it for her.'

'About right,' said Coffin. 'More or less how it was.'

Archie Young was carefully avoiding Coffin's eyes. He went on: 'She gave the Spinnergate address, so the Newcastle police rang us to do the home-news bit...and one of the uniformed lot recognized the district.'

Read on from there, Coffin thought.

'Does that mean that Eden knows?' asked Stella. 'They shared the Spinnergate flat.'

'No, not yet. She wasn't there, no one was.'

So the uniformed chap sent with the sad message came gratefully back, spared the task that no one liked.

'I'm glad to have heard so soon.' Coffin was aware that

Archie Young was discreetly asking no questions about why and how Phoebe Astley had been sent off to Newcastle.

'Phoebe was having a few days' leave, apparently,' said Archie, again with that careful disinterest that showed Coffin he either knew or guessed a lot. He knew that Phoebe had Coffin's confidence, and saw that he himself would have to wait until he was told much. Should have got on to Phoebe myself before the dear girl went, he thought.

Stella offered Archie Young a drink. 'Coffee, or wine or whisky?'

He accepted the coffee. 'There should be more news soon. I just thought I'd drop round and tell you what I knew.'

Coffin nodded. 'Thanks, Archie. I will tell you more about why Phoebe was there, but later. Not now.' He accepted some more whisky and gave a sharp kick at the sofa.

Gus looked relieved that the kick was not at him, but he moved away to sit under the table in a prudent withdrawal.

'Not anger, dog,' Stella told him, 'just misery.' But she thought there was a touch of anger, that most painful of angers: anger at self. No way out, my darling, she told herself, you are just going to have to live through this.

'Of course it's anger,' said Coffin. 'I'm angry with the sod who put the bomb there, and I'm angry with myself for letting Phoebe in for it. I'm even angry with Phoebe for being there and getting herself blown up. No one's grateful for the victim and don't you think it. I'm in a rotten mood, and the dog is quite right to be frightened of me.'

'I'll be frightened of you myself if you go on like that,' said Stella.

Archie Young finished his coffee and observed that he would join the dog under the table if he thought he could get under. 'Being a big man, I can't.'

A small laugh rippled round all three of them, lightening the mood.

'I'm off then,' said the chief superintendent. 'Don't bother to come down the stairs.'

'I'll come. That door can be tricky. Part of the old church and warped.' Coffin was brisk. 'But we love it.'

'Sure you do.' Archie thought if it had been his, he would have had it removed and something new that worked better put in its place. You could get very nice plastic doors that looked old and had some style. 'Perhaps you could fit a steel sheet behind it. Just for protection.'

They walked down the staircase in silence till they got to the great old door. It did have security locks, Archie observed.

'I have something for you,' Archie began. 'It's from Phoebe…a letter…'

'A letter?' Coffin's expression changed, and then he said quickly, 'Thanks for bringing it.'

'She gave it to me before she left, said to give it to you if she got into trouble…'

'And you did. Thanks, Archie.'

The chief superintendent hesitated as he stepped out into the dark. 'You haven't had any more intruders hanging round?'

Coffin shook his head. 'No. I'd have let you know. No one was found.'

'Perhaps we should have done a proper search at the time?'

'Not worth calling out a full search crew plus helicopter with heat-sensitive equipment. Couldn't justify it.'

He watched Archie Young walk away, then he went back up the staircase to Stella.

'Did he have anything else to say? You were a long time there at the bottom of the stairs.'

Coffin was evasive. 'Oh, you know Archie, he can be long-winded sometimes…'

Stella took his hand, which felt cold and dry as if the warmth had gone out of him. 'I don't know what to say about Phoebe, except that I am very, very sorry and will do anything I can to help Eden. Did Phoebe have'—she hesitated—'a lover or any man close to her?'

'Eden will know,' said Coffin.

'Right. Then Eden will tell him. Or her?'

'Phoebe liked men, not women, as far as I know.'

'I'm not being prurient, or probing, it's just it's easier to do the right thing if you know a few details.'

'I think you always do the right thing, Stella,' said Coffin with love. 'I'm glad...' He stopped there.

With some amusement, Stella said: 'What are you glad about?'

'I'm glad I have you.'

'Something happening like this, Phoebe dying, makes you cling to what you've got. I feel the same. You realize that all the time what felt like solid ground to walk on is just a crust that could open up at any time. Often does, too,' she added, 'and when one person falls into the hole, you know you could be the next. I've been in a hole and climbed out. So have you. But the black hole that got Phoebe, that's different, hard to climb out of, that one.'

'I'll hold on to you,' said Coffin. 'Stop you going over the edge.'

'Do the same for you.'

'Thanks.' He studied her face, the eyes shadowed with fatigue. 'You go to bed. I'll clear up down here.'

Stella yawned. 'Leave it till tomorrow.'

'I feel restless, I think I'll go for a walk.'

'Taking Gus?'

Coffin knew he would have to, the dog was already wagging his tail, white and elegant like a plume.

'Watch out for the prowler. I suppose Gus will protect you,' she said doubtfully, for although Gus had a splendid bark and was always keen to attack, he was small. If he was a lion dog, then it was a very small lion. He would fight, though.

'I don't suppose he is still around, but I will be careful.'

Stella listened until she heard the front door close behind him, then she went to the window to look out. There was no moon, and the darkness soon swallowed up the two figures. At intervals, she caught a flash of light.

So he had taken a torch with him.

Sensible. But was good sense the only reason?

Sometimes I distrust the motives of my darling husband.

COFFIN WALKED TOWARDS a corner where there was the stump of an old tree which had been turned into a seat in honour of an aged actor, Henry Ascot. There was a brass plaque bearing his name.

Coffin sat on the seat, Gus beside him. He opened the letter which Archie Young had brought him. He knew this was the real reason for the chief superintendent's visit.

He hesitated for a moment, looking at the envelope, which was thick and white with his name typed on it. He did wonder a bit about the circumstances in which it had been handed over to Archie Young, but he knew that Phoebe and Archie had a friendly relationship. Nothing more than that, they liked each other and worked together well.

Gus was giving a soft bark. 'Cool it, Gus,' he said absently as he opened the envelope, managing to cast light on the letter with the torch at the same time. It took some juggling, but he did it.

Dear John,

I knew the day would come when I would write this letter. I think I knew you were dangerous from the first moment I worked with you. Intuition, I suppose, or pre-cognition—I did have an Irish grandmother. Of course, I did not know the exact nature of that danger, I guess I thought it might be emotional. Well, I daresay you knew it was that too. We came very close, in those days before Stella came back into your life, to love.

I did anyway, but I realized very soon when I came to work in the Second City that I must not show it. It was not spiritual, this love of mine, very physical, which made it all the harder to hide. I was never sure if I did.

When you sent me off on this job, I smelt danger, phys-ical this time. Well, you more or less told me of it. I decided if I did not come back, I would send you my love.

Love and love,
Phoebe

He put the letter back in the envelope, then he turned off the torch to sit there in the darkness. He sat there for some time trying not to think, while wishing he was back in the days when you took a cigarette out of the packet and lit it, then sat there puffing it. This did not take your troubles away but it gave your body something to do while you were miserable.

Just for a moment he felt a flash of anger: what a number of ways women had of making a man feel ashamed.

Phoebe had stuck a knife in which she had offered with love, but had meant it to hurt.

Then he was ashamed again: she hadn't meant it that way, she just wanted to tell him that she loved him. And he had loved Phoebe. But only in the small, limited way that was all he had been capable of in those days.

They had met in disgusting circumstances at one of the messiest and bloodiest killings he had ever seen, a kind of butcher's shop. Phoebe, a young and raw detective, had gone outside to be sick.

Why this should have endeared her to Coffin was not clear to him, but he had been both touched and sorry for her, not usual states of mind for him in those rough days when he hated himself and the people next to him in that order.

And to that younger, unhappy, unpleasing Coffin, the best way to comfort a woman was to take her to bed. Pleasure for you and sympathy for her.

Looking back, he was not proud of that young fellow, not so young, either; old enough to have better manners.

And the thing was, she had laughed at him. If he had thought he was the great consoler, he wasn't.

Not an episode he was proud of.

He had buried the memory, forgotten it, he thought; he had become Phoebe's superior officer, promoted her, praised her, and rebuilt their relationship as friendship. Not even close friendship, but a detached, respectful relationship because he respected her professional skill. And Phoebe? Well, if it wasn't quite what she expected, he had just taken it for granted she did.

With pain you can either smile and pretend it isn't there, burst into tears, or sit there and think about it.

Coffin sat there to think about it, while Gus grumbled quietly at his feet. The most difficult thing was that he could never share the pain with Stella. They had reserves, the sort of marriage where you 'tell each other everything' would have been intolerable to both of them. But the Catholics had it right, he thought: the purging of guilt by confession gave easement to the spirit.

'Shall I confess to you, Gus, will that do? Shall I say to you that I regret my selfish, boorish, masculine self-satisfaction?'

Gus, pleased to be addressed, wagged his tail. Thinking, as any dog would, that this was a preamble to a walk, he got up.

Coffin obliged him. 'Right, let's walk.' Together, they walked towards the road, dimly lighted by Victorian lamplights which the preservationists had insisted upon retaining. Beyond, lay the old churchyard which was even more dimly lit. This park was one of Gus's most enjoyed walks. The smells there were ancient, varied and luscious. A bouquet on them that he found nowhere else in the Second City, except for an interesting area around Spinnergate tube station to which he rarely got, so that exact analysis was not easy to him. The smells there were not as ancient as in the old churchyard, sometimes vividly new, but none the worse for that.

Gus ran ahead into the darkness where Coffin followed him, occasionally flicking on his torch, still thinking. Under one of the big trees which still loomed above the tombs, Gus was sniffing at a branch that was on the ground. The trees were old, and since several winter gales, needed the attention of a good forester. It looked a big branch to have come down.

'Come on, Gus,' Coffin called, walking forward. The moon was up and a soft wind was blowing the clouds apart, making it easier to see where he was going.

Beyond the churchyard wall the ground sloped first gently and then as if gathering speed more sharply to the canal. There were several holes in the wall where it had crumbled away. It looked romantic and was probably dangerous.

Coffin stood there at the wall looking down at the water which was moving sluggishly in the wind. His thoughts were not cheerful.

On the muddy path which led to the wharf, with its old buildings now crumbling like the wall, there were a few tracks.

Those bloody children on their skateboards, but no, surely not. They'd be in the water and drowned before they could stop. Perhaps they had, perhaps there was a dead child floating in the water. He had death too much on his mind.

Harry Seton gone, Phoebe dead. Who next?

He was the obvious candidate because he now knew who was at the heart of much of the terrible happenings all around him. And with the name, he knew the motive. He knew why he had been sent off on the enquiry.

Ask Coffin, he thought sardonically.

He couldn't prove it, but he knew, and was suspected of knowing. Hence the attack on Phoebe.

'I felt danger but let her go anyway,' he said to himself.

Ahead, down the slope, he saw Gus going towards the canal. He liked to swim and the muddier the water the better he liked it.

'Come back, Gus.'

Gus trotted on, usually he disregarded a command that did not fit in with his plans. At the moment, the idea was for a lovely, squishy dip. He was a good swimmer and he knew from experience that he could climb up the bank or even leap on to the old wooden wharf where the barges had unloaded. Afterwards, he would need someone to dry his coat and comb it out, but someone always came forward.

Coffin saw Gus moving on fast, he marvelled at the speed those short legs could manage. Then Gus stopped. He was sniffing the ground.

Oh, please, God, not a dead child here.

He quickened his pace towards the dog who was still snuffling around. Then the dog slid forward, his belly on the ground, a sure sign of intense interest combined with fear.

Coffin went after him. Then he stopped, and stood there smelling the air.

That smell, the smell of the man who had hung about in St Luke's, he who had terrified Stella. The sickly yet sour, stale smell. It was a soiled, dirty smell.

Gus crawled forward, a low noise in the back of his throat.

He was taking himself into the old wharf building, a decaying wooden structure.

Coffin shone his torch inside. Gus was silent now, but standing up, baring his teeth.

There was a figure crouched just inside the door. Gus leapt forward, but Coffin grabbed his collar.

'Get up, whoever you are.'

If you are alive and have limbs that can move.

The figure stumbled to its feet. A muddy, bloodstained face with a great bruise down the side, clothes dirty with leaves and earth spattered here and there. And the smell, there and present in good force.

A length of rope hung round the neck, still knotted but torn in two. Not cut, torn apart.

'Thank God it's you, sir. It's you I was looking for.' A hand came out to steady himself against the wall. 'Don't you know me, sir? It's Jeff Diver.'

Coffin stared.

'I knew you would understand, sir.'

Coffin wasn't sure if he did understand.

'I tried to hang myself, but the rope broke and the branch with it. And I pissed myself and soiled myself. You do that when you are hanged, sir, did you know that?'

'I know,' Coffin admitted.

Diver was crying. 'And I can't get the rope off.'

He's still on the tree, Coffin thought, looking at the figure leaning against the wall, in the wood. Out of his mind.

'I thought it would be easier for my wife, that she'd forgive me if I was dead.'

And you are and she hasn't. But it's my job to bring you back to life.

Gus had retreated behind his master's legs, which seemed a safer area. He looked up as the telephone rang in Coffin's pocket.

Cursing, Coffin answered it. 'Hello?'

'Where the hell are you?' demanded Stella.

'Not far away, I'll tell you later. Sorry.' And he rang off.

Jeff Diver was muttering: 'I knew it was wrong what I did,

but I thought if I was dead, my evil would be wiped out.' He slid to the ground.

'Get up, man,' ordered Coffin sharply. Was he listening to a confession of the murder of the boys?

'Sins of the flesh.' Diver's lips were dry. He dragged himself to his feet, staggering forward. Gus growled in a low, menacing rumble

'Shut up, dog.' The man was sick, in mind and body.

Coffin rang for an ambulance, gave the directions and waited. 'Where have you been all the time?'

'Here, the old wharf. My dad used to work here. But I was going to kill myself. I thought drown first...' His voice tailed away. 'Came looking for you.'

'I know... What have you been living on?'

Diver looked vague. 'Crisps, chocolate...'

'Did you bring that with you?' It cast doubt on the idea of suicide. You don't take a bag of crisps on a suicide trip.

'No... Found them. Here.'

A kind of Robinson Crusoe, thought Coffin.

'Thirsty, though.' Diver licked his lips. 'Could do with a drink.'

Coffin shook his head. He was still up the tree with the birds. 'We'll get you something.' He could see the lights of the ambulance and the police car with it. If the Chief Commander telephones for help, you come with all force. 'Come on,' he held out a steadying hand, flinching from the smell. Not the smell of death, after all, the smell of Dachau and Belsen. Death was there, but degradation first. He made his voice gentle: 'Walk with me to the road.'

Slowly, the little procession—Diver first, then Coffin, and behind them the dog—made their way through the old church-yard.

The ambulance drew up to the kerb, the road was very narrow just there, the crew jumping out ready for action as Coffin led his captive up.

From the police car behind came Inspector Devlin. She came running. 'You all right, sir?'

'I didn't expect you,' said Coffin.

'I happened to be around when your call came through.' In fact, she had been with Sergeant Tittleton, talking over the death of Phoebe Astley. Archie Young, who had been there, had been called away by an urgent call, something to do with Astley, they suspected. 'Thought I might be needed.' Her eyes flicked towards Jeff Diver, who was muttering about confessing in a monotone. 'My, my, what have you got there?' There was a triumphalism in her voice that Coffin knocked away at once.

'He's confessing to something, but I don't think to the murders of the boys. Or anything to do with them. I think he is confessing to sexual relations with men.'

Paddy Devlin raised a cynical eyebrow.

'I think he had a strict mother and father,' said Coffin dryly.

As they talked, the ambulance men were dealing with Diver, who had slumped to the ground; he was helped on to a stretcher while the rope was cut from his throat.

'Suicide attempt?' queried Devlin.

'He is half starved, dehydrated, and in the middle of a breakdown. Yes, he did try to kill himself. He tried to hang himself, only the rope broke. And the branch of the tree.'

The mobile telephone in his pocket started to ring again; he reached in to turn it off. Not even Stella could be talked to just at the moment.

'Follow him to the hospital, will you? He might have something useful to say, although I doubt it.'

Devlin nodded and turned back to her car, saying that the air was fresher there, and why did he stink like a sewer?

Coffin shook his head. 'You'll find out, and remember, if you are ever trying to hang yourself, choose a tree with branches that aren't rotten. Oh, and a good bit of rope.'

Some joke, said Devlin to herself as she got in her car.

Coffin called her back: 'You'll have a man sitting by him in hospital, when he starts to be a bit more rational, ask him where he got the food—crisps and chocolate—that he ate. I want to know.'

Important, is it? Devlin asked herself. Well, the Big Man thinks so. She sprayed the inside of the car with air-freshener,

emon-scented; she seemed to have brought the stink of poor
Diver with her.

The ambulance men were muttering something about a bath
being needed, but were doing their job with skill and kindness.
'Come on, mate,' Coffin heard, 'relax a bit and we will be on
our way.'

They drove off, Devlin behind again, and Coffin went back
to his own home.

Stella was walking up and down the sitting room when he
arrived.

'My God, where have you been?'

'Was that you on the mobile just now?'

She stared as if she didn't take in what he said, then shook
her head. 'No, only the once.'

'Someone rang.'

She took a deep breath. 'It might have been...it probably
was—' She was interrupted by the phone in the room. 'You
take it,' she said to Coffin. 'It'll be for you. I told her to keep
ringing.'

Coffin picked up the phone. 'Hello.'

'Phoebe here.'

TWELVE

'My God you gave me a fright.' Coffin gripped the telephon[e]
hard, while his hand reached out for the whisky that Stella ha[d]
poured for him.

'What do you think it did for me? Being called dead, I ha[d]
a job to convince the hotel I was alive. Go off for a quie[t]
evening with an old college friend and come back to find yo[u]
are dead,' Phoebe said savagely. 'Not to mention the poor in[-]
nocent who went to put an extra pillow on the bed and got he[r]
head blown off.'

'I am sorry.'

'You let me know it was dangerous but you didn't mentio[n]
explosives...'

Stella came up to study her husband's face; there was a ques[-]
tion in her eyes, but it was Phoebe who put the query direct t[o]
him.

'Do you think you know who did it?'

'Yes, I'm pretty sure... In fact, what happened to you con[-]
firms it.'

'Oh, thanks a lot.'

'Are you coming back?'

'Yes, I bloody am.' Phoebe was still in a state of shock. 'Thi[s]
very night.'

'I want to see you as soon as you get back.'

'Yes, sir,' said Phoebe briskly, but with an edge.

Stella came up to confront her husband. 'I heard enough o[f]
that conversation to know you won't tell me any more.'

'Not yet.'

'Not ever unless I make you.'

'I'm not as bad as that.' He put his arm round her and le[d]
her back to the sofa. 'Sit down.'

'If you tell me I look exhausted, I shall probably bite. B[ut]
you can tell me why you were so long on that walk. Gus is a[

muddy, too.' Hearing his name, Gus wagged his tail, which was festooned in a necklace of dead leaves stuck together with mud. It looked like a tiara or a crown worn on the wrong end. It fell to the ground as he wagged.

'Down to the canal...' He stopped. The warmth of the room had brought a faint whiff from Gus's tail, reminiscent of he knew what.

Stella gave a sniff. 'I know that smell...' She looked from the dog to her husband. 'You both smell.'

'Oh God, me too?' said Coffin in alarm. He raised his arm to sniff the tweed. Yes, there it was, faint but pervasive. He groaned. 'I found our intruder of last night...well, Gus found him first.' Gus wagged his tail again and the scent was stronger...he would have to be bathed and soon. 'It was Jeff Diver...he had tried to hang himself. He was living rough.'

And apparently longing to unburden himself of his guilt to the Chief Commander.

'Is he—?' Stella stopped, holding her handkerchief to her nose with one hand and pushing Gus away with the other.

'No, I don't think so. Not the murderer of the boys. But I can't be certain. I think he tried to die, but really wants to live.'

He moved closer to Stella. 'Can I have a whiff of l'Heure Bleu to clear my nose. And yes, you needn't say it, I will have a bath before I come to bed.'

'I'm not sure I'm going to let you anywhere near the bed.'

'Yes, you will, we both need comfort tonight.' He had been too near death twice that night, what with Phoebe and Jeff Diver; he needed to feel alive, and there was a very good way of achieving that end.

Gus slid under the sofa, he had no intention of having a bath tonight. Besides, he liked his smell, it was interesting.

THE CHIEF COMMANDER was early in his office next morning. He worked fast, talking to Paul Masters about the engagements in his diary, and signing letters already prepared for him. There was also a report, provisionally drafted, to read through and check.

He was halfway through the morning's work when Ed Saxon phoned.

'Wondered when you would,' he said.

'Thought you might phone me.'

'Two minds with but a single thought.' But Coffin had to admit he rather thought not. What he was thinking, he trusted Ed Saxon was not.

Ed Saxon picked up something, but was unsure what it was. 'What's the matter with you? I didn't like what happened to Phoebe Astley.'

'Who does? You know all about it?'

'Yes, sure. As soon as I got wind of it, and word got around soon, John, I checked up. I'm relieved she's all right. But it shouldn't have been her. It should have been you.'

'Yes, you are right, Ed. But I don't suppose you mean to put it quite like that.'

'What? No, of course not. Don't misunderstand me.'

'I don't, Ed. It should have been me, I know that.'

'You're a difficult cuss when you like, John.'

'I didn't save my life on purpose to spite you.'

Saxon changed gear. 'Are you getting anywhere on the main question?'

'Oh yes, I think so, yes. I really think so, Ed.'

'Oh?' The query was there and Coffin got some satisfaction in spurning it.

'You won't mind if I don't go into it now, Ed? But I'd like a chance to talk things over later.'

There was a pause, during which Coffin could hear Ed Saxon breathing. Perhaps he had a cold. 'Give me a ring,' he said at last.

'I will do. Of course I will,' Coffin said cheerily. He found himself feeling more pleased than all the morning so far. 'Oh, and Ed, any progress on Harry's death?'

Slowly and as if reluctantly, Ed said: 'Davenport says it was a contract killing.'

'I've heard that.'

'He's putting forward a few names.'

'What about the name behind the contract?'

'He did fancy the wife.'

'I know, I know.' Coffin was impatient. 'I should think he has given up that notion, hasn't he?' It was an interesting idea which he had explored himself, but unacceptable.

'Yes…so he says. Never had much cred. Don't know who is on the new list…he's keeping very quiet. Someone from the pharmaceutical world, I guess.' Saxon sounded more hopeful than convinced. 'May be a crime that is never solved.'

'You mean we will know the answer but never get a conviction?'

Reluctantly, Ed Saxon admitted that he supposed he did mean that.

They promised each other to keep in touch, which was a halfway house to promising nothing.

'Don't think Ed likes me,' said Coffin to himself, 'but then he never did.' He wondered what Mary Seton made of it all.

He did not have long to wait. He had written two letters and read half a report when she was on the telephone. Within the hour he had spoken to Ed Saxon and was now talking to Mary Seton.

Coincidence? Or they did communicate?

She had rung with a complaint. 'I thought you might have rung to let me know how you were getting on. I can't get anything out of Davenport or Ed Saxon, but I thought you were the sort of person who told one things.'

All right, she did not communicate with Ed Saxon. If she was telling the truth.

'I don't know anything that you won't know about Harry's death,' he said mildly. He could make some guesses though, which he would not pass on.

'I bet you know that I was prime suspect for a bit. Vicious, wasn't it?'

Coffin kept quiet.

'Anyway, I am finding out things about Ed Saxon, and it might be *me* that tells *you* things.'

Coffin expressed interest.

'No, it's a trade; you have something for me first.'

She put the telephone down with a bang.

For a second, Coffin sat considering. He realized he had been stupid not to consider Mary Seton as a source.

Voices in the anteroom, louder than normal, attracted his attention. Paul Masters and a woman.

Coffin stood up. Phoebe: she was there.

She was defiantly, strongly and definitely there. She came in as if at the head of an army. Paul Masters, a tall man, looked diminished behind her by the strength of her entry.

Coffin held out his hand. 'Phoebe, there you are.'

'Yes, here I am.'

Paul Masters melted away in tactful retreat.

Coffin took command of the situation. He knew from experience, that it did not do to let Phoebe take command of the scene. 'Have a drink, then we can talk.' He went to the cabinet against the wall where he kept some whisky.

'You're glad to see me back?' demanded Phoebe with some irony. 'I must admit there was a moment when I thought you wanted me dead.' But she accepted the whisky. Coffin was not known for being liberal with his whisky, saying that he preferred his officers sober rather than drunk. You had to be very successful, or very ill, or about to get the boot, to be offered strong drink.

'Now tell me about last night. I only know the bare outline.' In fact, he knew a bit more than that, having been fully informed by his counterpart in Newcastle, but he wanted to hear what Phoebe had to say.

'I booked in to the room. I told them that it had been reserved in your name but it was really for me. They may have thought it odd, but they did not question it. After all, here was a paying customer checking in and signing the register...in my own name, of course. I unpacked, not that I had much, then I went out to dinner with a friend.'

Coffin did not ask her who the friend was. He might ask later.

'Well, couldn't do much that night,' she said defensively.

'No, of course not.'

'So I went out. Before I went, I asked for another pillow for my room and was told one would be taken up. Then I went

out to dinner with Albie...we were at police college together...he is very clever, on the scientific side. I thought he
might be helpful, know people and places. So I told him a bit
about what brought me to Newcastle.'

'And was he helpful?'

'Not then, but I think he will be. It turned out he knew about
it.'

'Did he indeed?'

'Oh, Albie always knows everything. He is definitely not one
of your scientists working in an ivory tower. Albie is plugged
in.'

When Albie is unplugged, I hope he is helpful to us, Coffin
thought. He nodded. 'So?'

'So we had dinner and I went back. I nearly got arrested. I
had the greatest difficulty in convincing them that I was who I
claimed to be and still alive. But then they decided I must have
brought the bomb with me. They weren't sure if I was a bomber
with bad timing or the victim. In the end, Archie Young convinced them.'

The memory of Archie Young gave her pause for thought
before she moved on. 'Be nice if Albie comes up with something. That woman who died deserves justice. You realize what
it means? Someone wants to wipe you out. So you were getting
close to something. Only were you? All the signs are that there
isn't much to get close to. Not out there in what used to be
called the provinces. The operations close down, then start up
again. All right, there is someone planted somewhere inside the
operation who talks to the suppliers, even the producers, perhaps, so they just move on and out. Always in a small way,
but getting bigger, or anyway on a wider scale and making a
profit for someone...'

It was quite a speech for Phoebe, so Coffin refilled her glass.

'I agree with every word you say.'

'Oh.' She was taken aback.

'And I know where I am. Well, more or less. There are things
to be tidied up.' Like H. Pennyfeather. 'But I shall get there,
especially if Albie comes in with anything.'

'If he does, I'll let you know.' Phoebe stood up. 'Thanks for the drink.' She moved to the door, then remembered what was worrying her.

'Did Archie Young give you a letter?'

Coffin said gravely, because a smile would not do, 'Yes, yes, he did.'

Phoebe took a deep breath, and covered her face with both hands.

'Ever been embarrassed?'

He said nothing further to Phoebe on the subject of the letter. Silence is always best. Or it suited Coffin to believe so.

He gave Phoebe her letter back, sealed. If she looked at it carefully she would see that it had been opened and then closed.

To Stella, he said nothing at all. No need.

He did, however, telephone the hospital to find out how Jeff Diver was.

Sedated, was the answer. He was on a drip because he had been so dehydrated, which possibly accounted for some of his mental state. More would be known about that when he was conscious.

Meanwhile his wife had been in to see him, showing signs of affection and forgiveness. There was also a police constable sitting by his bed.

He then rang Inspector Devlin. 'Did you get anything out of Diver about how he got food?'

'Not really. He seemed to think the fairies left it for him. Or the birds. He was not coherent.'

'Let me know if you get anything more rational.'

'Yes, of course, sir, but I don't hold out hopes.'

'I'd like to talk to him myself when he can talk.'

'Of course sir. I'll let you know.'

He could tell she wondered what all this was about. A nice woman, good at what she did, lacking in imagination, perhaps.

Coffin put the telephone down. He had a good imagination himself which seemed to have got better with the years. It was very useful when he had to deal with children. He had never used rollerskates or rollerblades himself, nor had the rollerblades existed when he was a kid, but he could see the use of them and imagine more.

He ate a solitary lunch of a sandwich and a cup of coffee at his desk. Stella, he knew, was busy at the National, seeing this person and that and working out plans. It was the real reason she had come back to the Second City, he felt sure of it, whatever else she claimed.

She had been very loving and comforting over what he called to himself 'the affair Phoebe': Phoebe's reported death. Be nice to hear her voice. He reached out his hand to telephone her. Then he drew back. No, let her get in touch if she wanted to, bless her.

There had been a bad time, not so long ago, when he had been obliged to investigate her relationship with one of her friends. That was in the past. Let her feel free now, not to feel he was always behind her back, watching and checking.

The fact that he still did this automatically was a fact he was trying to change, but had not quite managed. He knew, for instance, that she had not been all the day at the National yesterday.

And how did he know this? He knew it because, being his wife, the number of her car was known and its whereabouts recorded. She was on video leaving her car in Turk Street, Soho. Reports of such things came his way as a matter of course. Security, they called it. He did not dare ask what Stella would call it.

He had better stop thinking about Stella.

On cue, the telephone rang. He was shocked how eager he was to hear her voice. Shocked at himself, because he had made a vow long ago, now broken every day, not to hang on to Stella.

The call was not from Stella, though, but from the secretary of a committee he was chairing. Yes, he would be at the next meeting, and yes, he had read and approved the minutes.

He put the telephone down and took a deep breath.

There were some papers he needed which had been left at home in St Luke's; he decided to take Gus, walk home and collect them.

Stella might, after all, be there, and perhaps he could say: 'What were you doing in Turk Street yesterday, my love?' And perhaps she would smilingly reply: 'Mind your own bloody business.'

He set off down the stairs, avoiding the lift, deciding it was certainly better to say nothing.

Followed by the dog, he walked briskly towards the main entrance. As he passed through, he saw a short man wearing thick, dark spectacles, and a hat and a heavy coat talking to the constable on duty. A small, thin dog, a terrier of no pedigree, was attached to him on a string.

Gus showed signs of interest, but Coffin let him linger for only a moment then urged him on. Together they passed out into the sunlight, which was certainly glaring enough to need dark spectacles.

He enjoyed the walk through the streets of the Second City; he felt he had made an escape, leaving Paul Masters and the two secretaries behind. It was no great distance to St Luke's, indeed he could see the tower already.

Gus trotted ahead, but not too far, he liked to keep in safe touch with Coffin. Master and dog got different pleasures from a walk through the Spinnergate streets. Gus liked to appraise the smells of the streets, many of which he knew of old but which required a sniff to see what the days had added. Some smells dried out and lost his interest, these he departed from quickly, others had a new lustre and demanded his lingering attention.

Coffin, on the other hand, used his eyes to watch the people walking, the traffic passing, the cars parked at the kerb, the cyclists pushing their way through any hold-up—frequent in the crowded streets. It was his city.

School was out, a group of rollerbladers, fast and expert considering their youth, were skimming along the pavements, weaving in and out of pedestrians in a dangerous fashion. From behind a pair of skaters swooped past him on the other side, then crossed in front of him.

Coffin stepped back quickly, while Gus barked in alarm. He had not been hurt, but that never counted with Gus: don't wait to be hurt, complain first.

Coffin swung round and grabbed each lad by the shoulder; he had moved faster than they expected.

He stared into each face: 'I shall know you again,' he said in a hard voice.

They were young lads, he found it hard to judge their age, but no more than nine or ten. Both were still short in height, so obviously the puberty growing period had not set in, but they were sturdily built, one with shining dark hair and the other with curly fair hair worn very short. Each had a brightly coloured jerkin with strange jokes across the chest, while the dark lad had an expensive-looking jacket on top. Come to think of it, those skates were not cheap.

The boys stared at him without a word, blue eyes and brown surveyed him boldly, then they linked arms as they skated away. 'Off, off, off,' they chanted as they went.

They had not been frightened by his anger, or daunted by his threat. Coffin walked on, a conviction dripping into his mind like cold water: They want me to know them again.

He continued walking, assessing what this meant in his picture of the life of the Second City. These kids seemed to use their rollerblades as a means of communication.

So what were they trying to say to him?

'What do you think, Gus?'

Gus never answered, it was one of the nice things about him that you never got, and never expected, a reply. It was a comfort in a world which so often answered back.

The walk through the unheeding crowds, in the mixture of sun and rain which was the Second City's allotment of weather at the moment, freed his mind for thinking. Every detective needed a Dr Watson figure, he believed, to whom he could pose intriguing questions and get innocent answers which were valuable. He had a highly efficient and sophisticated detective force which did not fulfil this function.

He walked on, letting his mind roam, sometimes looking at the clouds moving across the sky, sometimes watching his feet on the uneven pavements.

His thoughts fell into two parts. A and B groups, you could call them, although they overlapped.

He believed he knew who was behind the pharmaceutical affair, he believed he knew why he had been chosen to investigate it. This was A, or part of it. He did not know who had killed Harry Seton, but he believed he could leave that to Inspector Davenport—it was his job, and from what Coffin had heard from him, he was the man to do it.

Coffin was convinced he understood why he had been chosen to investigate the pharmaceutical mole, informer, call the person what you will. He knew who the informer was and how that part of the game was managed. Proving it might be tough, even painful, but he meant to do it. The actual manufacturing side was another problem, but he believed he knew how this was done. He did not yet know where, but he could guess at who and the rest would follow. The game would move on, of course, and never be quite resolved.

Yes, he felt confident about the pharmaceuticals, but this was where Dr Watson would be so useful. He could be told and say: How clever, Holmes.

You don't have to be clever, Coffin-Holmes would say, you just have to see things. He, Coffin, had seen, and he would not be risking his life or Phoebe's any further.

Now for B. B was buggery and murder. Inspector Devlin was a good detective, but she was probably not enthusiastic about his intervention. Let's not call it interference, he told himself, although she might do.

He paced on, slowing down as he assembled his thoughts: four dead boys, all friends, all much of an age, all went to the same school on the same bus.

One of their friends, Louie, said he had seen the first boy go off with a policeman... He was vague on details, but manifestly earnest and doing his best. Not a joker. That was the considered judgement on him and his evidence.

So they look for a policeman: one goes missing after he claimed he was guilty. But guilty of what? Because when he is found he says to Devlin from his hospital bed that his guilt was an affair with another man. Or possibly two, or possibly more. Anyway, he felt bad enough to try to hang himself, but was not efficient enough to do so.

Judgement open here. Probably not guilty.

No evidence to be found against the driver, although he was under suspicion, and knew it. But the thought of the driver brought up the query of how the bodies were transported. He would like to have thought it was in the school bus, but such tyre marks as could be traced did not match those of the bus. No forensic traces of blood etcetera in the bus either, although constant use made examination unreliable.

There was blood on the clothes found with Archie Chinner, one patch of which was possibly from his killer. This blood had traces of an oral morphine solution, a slow-release pain-killer which metabolizes in the blood. We can test Jeff Diver, but his wife says he was not on a painkiller.

What about the bus driver? Said Dr Watson.

Worth thinking about, says detective Coffin. And also, no doubt, Inspector Devlin. She must be asked if she has tested him. Devlin was very occupied with checking on all the deviants and pederasts known or suspected on her list, widening the scope every day, contacting Dutch, Belgian and German police. Not the French, because they were contacting her, having troubles of their own with a series of child sex and murder cases in Calais.

'Those frogs are badgering me,' she had said indignantly— she was not Europhile. 'As if we've got their paedophile. We bloody haven't; our man is British.'

There were some more thoughts moving around at the back of his mind but he hadn't got them sorted yet.

He walked on. If he took the right route and didn't mind the extra walk, then he could go past H. Pennyfeather's chemist shop with its golden, green and sapphire-blue bottles. Unconsciously, his pace quickened, not to the pleasure of Gus who was panting behind.

Along the road on his left, he could see the small row of shops, one of which was H. Pennyfeather. He strolled that way, followed by Gus, who was tired but game. Felicity Street was a short street with a terrace of small modern houses, together with six shops. Its name had nothing to do with any happiness of the inhabitants, but was the name of one of the three daughters of a former town councillor on the housing committee. The next street was Iris Street and round the corner was Rosamund Street.

It was not a rich part of Spinnergate, as the row of shops revealed. Whatever the builders had had in mind when they ran them up—Coffin used the words advisedly since the shops looked to be put together in a hurry and with no design beyond a big glass window and a door—the shops now housed a Chinese takeaway, a curry restaurant, the window carefully veiled in off-white net, and a betting shop—here the window was coloured green to remind you of race tracks and horses, not the cigarette smoke and the television screen, which Coffin knew was inside. There was a cut-price grocers, and next to it, like a peacock in a chicken run, the shining, radiant, chemist shop.

Gus advanced to the only shop that offered him the smell of what he fancied: oily chicken.

'You won't get anything there, boy,' Coffin told him. 'No free chicken legs for you.'

Events proved him wrong: a boy came out of the takeaway with a paper bag under his arm while he chewed on a chicken joint. He met Gus's envious eyes and threw it to him. 'Here you are, feller.'

Gus grabbed it to carry away to the gutter where he began to gnaw it. He wagged his tail at the same time. Dogs win, it said.

The sight of Gus working away at the bone reminded Coffin uncomfortably of what had happened to Harry Seton's body, and brought back a memory of the leg in Archie Chinner's grave.

Had an animal buried it for future use?

'You beast,' he said sadly to Gus. 'But we are all beasts, aren't we? And one way and another, we eat each other.' His back molar gave a twinge, reminding him that men were that sort of beast too.

Along the road, two young women with prams were stopping outside H. Pennyfeather's for a gossip. Then an elderly couple came out together and stopped to talk to the children. The phar-

macist's assistant in her white coat came out to hand something
to one of the mothers that she had forgotten.

'You forgot to take the calcium tablets, Mrs Cook.'

Mrs Cook extracted herself from her deep conversation over
her pram. 'Oh Lord, yes, thank you, Isobel. Forget my own
head next.'

'You don't want to bother with those tablets,' said the old
lady. 'Drink a lot of milk.'

'A tablet is quicker to swallow. And it doesn't put the weight
on, Mrs Armstrong.'

Mrs Cook's friend touched her arm. 'Come on, Bea, we
won't get to our exercise class if we don't move.'

'Should think you got enough exercise looking after the family,' said Mrs Armstrong.

'That's work, that leaves you tired,' was the tart response.
'Exercise makes you feel better.'

Mrs Armstrong had no answer for this, although obviously
searching her brain for one, and removed her silent husband
with the order to stop looking at the girls' legs.

Coffin came up with Gus in time to hear Mrs Cook's comment to her friend that everyone knew the old boy was as blind
as a bat and couldn't see beyond his nose. But the best bum-
pincher in the road, responded her friend with a guffaw.

Both of them were laughing as Coffin walked towards the
door of the shop. He tried the handle, which did not give. The
two women watched him.

Mrs Cook spoke up. 'You won't get in. Mr Barley closes at
one sharp.'

'He opens again at two,' said her friend. 'Then closes again
at five sharp.' They were enjoying observing him, he was a
new fish in their pool.

Was he in pain? Did he need a painkiller? 'Boots down the
hill is always open. Till midnight,' she volunteered.

'Yes, thank you.' Coffin was looking through the door into
the shop where he could see an elderly man with a crest of
greying hair, in a black jacket with a stiff white collar. No
nonsense about wearing white here, this was a professional
man, like a banker. 'No, I'm all right.'

There was a strangled noise behind him.

'Your dog's being sick,' observed both women with one voice.

He turned round to see Gus heaving and straining, disgusting wretch, in the gutter, where he was depositing the remains of the chicken leg. He looked up at Coffin with sad, repentant eyes.

'Damn you,' said Coffin.

'INSPECTOR DEVLIN HERE, sir. I thought you would like to hear a bit of news.'

He had walked home quickly to St Luke's Tower, tidied up Gus, then made himself another sandwich, barely tasting it. After which, he had ordered a car to meet him and take him back to his office. Ruthlessly, he had left Gus behind, pointing out that he still smelt.

Almost as soon as he arrived, Devlin had telephoned.

'I hope it's good news.'

'Neutral, I'd say, sir, but something we needed. The man who first saw where the Chinner boy was buried has come forward. He came into Spinnergate, said he had heard we wanted him. Then he made a statement.'

'I'd like to see it.'

'Of course, sir. The sergeant on duty took it, got the man's name and address and checked it was OK on the computer.'

'So what do we know?'

'He is Arthur Henry Killen, aged fifty-two, he lives at twelve, Dimsey Gardens, East Hythe. No sort of record. Oh, and brought the dog.'

'Did he say why he went off?'

'Said he felt sick...and has since been away, came as soon as he got back.'

'Right.' Then he asked: 'Have you spoken again to the young couple?'

'Mr and Mrs Foster? No, sir, not yet. After the inquest and funeral they went off again for the rest of their honeymoon. Expected back soon.'

'Let me know what there is.' If anything, he thought.

Coffin sat in quiet reflection. 'The man was there at the front desk when I went through. I saw him. If I hadn't been in such a rotten mood I might have stopped and spoken to him myself.'

INSPECTOR DEVLIN PUT THE telephone down, before turning back to Tony Tittleton. She grimaced at him.

'The Big Man breathing down your neck again?'

'Yes,' she said shortly.

'Bear with him. He's great at seeing through a problem.'

So am I, thought Devlin. Just give me space. I am not clear where I am going at the moment, I admit it, but I will get there.

Tittleton looked at her with sympathy and amusement. You'll get there, but the Big Man will be holding your hand. Won't he?

But he did not say this out loud.

THIRTEEN

TIME FOR THOUGHT was rare in Coffin's working life, although when Stella was off on one of her trips he found plenty of time for it in his private life. Did Stella think about him when they were apart? Sometimes he wondered.

Ed Saxon was still sulking in his cage, he would have to be dug out, a problem for the future, but for the moment Coffin was thinking about the deaths of the four boys.

The same questions were going round and round in his mind. He wished he had spoken to the man—what was he called... Arthur Killen?—himself. He looked at the address scribbled on a pad in front of him: 12, Dimsey Gardens. He knew where that was; the row of little dwellings had housed a serious arsonist, now dead, whose house he had inspected himself. The arsonist had died of smoke inhalation while trapped at one of his own fires, which was justice enough.

Might go round to the Killen house himself. With Inspector Devlin, he added quickly, must not step too briskly and heavily into her territory, although he was seriously tempted.

Where would that get him if he did go there? Well, it was just possible the man had seen someone and something that might help. No doubt Devlin had already considered it.

Then there was the young couple who had actually got in touch with the police. They might have more information tucked away without knowing it. They were away on their interrupted honeymoon, but Paddy Devlin would be round there too.

He was drawing circles round and round on the pad.

There was a neat forensic aid in the form of the blood test, loaded with painkiller, but you first had to find the owner of the blood.

He had noticed that the bus driver, Peter Perry had limped away. What about suggesting to Devlin that he be asked for a blood sample?

Once again, she might have thought of it, but if so, she had not said anything about it. On the other hand, would you have done so, he asked himself, at her age? This was another occasion on which a Dr Watson figure would be useful, he could be sent round asking questions.

He finished reading a report, signed it, then picked up another. You had to be a quick reader in this job, a skill he had learnt.

A knock at the door and Paul Masters came in. 'Inspector Davenport rang while you were out at lunch, I took the call myself.'

'Did he say what he wanted?'

'No, but he will ring back this afternoon.'

Masters looked round the room. 'No dog?'

'He's home in disgrace...he ate a leg of chicken and couldn't digest it.'

'A bone might have got stuck, sir. Don't you think he ought to see a vet?'

Coffin summoned up the picture of what had happened in Felicity Street. 'I don't think anything got stuck in Gus,' he said dryly. 'I think he dealt with it himself.'

'I like the little fellow,' said Masters by way of apology.

'We all do, we all do. But he can be a pain.' Coffin looked at his watch. 'I hope Davenport rings soon, I might have to go out again.'

The phone on his desk rang, as if prompted.

'That'll be him, sir,' said Inspector Masters, taking himself off. Beyond the door, he thought, pity about the dog. I hope he is all right. He often looked after Gus when the Chief Commander had to be away for some hours, and felt that the dog needed more from life than following around an abstracted Coffin.

Davenport never wasted any time. 'I thought you would like to know that we've got a man for the murder of Harry Seton. A known criminal, one George Hopkins, known to us, Georgy is, never done anything big before, this is a first. And last, I trust.'

'Good.'

'Case isn't quite tied up; he denies it's him, and claims an alibi. But there is solid forensic evidence on his clothes, on the van he used for transport and,' he added, 'in his bank account, where there is over a thousand that shouldn't be there by rights.'

'Foolish of him not to take cash.'

'Oh, he did, but then he went and opened a bank account.' Davenport gave a snort of laughter. 'Not a bright boy. I'll break that alibi.'

'And do you know who is behind it?'

Davenport was silent for a second. 'I will have to go careful there. Can't say for sure. I did suspect the wife, as you know… I'll get it out of Georgy boy, don't worry about that. Few hours of questioning and he will talk.' Davenport added speedily: 'And then, of course, I will let you know, sir.'

'Superintendent Saxon will want to know too,' Coffin reminded him.

'And he shall do, of course.'

'Tell him first,' said Coffin. 'That's the right way round.'

'Wouldn't do it any other way, sir,' said Inspector Davenport with satisfaction. There's a job there for me, he thought, if I don't get promotion here and I fancy a move.

Paul Masters waited until he heard the telephone replaced before coming in with a batch of letters to sign.

'All well, sir?'

'Yes. He's a competent but slippery bugger, Davenport, but I think he's done well here.'

Coffin signed the letters quickly, before looking at his watch.

'Can I bring you a cup of tea, sir?' Masters spoke from the door.

'No, I will be out for about an hour.'

He went down in the lift. This time there was a plump elderly woman at the desk. She was in tears.

'Lost her dog, sir,' said the constable at the door.

'Oh, I'm sorry.' Coffin went over to speak to her. 'I am sorry, madam. Has he been gone long.'

'She. She's a bitch, a mongrel terrier. I just left her outside a shop…dogs aren't allowed in our post office, which I think is wrong, not like a food shop where I would never take Freda.' Her tears had dried as anger took its place.

From behind his protective glass panel, the constable on duty said he was sure the dog would come back.

'She's been stolen,' said the woman with conviction. 'Freda would never leave me.'

'Has she got her name and address on her collar?' asked Coffin.

The constable said he had asked and she had. 'I reckon she'll be back under her own steam, Mrs Darby. She was last time, remember?'

'That time she was frightened, she ran...'

Coffin thought it time to go himself. Mrs Darby did not notice his departure, engaged as she was in defending Freda's virtue. 'The puppies were planned,' he heard her say with emphasis.

COFFIN DROVE THIS TIME to Felicity Street, his desire for a walk having been quenched. He parked on a double yellow line outside H. Pennyfeather, Chemist.

Mr Barley was behind the shop counter, while the white-coated assistant arranged boxes of tissues on the shelves by the door.

'Good afternoon, sir.'

'Afternoon, Mr Barley,' said Coffin casually, as if he was a frequent customer.

'What is it you need, sir?'

'I've got a headache, so aspirin, I think.'

Mr Barley nodded. 'Oh, I can give you something better than that.' He reached underneath the counter and produced a white and blue packet. 'Codeine...more powerful, sir.'

'I didn't think you could buy that now,' said Coffin, feeling for money. The price on the packet was high.

'Oh yes, indeed, sir. I always keep a little. Just take what it says and don't overdo it.'

Coffin was reading the packet, which seemed to be in German on one side with English on the other. English, of a kind, not perhaps as she was spoken. The trade name seemed to be Felixacan.

'No, I certainly won't do that...' He touched his head. 'I think I have an infection...a sort of flu, I think.'

'Any other symptoms, sir? Throat? Cough?'

'A bit of a throat, no cough, but a general all-over ache.'

Mr Barley nodded appraisingly. 'Well, you'd better take this.' He produced a bottle of yellow capsules. 'Two, three times a day, and no alcohol. Just for three days. Don't let it run on. Come back if it hasn't worked.'

'Oh, I will,' promised Coffin. He paid for the antibiotics, which was what he assumed the capsules to be. Antiveron was the name, and like the painkiller, they seemed to be bilingual. This time they were not expensive if they did what Mr Barley said they did.

He stood on the other side of the counter, grey-white hair, neatly combed, respectable, and confident.

He's mad, Coffin thought, I could probably arrest him on the spot and close the shop, but I shan't—I want more.

'You have a good stock,' he said, to start the conversation going.

'Haven't I, indeed?' There was a kind of innocent pride in Mr Barley's tone, like the parent of a particularly promising infant.

'And reasonable prices too.'

'It is, it is. But this is a poorish neighbourhood, sometimes people cannot afford what the doctor prescribes... So I fill a need, sir.' The old man nodded his head like an ancient, well-meaning sage, not at all like a man who is selling counterfeit medicines. 'Yes, I fill a need.'

Coffin would have liked to ask him who supplied him, and devoted a second to thinking how to put it. But Mr Barley spared him the trouble.

'My son,' he said, 'my son understands how I feel about the poorer people and is a great help to me. He is a chemist, you see, and a very good one. He works in the university, the one down in Spinnergate; there is at least one other now,' he said, his voice suddenly going vague, as if universities now grew like trees and might sprout anywhere.

Mr Barley looked around him with pride: 'He built this shop for me, or rebuilt it, would be fairer. I remembered how chemist shops looked when I was young. Beautiful in their way with the bottles of liquid medicines and great china urns of pills and powders...some chemist's still made their own pills.'

How old is he? Coffin asked himself. Surely not so old as that? He is dreaming of a world he did not live in, never had lived in.

Coffin looked round the shop with its gleaming mahogany shelves, the rows of drawers beneath with the name of the drugs they contained painted in gold in a flowing hand. The shelves were lined with bottles and white pots, all carefully labelled by hand.

'It is beautiful,' he said, with truth. Some of the preparations looked pretty lethal. What did you do with Mordpearl or Shellaura? Did you eat them, swallow them with water, or bury them in the garden and say a prayer?

'Old-fashioned, but my customers enjoy it.'

I daresay, Coffin thought, if they are getting cut-price drugs. 'It's got a nice atmosphere,' he said, and meant it. It was very clear that a lot of intelligent research had gone into this recreation of an apothecary's shop from the past.

'I knew what I wanted, I had a picture in my mind, I didn't just take the money.' He shook his head gently, smiling. 'You could call it rent from a son. Or in this case, he did all this in lieu of rent. *My* vision, and he paid.'

'A good idea.' Coffin had no idea what Mr Barley was talking about.

'Come through to the back, and I will show you something. I can see you are interested.' He led the way through a door to a back room. Over his shoulder, he called to his assistant: 'Lock up, Isobel, dear.'

'Mr Barley...' she called after him.

'Just lock up, dear.' He nodded to Coffin. 'I sometimes close early, as it suits me.'

He drew Coffin into the room, it was part sitting room, part office, not particularly tidy but with comfort as the key everywhere. A big soft sofa by the fire, an armchair facing it. The window curtains were thick, heavy, dark-red velvet. Coffin thought it was quite likely that the room had not been dusted or swept for weeks, perhaps even longer. On a table by the fireplace there was a tray with a teapot and a used cup.

'I look after myself,' said Mr Barley, 'as you can see. The girl is good but she works only in the shop.' He looked round the room, his expression vague. 'There was a woman who used to come in to clean but she got ill and I have never seen her again. She may have died; people do not always tell you.'

'That's true,' agreed Coffin.

Mr Barley led him to the window which overlooked not a garden, as he might have expected, but a cemented slope which led down to a large low shed-like building. Beyond the shed was the glint of water.

'Minger's Canal,' said Mr Barley, seeing Coffin's surprise. 'Minger had a factory here in about eighteen eighty; he made tin baths and tin trunks... Minger went on till about nineteen forty, bombed out then. You need to know the history of this part of Spinnergate to understand what you see.'

'I know,' agreed Coffin. 'What's the building there now?'

'My son works there,' said Mr Barley proudly. 'He lectures in the university but this is his private enterprise. He is very successful, which is why he could afford to help me create my shop. I was not a success, myself, you see.'

Behind every successful son is an unsuccessful father, Coffin thought.

'What does he do there?'

'Not make tin baths,' said Mr Barley with a touch of humour. 'He tries for new drugs, when they are good, he can sell the recipe for them to big drug companies...he has the copyright, you might say.'

'I am glad to see it. It interests me,' said Coffin with truth. 'How is it inside?'

'Never seen it.' Mr Barley was regretful. 'Visitors not allowed. Hygiene, you know. Mustn't take dirt in, or bacteria.'

In the shop outside, there were sounds of the assistant closing up.

Mr Barley showed Coffin out. 'I always like a visitor, but a man of education such as yourself does not come often.'

He ushered Coffin through the shop and bowed him to the

door. 'Thank you for showing me round,' said Coffin politely. He thought he would be back.

The door was locked and bolted behind him with some ceremony, as Mr Barley explained that vandals and villains were rife in Felicity Street. 'My son has very good security which protects me a little. By the way, Felicity Street, we are in Felicity Street, you notice. I believe the original Felicity was one of the Minger daughters.'

Out in the street, absorbing the information thrust at him, Coffin stood drawing breath. He had enjoyed Mr Barley.

A few yards away, her hands on her bicycle, the girl Isobel was waiting for him. She held out a hand. 'Isobel Dutton.'

Coffin shook her hand.

'I wanted to talk to you. I could see you looking around…he's all right, you know. Lives in the past, but quite happily. I run the shop, I am the qualified pharmacist there and make up the prescriptions from the doctors. I saw you were thinking about it all… I know nothing about the cheap drugs.'

Coffin nodded.

'If it hadn't been that someone must look after Mr Barley, I would have been gone long ago, but he was kind to me as a child, I owe him something. He wasn't always like this, you know.'

'So I supposed. He was talking to me about his son,' said Coffin. 'Seems to rely on him a lot.'

Isobel Dutton looked straight at Coffin. 'Ah yes, his son. Sometimes, you know, he says he hasn't got a son. Sometimes that his son was killed in the Falklands. He works in the university with Sir Jessimond's son.' She did not say more with her tongue, but her eyes said that he was the one running the scam. Clever lad, but greedy.

Then she got on her bike and pedalled off, fast.

FOURTEEN

COFFIN WENT STRAIGHT BACK to his office. He thought one of his puzzles was on the point of being explained.

When he had first been asked to aid in the matter of the counterfeit drugs by a higher official than Ed Saxon, he had been told because it was believed that the centre for the drug production was in the Second City.

He thought he now knew where it was. Or at least where the formulas for the drugs to be copied were worked out and, as Mr Barley had said, given a 'copyright'. It was his opinion that there were many centres, and moveable. But it might be that the Second City had the honour of being the home of the mother of them all.

He walked from the car park to the office; walking cleared the mind and promoted the imagination. It also made you hungry: for various reasons, a dinner at Max's tonight seemed a good idea.

As he walked into the forecourt, he saw the sturdy, tweed-coated figure of the owner of the lost dog walking away. But the dog was not lost, she was trotting by her side at the end of her lead. She too looked a familiar figure—it was amazing how one mongrel terrier resembled another.

He spoke to the constable on duty. 'I see she's got her dog back.'

The man grinned. 'Yes, sir. Either knew the way here herself or an unknown hand delivered him, but she turned up near the chief superintendent's car, and he brought her in. I phoned the lady and she came to collect her. Put a good donation in our charity box as a thank-you. But we didn't find her, she did the job herself.'

ONCE IN THE OFFICE, Coffin rang up Superintendent Simpson, who liaised with him and the Drugs Control Committee from the Home Office on this matter of the counterfeit drugs, and told him to get the appropriate squad round to the building behind Felicity Street and turn it over. No, not to tell the Met yet.

He was afraid that Mr Barley was in for a bad time. It was a good thing that the girl Isobel Dutton had pedalled away. He didn't see much future for a pharmacist who had worked in that shop. He had liked both her and Barley.

What is innocence? he asked himself. Hard to prove and, alas, even harder to believe in.

Inspector Paul Masters, who was there as Coffin made the call to Gregory Simpson, managed to look knowledgeable, questioning and incredibly discreet all at the same time.

'Just a dirty rotten business,' said Coffin. 'I believe it is almost sorted. Still a few ends to tie in.'

'Your wife telephoned,' said the inspector. 'She wants you to ring her.'

Coffin agreed that he would do so when he had a moment: he could guess what it was about, the dog and why did he need a bath? He hoped she was giving Gus one.

'Oh yes, I'll ring back when I have time.' Which would be soon, it did not do to keep Stella waiting. He might find she had fled the country without leaving a note and taking all the family with her. Except there was not much of that.

Paul Masters made a sort of mini bow that he had perfected, and bowed himself out. He ought to be in the royal service, thought Coffin, with that obeisance. Perhaps he was training himself for it?

He ought to know more about Masters than he did, but on the other hand, you sometimes learnt things that you didn't want to know if you probed around.

Like an iceberg rising above the water, his other worry surfaced, silently and coldly.

Another moment when a Dr Watson figure would be useful to send out on the town, observing and listening. But then, Inspector Devlin had a kind of Watson in the specially programmed computer. He hoped that this machine was even now printing out the names and addresses of all males who had come in contact with the four boys.

He rang her to find out what was on the list, probably half of Spinnergate and further east. But Inspector Devlin was out; yes, she would call him back.

Time then to telephone Stella.

She launched at once into the attack. 'What happened to Gus?'

He could hear a sound of rushing water: Gus was obviously for it. 'You're bathing him.'

'I certainly am. He's under the shower so the smell runs away quickly.'

'How are you managing that?' He could imagine the struggle with an angry wet dog.

'I'm in there with him,' she said grimly. 'But what *happened* to him?'

Coffin explained. 'Greed, really. Serve him right. Not you, though. I'll come hurrying home to take you both out to dinner.' He wanted to go to Max's, he needed to see the boy Louie again.

'You can take me, but not Gus.'

He promised again to hurry home, knowing even as he did so that he might not keep the promise, that was the way his life went.

As he finished speaking to Stella, Inspector Devlin returned his call. He asked her what was coming through on the computer.

'All males over ten and under ninety who came into contact with the four boys. Practically all Spinnergate with a selection from East Hythe,' she said wearily. 'You'd be surprised how many men have some connection with either the police or uniforms. Of course, the driver Peter Perry is on the list, but we have absolutely no positive evidence. We have had him in and talked to him again, but still nothing.'

'Have you talked to the children who knew the dead boys?'

There was a pause. 'Yes, and once again the results are null and void.'

'But it worries you?'

'Yes, there is something shifty about them. We can't appear to bully, though.'

Coffin thought about it; he meant to speak to young Louie. In a kindly way, of course.

Devlin went on: 'We are just about to build in other factors to see what we get.'

'How is Jeff Diver?'

'Recovering. Ashamed and miserable. Some people have shame and guilt built into them and I think he is one of them.'

'That's sharp.'

A sigh down the line. 'You get sharp in this job.'

'Does he still think the birds and fairies fed him?'

She laughed. 'No, he says some kids threw their bags of crisps away and he ate those. He's thinking about resigning and going into private-eye work. He has illusions, still, you see.'

Coffin thought about the rollerbladers who had shown such an interest in him. 'Ask the computer to build in play and leisure activities.'

'Yes, I thought of that myself.'

'And there is one other thing.' It might be far out, mad, but he would try. 'I want to see the young couple, the Fosters. With you, of course.' Mustn't tread on too many toes; he had enough enemies as it was in the Met. 'Are they back from their extended honeymoon?'

'I'll find out.' She was polite and anxious to cooperate, but puzzled. However, not only was he the boss from whom all promotions flowed, but, as Sergeant Tittleton had pointed out, he often saw further into the wood than most.

No TABLE HAD BEEN BOOKED at Max's, but the Chief Commander and Miss Pinero were never turned away, even if tables had to be shuffled around.

But tonight was easy for Max. 'A nice table by the window?' The occupants of that table had eaten fast and left early. Trouble there, the cynical Max suspected. They dined with him often, very loving to each other on the first few visits, then working through a touch of detachment to downright quarrelling as tonight. He wouldn't see them again, or not with each other. The man worked in a big American bank not long moved into the Second City, but what she did, Max did not know, except spend money on clothes. Some sort of a scientist, he had concluded from the way she spoke. Not married, or not to the banker.

Max spared them his usual guide to the menu; they were all old friends.

'How's your grandson?' Coffin asked over the smoked trout. 'Young Louie.'

'He's out back tonight, his mother's at a class.' Max frowned. 'She is studying law...going to be a solicitor.' He did not quite approve. She was the Beauty Daughter, and that ought to have been enough for her, but with one broken marriage behind her perhaps she did need something else. 'We look after him.' More and more, he was the grandparent, even if his wife did most of the grandparenting.

'I'd like to have a talk with him,' said Coffin.

'Surely, surely. I bring him through.'

Max was called away to another table, and Stella turned on Coffin. 'So that's why we came here.'

'I didn't know the boy was here,' protested Coffin.

'Well, it will cost you a bottle of champagne.'

The boy Louie duly appeared with the pudding, he was neat in jeans and a shirt with the words 'Grinding and Grooving' on it; he looked quiet but cheerful, in expectation of ice cream or something good to eat.

As Louie spooned up ice cream and mixed fruit, Coffin asked, 'Remember what you told us earlier about seeing Dick Neville go off with a man you thought to be a policeman?'

Louie did remember and did not seem particularly disturbed at being reminded of it. Bored, possibly, and distancing himself a little, but he had done that before.

'Was that what you thought yourself?'

Louie said it was. He lifted the ice cream spoon.

'Did you all think it?' asked Coffin softly. He put his hand on Louie's hand over the spoon.

Louie considered. 'Yes,' he said after a while. 'All of us.'

'All of you?'

Louie considered again: he couldn't see any harm in this. All agreed that the Chief Commander was a good chap who could be a help.

'All of Group Four of the rollers. We will probably push Group Three aside,' he said appraisingly, 'and be Group Three...top group after a bit, probably. We are getting better all the time.'

'And where were Group Four at the time you saw Dick Neville with the man you thought was a policeman?'

'Rolling up and down the road,' said Louie, surprised at the question. Self-evident, wasn't it? Where else were rollers?

'And who tried to feed Constable Diver?'

Stella gave a surprised sound; she gave her husband a quick look but she said nothing.

Louie thought for a moment. Then: 'We did when we saw him.' He returned to his ice cream with a feeling that he had done well.

After he had finished his ice cream and returned to his grandfather, Coffin said: 'They did see someone, and it wasn't Diver, it was another man. One they thought they knew. Perhaps were not sure. I believe it was what you might call an imaginary portrait...they built it up from what they knew.'

'I don't understand.'

'People looked different out of context.'

'But the boy Dick must have known him?'

'Oh yes,' said Coffin. 'He knew him, and trusted him. We must find out why. I think they know the killer, trusted him once, now fear him, and who can blame them? So they hint, rather than speak out.'

The rollerbladers had given him the key to open the door, he thought.

AFTER THE QUIET domestic evening which Stella had decreed and to which a humbled and newly fresh Gus quite concurred, Coffin was early to start work.

Stella stumbled down the stairs to share his coffee and toast. 'I'm off to the National this morning, then making travel plans.'

'I shall miss you, but I'm glad you're back for a bit, even if I don't know why.'

'To see you,' she said firmly.

'And the offer from the National?'

'That too,' she admitted without guilt.

I'm the only one around here who feels guilt, Coffin told himself, as he poured her some coffee, and I feel it for Gus as well.

'What about the nose job?' Was it to be done or not?

She was bland. 'Still on hold.' Now it was his turn to get the questions. 'I get the feeling that things are coming to a head. I mean, after that talk with Louie last night, you looked satisfied.'

'Perceptive of you.'

'And what about Phoebe Astley?'

'That business? Yes, I think that is drawing to a close.'

'So I can safely go away and leave you?'

They faced each other, two protagonists, equally matched.

'Is that how it seems?' asked Coffin.

'More or less.'

Then Coffin leaned across the table to kiss her on the lips. 'I might come out and join you in Los Angeles. But mind you, no nose surgery.'

COFFIN'S FIRST NEWS in the office, where Gus had trailed him, was from Superintendent Simpson.

'We went into the premises on the wharf. One sterile area where some experimental work was going on; the rest full of women, few men, packing and labelling various substances. Illegal immigrants, I should say, a problem in themselves. Accommodated on the site, a real health hazard. The boss figure was not there…in the university lecturing, but we are on the way over. He won't run.'

'There might be some link-up with Oxford.'

'It'll be checked.'

'And what about Mr Barley and his assistant?'

'The girl hasn't appeared, but we shall find her. The old man claims he knew of nothing wrong…hard to believe.'

'I'm afraid so.' Coffin went on: 'Keep it as quiet as you can in the Second City. I will deal with the inner London side.'

He sat for a moment thinking, the steady weight of Gus on his feet as usual. Then he telephoned Phoebe Astley.

'It's all over here. For the moment, anyway.' Not gone forever. Some other eager hands would start it up again. It was too good a business to let rest, too profitable. 'You can come out of hiding.'

'I wasn't hiding.' She was indignant. 'Just resting.'

'Right, you can stop resting. Have your holiday or come back to work. You can choose.'

He knew which she would choose. She would be back tomorrow.

There was the usual routine of work with Paul Masters, then he had a meeting with some senior officers on various matters like promotions and rescaling of units.

Before they broke for lunch, Inspector Devlin telephoned. 'Hang on a minute,' said Coffin, 'while I wind up here.' In a minute he was back: 'So?'

'I've got the young Fosters for you. They came home yesterday and they are willing to see you at once. They say they have nothing to add but want to help.'

'Good.'

'Shall I bring them round to you, or will you go there? I am speaking from their flat. By the way, I had better warn you, they have a cat, so dogs are not welcome.'

'I will come round.' He looked at Gus. 'You are not on this trip.'

The young Fosters had a flat in the western part of Spinnergate, not far from where Mimsie Marker, the all-seeing gossip and sage of the Second City, sold newspapers and observed the world go by. Almost certainly she had seen Coffin drive past and go towards MayDay Drive.

Coffin was met at the door by a large and hostile tabby cat. Mrs Foster held the door open, explaining that the cat was hers, that she had had him before she knew Giles, her husband, and the cat had not, as yet, accepted him.

'Nor anyone else much,' she apologized, removing the bright-eyed beast, who was growling in a quiet mutter.

'It's very kind of you to see me.'

'We want to help, but I don't know what we can tell you.'

Coffin took them through the whole episode again. Mrs Foster did most of the talking, her husband sitting on the arm of her chair.

Mrs Foster blushed slightly as she skirted round why they had gone there that night. 'We went up there. I think we were laughing, weren't we, darling?' Her husband nodded. 'And then we saw the man...'

'What was he doing?'

She frowned, summoning back a picture of that scene. 'Just looking down at the ground...then he saw us, and came across.'

'At once?'

'No, no, we stared at him and he stared back, then he came to show us.' She swallowed; her husband put his arm round her shoulders. 'It's all right, Giles.'

'You are being very brave, Mrs Foster.'

'I don't mind with everyone here... He came across, and we went to look...well, you know about that.'

'And he said he was out walking his dog?'

She nodded.

'Did you see the dog?'

Mrs Foster frowned. 'Well, I did see a dog, thought it was with him, only the dog acted more detached, as if the man was not its owner. Giles phoned the police and when we looked round he had gone. Have you found him?'

'Oh yes, he came in to tell us exactly what you have told us. Said he felt ill. Sick.'

Giles Foster said he could understand it, felt the same himself.

'And you didn't see him again?'

'No, I think I heard a car drive off...probably him.'

'Yes, and what about the dog, did you see the dog?'

The two Fosters looked at each other. Mrs Foster answered: 'Not sure what happened to the dog.' She sounded troubled. Paddy Devlin, who had remained silent but watchful, followed him out.

'You got what you wanted?'

'You can read my face? I think so, or shall we say I got what I suspected. I think we go and see Mr Arthur Killen at twelve, Dimsey Gardens.'

DIMSEY GARDENS WAS A line of small detached houses with carefully tended gardens. The garden of number twelve looked a little less cared for than its neighbours. The grass was ragged, the dandelions rampant, and a row of geraniums looked thirsty.

'No gardener,' said Paddy Devlin. She walked up the short path, waved cheerfully to the woman next door, who was watering her lawn, then she rang the doorbell.

Coffin followed behind. The inspector turned round and shrugged.

'No answer? Try again.'

Devlin both rang and banged on the door. 'Of course, he didn't know we were coming.'

'I think he guessed we might.'

He stepped back to look up at the windows of the house, the curtains were not drawn but no one was moving around inside.

He became aware that the woman next door was leaning over the fence.

'You're wasting your time ringing there. You won't get Arthur.'

'No?'

'No, Arthur's in Australia, went out there last month to see his son, he won't be back till the autumn.'

Inspector Devlin walked back down the path to stand beside the Chief Commander. 'Are you sure of that?'

'Saw him off, didn't we? My husband drove him to the airport. And he phoned us from Perth only last night. Having a lovely time.'

Coffin thanked her, and got back into the car.

So who was the man who had gone to the police station with his borrowed dog?

The same man whom the young Fosters had seen finding the body.

Only not finding but burying.

He turned to Inspector Devlin: 'Ask your computer to build into its list all the men who not only fulfilled the other criteria but who could have known that Arthur Killen was away.'

COMPUTERS WORK VERY FAST when given the right questions. By that very evening, Inspector Devlin was back with a list.

She handed it over to the Chief Commander: 'This is the list of the men who would have come across the boys through school, sports, swimming and skating, and other activities, church, choir.

'James Ady, Edward Brother, Bruce Bowen, Will Canter, Oliver Deccon, Philip Gant, Jim Hand, John Indy, Ross Jenkins, Ted Kelly, Robert Mackay, Peter Perry, Alan Rinten and John Salmon.

'The last is the vicar, but we don't rule the cloth out, do we?'

Coffin shook his head.

'Then we added Arthur Killen to the list. We knew already that the boys went swimming, and that Peter Perry drove the bus to the pool once a week. A private arrangement, the boys paid extra. But attached to the pool is a very fine small skating rink, and a group of the boys went there after a swim. Arthur Killen also skated.'

She handed him the second list, much shorter.

Edward Brother, Oliver Deccon, Robert Mackay, Peter Perry, Alan Rinten, John Salmon.

'The vicar is a keen swimmer and skater. But he has no other connection with the school or the boys. Nor was he ever in any police force, not even as a cadet. All the names here had some connection with the swimming pool or the skating, as had Arthur Killen, but when we added the police connection…'

Coffin said: 'We are left with Peter Perry who is on the list, on every list that touches the boys, and Oliver Deccon, once a police cadet, then moved over to the physical training side till he retired early.' Or was retired, there might be a story there.

Inspector Devlin nodded.

'What does Deccon do now?'

'Drives a bus as replacement, helps in the pool, and assists in the skating rink. He was a champion as a kid but fell away afterwards. Still skates and teaches. Perry, even although lame, was learning.'

'Get them both in,' ordered Coffin.
'And then what?'
'Like Dracula we go for their blood.

FIFTEEN

'HE DIDN'T SAY and do it pretty damn quick,' said Inspector Devlin to Sergeant Tittleton. 'But I got the message.'

'Cut every corner,' advised the sergeant sagely.

'I am.'

'He's pretty twitchy. I heard his wife has left him. Taken a job at the National Theatre and is moving out.'

Gossip about Coffin and his illustrious wife sped about the Second City all the time.

'I don't believe it,' said Devlin, 'but I am taking Perry and Deccon in and you can come with me to do it.'

PETER PERRY WAS CLEANING out the school bus when they arrived in the early evening. He had done his school trips and was looking forward to a quiet evening watching television.

'Oh, leave me be,' he groaned, 'I haven't done anything. You've asked me questions and I've answered them. Don't forget I've been one of you and I know you are just dredging around because you haven't got a strong lead or any evidence.'

'Have you got a dog?' asked Tittleton, who had been staring at the wall of the shed where the bus and other vehicles were housed.

'No, I haven't,' snapped Perry.

'So what's the dog lead doing there, hanging on the wall?'

'I had a dog once.'

'It looks like a new lead.'

'Well, I don't know anything about it.'

But he made not much fuss about being taken into the Spinnergate headquarters where Devlin had set up her incident room, only saying he must let his girlfriend know or she would wonder where he was.

'We'll tell her,' said Tittleton brusquely. 'You just come along with us.'

Devlin had not said much, but had prowled around the garage, inspecting the cars and showing some interest in the white van parked behind the second bus.

'Whose is that van?'

'Communal,' said Perry. 'All of us own it. And use it.' His mood was sour, changing him from the jolly figure the boys knew as he drove the school bus to someone darker. 'Three of us: me, my brother and Ollie Deccon. Also, anyone we might lend it to. So put that in your pipe, Inspector, and smoke it.' He had never liked women in the police.

But he was quiet as he limped out to the car and was driven away.

Ollie Deccon was taken in next. He did not know that Peter Perry was there before him, nor was he told. He had been working at the sports centre, taking a group of ladies in their first swimming class. He was a popular teacher because he was kind, quiet and seemed virtually sexless. 'Which is what you want with someone who is in the water with you showing you breast-stroke.'

The girls—Ollie called them his girls, although their average age was usually nearer thirty—gathered around him protectively in the water like a circle of swans as Inspector Devlin summoned him out.

'See you back soon,' they called after him, before retiring to shower, sauna and dress while discussing with interest what their teacher had been taken in for.

But he did not answer the shout of support, seeming more depressed than cheered by it, but he went with Devlin and Tittleton quietly enough, pointing out that he only did the school run as a relief driver.

The sergeant watched him while he dressed. 'Nasty bruise you've got there.' A long streak of purple stretched down Deccon's leg. He shrugged. 'Did that ages ago, weeks—had a fall.'

'Must have hurt.'

'Still does at night.' He was shrugging himself into jeans and sweater.

'Your face as well…you might have cracked your cheekbone, now I bet *that* hurt.'

'So what?' Sympathy from Tittleton was not needed; he had worn the uniform himself and knew what sympathy meant: nothing, it was meant to make you talk more freely.

'What're those things?' Tittleton pointed to a pair of leather tubes, like leggings only much shorter.

Deccon barely looked at them. 'Should wear them when I skate, I don't always and that's how I got the bruise…ankle went over.'

'You might have broken it.'

Ollie did not answer, but followed the sergeant out to where Devlin was waiting in the car.

All she said as they drove off was: 'You were quick. Good.'

'I deserve more than that,' said Ollie. 'An apology or an explanation would not come amiss. I don't know what you are after.'

'Among other things, your blood,' returned Devlin. 'I know you will be glad to give us a drop. Or more.'

'Are you serious?'

'I am.'

'Then you are a bloody vulture.' And Deccon sank back in the car seat, saying he wanted a lawyer.

You can have one, thought Devlin, but let's get that blood from you first.

'It's my blood,' he called after them as he was shut into the interview room, 'and I'll keep it to myself.'

'He's not too pleased with us,' observed Sergeant Tittleton as the door closed.

'No, it's not him I'm worrying about. Let's get the ball rolling.'

She knew this case was important and one she must tidy up and quickly too. Those children deserved a quiet rest now which they could only get when their killer was found.

Apart from anything else, the man was a danger and might kill again. She saw this every time she met Chief Superintendent Young, who called in regularly to get the latest news. Dr Chinner was another caller, the most persistent of the parents whom he had organized into a group.

There was also the Chief, John Coffin, whose approval was very important to her. She did not agree with Tony Tittleton that his wife was about to leave him, although that story was spreading, but she could see he was troubled.

COFFIN WAS TROUBLED, not about Stella whose love he counted upon, whether she was here or across the Atlantic, although she could be delightfully, maddeningly elusive, but about the Ed Saxon–Harry Seton business.

So far he had not heard from Ed Saxon, but it would come and he must decide what to do. He had never admired Saxon but he had certainly respected his skills as a policeman. Yet his career had stalled.

Where was it now? It was hard to call his present appointment anything but a dead end. What had gone wrong? He had probably irritated a lot of the wrong people, but Coffin himself had done the same and he had come through, never drowning but swimming to the surface.

I must have a lot of my terrible old mother in me, he thought: the mother who had given birth to him, then dumped him and moved on, always making fresh worlds for herself. I am the same, he told himself, a fish, not a bird, I just swim on.

But Ed? Some men when disappointed dry up or join a club, but Coffin sensed in Ed some fire still alight.

'I think it's having you that's kept me afloat,' he said to Stella over breakfast the next day. 'Kept me right.'

'Because I'm always right?'

'No, as a matter of fact you are nearly always wrong.'

'Oh, thanks.'

'But there's an essential rightness about you.'

Stella was perplexed. 'Oh, but I am an actress and we just take colour from where we are.' She poured him some coffee. 'I like having breakfast together. Why are you so morbid today?'

'Not morbid...it's just that today I think I am about to find out that a man I thought a decent sort is a multiple murderer and that another man, whom I have certainly respected, is…' He did not go on. Leave Saxon alone for the moment.

There was much confusion and anger at the Clement Attlee School as the bus driven by Peter Perry did not arrive and assorted parents were obliged to drive their offspring to school.

The friends of Louie came together as a group and talked of what had happened. Something, they agreed, must be done.

COFFIN TOOK THE CALL he was expecting from Paddy Devlin in the early afternoon.

'We have the blood-test result. Negative for Oliver Deccon, although they share the same blood group, but strongly positive for Peter Perry. His blood was loaded with the drug found on clothes of Archie Chinner. No wound on Perry but we conclude it healed.'

'I am coming in to see him.'

Inspector Devlin met the Chief Commander on his way. 'He admits taking painkillers for what he calls "the screws" but denies killing the boys. He would, of course.'

'Have you found the drug on him?'

'No, but we searched the house and have found an unlabelled bottle with tablets which are being examined now. I don't know where he got the drug and he isn't saying. But possibly from Mr Barley who seems to have a liberal attitude to drugs. But you know all about that, sir.'

'I do. Anything else?'

'We had already been over his car but a fresh forensic test is being made on the white van where he garages the buses… I think we are getting something.'

'Good.'

'We haven't charged him yet, of course, and his girlfriend is outside complaining noisily.'

'Only to be expected.'

'She says he's an innocent man.'

Coffin sighed. He had met so many defensive wives and girlfriends of deeply guilty men.

Archie Young was waiting for Coffin. 'Can I come with you, sir?'

'Of course.'

The three of them, Coffin, Archie Young and Paddy, walked in together.'

Perry was sitting, indignant, and dejected. Denial personified. Sergeant Tittleton was leaning against the wall; he straightened up rapidly as the trio came in.

Perry too stood up. 'That's right, three of you, four if you count him.' He nodded towards Tittleton. 'Four against me, but it won't get you anywhere. I don't admit to anything. I didn't do it and you can't prove I did. I don't confess.'

'It's a powerful drug you took.'

'And I had a powerful pain. Look...' He hobbled round the room. 'That's the best I can do and that hurts. And it's one of my good days, no credit to you.'

They talked to him, but he stuck to what he had said about his innocence, and after a bit, he would not talk at all.

'We can hang on to him for a bit to see what forensics can come up with, but we can't charge him with what we've got.'

'No,' said Coffin thoughtfully. 'No, we can't.'

Archie Young said nothing, just shrugged and walked away.

'He's upset,' said Devlin.

'Of course he is. We all are.'

Coffin hovered at the door, still talking to Paddy Devlin on the matter of the drugs, but he was near enough to the constable on duty whose loud voice could be heard informing someone that he could not believe it of Peter Perry. 'Not boys,' he was saying. 'Never saw that his taste lay that way. Now if it had been girls, yes. The biggest womanizer in the unit, we used to say.'

Coffin heard and noted.

Back in his office, he rang up his own doctor, a distinguished physician with a title.

'Powerful drug, morphine solution. It's given to you for the sort of pain that makes you want to shuffle off this mortal coil. And frankly, if he was lame as you say...'

'He was hobbling. I suppose I noticed it. But not enough!'

'I don't believe he could have carried the bodies around.'

'Thanks for telling me. Stella says to say she wants you to come for dinner soon.'

Archie Young came into the office. 'I don't think he'd confess if we gave him fifty lashes.'

'He might,' said Coffin. 'I would myself, but it wouldn't mean he was guilty.' He stood up. 'Come round to St Luke's and have a drink. I don't know if Stella will be there. But there's me and Gus.'

As they walked across the car park to where Coffin's car stood in the shade, there came that rattling, gliding, banging sound that Coffin had got to know.

A group of rollerbladers came up, made a wide circle around them twice, then sped away.

They were silent and polite, but they carried a home-made banner which read: *Pete Perry is innocent, Pete Perry we like.*

Then they sped off. But when Coffin and Archie Young got to St Luke's there was another group, about six this time with Louie among them, waiting. They too had a banner with, this time, what looked like a photograph pinned on it.

Once again they circled round the two men, this time chanting: 'Not Pete, not Peter, not Pete.'

'Bloody kids,' said Archie Young. 'Clear off.'

'We've got rights,' one of them called out.

'No, not this time,' said Coffin. 'This is private land. Hop it. You've made your point, now go.'

Stella was there and kissed them both warmly. 'I hear everyone says I am leaving you so I must make a display of love.'

Coffin was annoyed. 'How did you hear that?'

'Oh, Mrs James let me know as she was hoovering. She's back on the job. She hears everything. Tells it, too.'

'I must remember that.'

Stella began to assemble the drinks, still talking away. 'She says Peter Perry couldn't have done it, she used to see him in the Rheumatism Clinic at the University Hospital when he could hardly walk...that's why he stopped being a policeman. She saw Ollie Deccon there too when his wife was dying...something nasty, she doesn't know where.'

'There are limits to her knowledge then.'

'A bit; she says Maggie Deccon went home to die.'

Coffin said thoughtfully: 'I ought to have spoken to Mrs James before.'

They had one drink, but Archie refused to stay. 'I promised to drop in on Geoffrey Chinner to tell him how things went.'

Coffin went with him down the stairs.

'He's not happy,' said Stella.

'Can you blame him? He wanted Perry hung, drawn and quartered.'

'And did you?'

Coffin shook his head. 'No.'

'What's that you've got in your hand?'

'It's a photograph. Someone dropped it through the door.' Stella stretched out her hand. 'Can I see?'

'Not yet. Later.' He finished his drink. 'Can I leave Gus with you? I don't want to take him where I am going.'

OLIVER DECCON LIVED IN a small, modern house, with two garages and several sheds, next to the sports centre, which had been built to house the groundsman, but he owned a house nearby and preferred to call that home without living there. It was a good investment, he said.

Ollie was not pleased to see John Coffin. 'So it's you lot again. Top brass this time. They let me out, didn't you know? I'm innocent. It's Peter Perry that's for it.'

'Supposing he is innocent?' said Coffin.

'Then we are both innocent. Thank you for coming, goodbye.' He prepared to shut the door. But Coffin put his foot there.

Ollie stood back, still holding the door. 'Trust a copper to put his big foot in it.'

'You were one yourself once.'

'Cadet only. So, what is it you want?'

'I thought if I came to see you myself, it might clear my mind. You know, of course, that you and Peter Perry are the two chief suspects for the murders?'

'Always have been, I suppose.'

'Very nearly always.' He advanced through the door. 'May I come in?'

'You already are.'

'It seemed to me that some of the young boys you helped to skate don't think Perry is guilty. And Killen is out of it too, you just found it handy to use his name. You've always used other people, haven't you? I think I would call you a devious chap. I believe the boys sensed that much.'

'What do boys know?' There was contempt in his voice.

Coffin looked at him. 'Only you know that, Ollie.' He handed him the snapshot. 'This is one of those quick pop-up photographs. Take a look.'

Deccon took it delicately with the fingertips of his right hand, as if touching it was dangerous. It showed a man wearing a policeman's uniform holding the hand of a boy.

The picture was blurred, as if taken from a distance, possibly even through a window.

The man's face was that of Ollie Deccon.

'You didn't know about this photograph, did you, Ollie? I think your mate Perry took this, as an insurance policy for himself.' Or possibly for a bit of blackmail. 'I think his girlfriend decided it was time for me to see it.'

Ollie was silent, but he stared at the photograph. He had always hated himself in that bloody uniform. Police!

'Who's the boy, Ollie? An early seduction scene, or one of the boys you killed?'

Ollie dropped the photograph, his face was changing. 'I didn't hurt him, only gave a little…stroking, asked nothing back.'

'Not that one,' said Coffin gravely. 'So what changed you?' He could see Ollie's face was sweating.

He was breathing heavily. 'The girl, the dead girl, I found her body. I used to go and look at it…her innocent deadness.' He slumped to the floor, and covered his face. 'I only did…that to them after they were dead.'

And the girl? Could he believe what Ollie said? For the girl must have been decayed, putrified.

Not true, thought Coffin, and his mood hardened, the dead do not bleed and bruise as these boys did.

'I used to visit her…before, you know what I mean, before I did anything… She was so like a boy, more like a boy than a girl as she lay there...a rat or a dog was savaging her... I cut off her leg, and buried it... I did it out of love for her.'

Ollie looked up. 'I feel better now I have told you.' This was not true, but he knew it was the sort of thing that they expected you to say.

Coffin was grimly satisfied. 'I don't want you to feel better, I want you to feel worse. And you will, Ollie, because we will prove all this.'

Ollie stared, his eyes pale and wary.

'There is the blood on the clothes where you buried Archie Chinner. Traces of dihydrocodeine in it, prescribed for your wife originally, but you used them for a painkiller. It's a slow-release morhpine, it metabolizes in the blood; it can be identified.' Coffin studied his face. 'That's a nasty injury you had there. It must have hurt, you took it then, I guess. Of course, it passes through the system and it was out of yours when you were tested. Perry had some, from you, but he wouldn't say. What hold did you have over him? Some trouble with a girl? Underage? It will all come out and Perry will talk.'

He put out his hand, and dragged Ollie to his feet by his collar. 'Stand up, you miserable, snivelling little sod. Don't think you will get away with anything. You and Perry both. You are back in the real world where there will be DNA testing of the blood, and where forensics will go over the white van in the garage, over this house, and have the skin off you if need be.'

'I kept them in the garage.' Suddenly he was willing to talk. Deccon pulled a small diary from his pocket. 'Here, you can have this...I wrote it all down. I'll tell you the code... WP means Wet Pants, they all wet themselves. S means sicko...a police connection didn't help them.' He gave a giggle which he tried to change into a cough.

'You chose them for the connection,' said Coffin, hating the man, holding his hands off him with an effort.

He reached in his pocket for his mobile phone. 'Thank God for science. It may not be a walk to the gallows for you, but you will feel the touch of the whip if I have anything to do with it.'

'You aren't meant to threaten, sir,' said a voice from the door. It was Archie Young. 'I followed you, sir.'

Coffin stood back from Deccon. 'Not a threat but a prophesy. We both know what happens to men like him in prison.' *If he doesn't hang himself first.*

STELLA WAS WAITING for him. 'You look sick.'

'I feel sick.' He bent to pat Gus's head. 'And an end to a lousy business and a bad day.'

'It's not over yet, I'm afraid.'

He looked up sharply. 'What's that?'

'While you were out there was a phone call for you from Mary Seton.'

'Ah.'

'Will you ring her, as soon as you can? She sounded very distressed.'

Stella handed him the phone. 'I'll leave you to it and take Gus for a walk.'

'No need for you to go.' He held out his hand to her.

She took his hand in a firm grip. 'I think there is. Come on, Gus.'

The phone felt heavy in his hand, this was a call he did not want to make. Mary Seton answered on the first ring. 'Thank God you have rung. Please come, you must come. I am terrified.'

'Now? Tonight? It's not easy.' Inspector Devlin would want to talk to him; Archie Young might yet be around again.

But he had realized that the searching of the whole pharmaceutical premises, shop and all, would be explosive. He had known too that some of the debris would be coming his way. It was just happening a bit sooner than he had expected.

Tonight, rather than tomorrow.

'I'll come. Where to?'

'My flat. You know where it is?' She explained how to get to her home in Battersea. Not Chelsea, but nearly. 'Just over the bridge, big block of flats, Conygham Rise. I am on the third floor.'

He could hear noises in the room with her. It sounded as if a chair had fallen over.

'I must go. See you.'

Coffin stood up as Stella came back into the room, bringing a rush of fresh air with her. 'You weren't gone long.'

'We didn't go far. I thought if I was away too long you might not be here when I got back. Wherever you are going tonight, I am coming too.'

'What makes you think I am going anywhere?'

Stella chose her words carefully. 'Let's just say that I've been around you a long time, and I have learnt to read the signs.' She looked down at the dog who had pressed himself against the door so it could not be opened without moving him. 'So, for that matter, has Gus.'

'Right, get your coat. But not Gus.'

IN THE CAR, Coffin said: 'I said not Gus.'

'He didn't hear you.'

'I don't know how he does it.'

'I don't know either,' said Stella placidly, lying, because she had smuggled Gus in under her coat.

Coffin undid his seat belt. 'Give me a minute, I've forgotten something.'

Stella sat quietly with Gus; she did not know exactly where they were going but she was determined to go with Coffin to Mary Seton. She was a little tired of all the women surrounding her husband, clamouring for his attention.

Coffin slid back into the driving seat. 'Sorry about that.'

He drove quickly and neatly out of the Second City and westwards towards Chelsea and then Battersea.

As he drove, he told her, first of all about Peter Perry and Oliver Deccon, and then about the pharmaceuticals affair. 'It's not the end of that business, it's like a field of mushrooms but as far as I am concerned it is over.'

'What about Ed Saxon?'

'It's wait-and-see time there, Stella.'

For the rest of the journey there was not much talk. Coffin was close to exhaustion, aware that he had neither eaten nor slept much for twenty-four hours. Not exactly insomnia, he told himself as they passed over Battersea Bridge, but a touch of nightmare.

He got lost trying to find where Mary Seton lived, but a passing cabby set him right.

'That's it,' he said, looking up at the redbrick block which had been new when the century was young. 'Third floor—you stay in the car, I will try to be quick.'

Stella ignored this advice, she was already opening the door of the car.

'Not Gus then.'

She nodded, putting the dog on the back seat. 'All right, not Gus.'

'I know he's a brave boy, but I don't want him killed.'

'What?' She was startled.

'You heard.' Coffin was already walking forward. In the big front entrance there was a panel of bells with entryphones. He pressed the bell under Mary's name, and she answered at once.

'Come up. I'll have the door open.'

There were three lifts in a row. Stella started towards one, but Coffin put his hand under her elbow. 'We'll walk.' At the third floor, Coffin stood looking about him.

Mary was standing by her door. 'It's good to see you...Stella.' She held out her hand. 'I didn't expect you.'

Less good to see me, Stella decided, but polite about it. Leaving Gus in the car was the right thing to do.

They went straight into the sitting room. Mary stood in the middle of the room; in the light there they could see a bruise on her cheek.

'How did you get that?' asked Coffin.

Mary did not answer. Another woman pushed open an inner door and stood looking at them. Her face was bloody and swollen, thick bruises were already lining up around her eyes and mouth.

'The same way she got those. You know Ed Saxon's wife, I take it?'

'He didn't know me this way, be surprised if he knows this face.' Laurie Saxon had a deep, husky voice.

'I know you, Laurie,' said Coffin. 'Did Ed do that to you?'

'Who else?'

'And he hit you too, Mary.' It was not a question and Mary Seton did not answer it. 'Why?'

'Not because he loves us, but because he is angry and when Ed is angry he has to hit someone. Preferably someone who can't hit back.'

Coffin turned to Mary. 'Is that why you sent for me?'

She licked her lips. 'He's very, very angry. I was frightened.'

'Where is he?'

The inner door opened. 'He's here,' said Ed Saxon. He stood, feet apart, looking large and dangerous. 'I'm glad you came; I thought you would if I got Mary to phone you. You always were a ladies' man. I see you've brought Stella with you. I wish you hadn't. Stella, you shouldn't have come.'

Coffin pushed Stella behind him.

'I don't want to spoil your pretty face...'

'I know all about you and TRANSPORT A to give it that name. I know you were the corrupt one in the middle, and this was why you sent me off on that wild-goose chase.'

'Aren't you the clever one?'

'You gave me those files so I would be inspired to get off to Coventry and Oxford, to get me out of the way, because you knew that Humphrey Gillow of the Home Office had put me on to investigate the whole business. I was meant to be killed. As you killed Harry Seton, because he didn't only suspect, he knew.'

'Mary and I didn't want that, did we, Mary?'

Something like a moan came through Laurie's swollen lips. Mary said nothing. Practically everything she had said and done had been false, a lie, Coffin thought. Everything began to look like a set-up now from the fire, which either Saxon or Mary or both had organized (she had certainly gone there to check up), to some of the file messages.

Not the Pennyfeather mention, though—that had to be a genuine contribution from Seton which had not been deleted by his killers.

Right, let's sum it up, a cynical question arising about the probity of that forensic search. But go on.

So it was Mary, Coffin thought, who had gone into Seton's

office, messed it up, and left confusing messages on the computer. A dear little traitor. And ASK COFFIN, that was her idea to intrigue me, spur me on, because I had liked Harry Seton.

'But I didn't kill Seton. Not me.'

'You paid. Or did Mary pay? Inspector Davenport suspects it was her.'

'Only because of you. Davenport couldn't see through a glass wall, sod him.'

Not drunk, Coffin decided, but high, wild on something.

'But you can all go together, a bullet each: you first Coffin, ladies afterward. Not Mary, I've grown attached to her face…quotation, you are not the only one who reads. Mary can come with me. But not my dear wife who has been helping herself to my money.'

He was drawing a gun from his pocket.

I wish I had brought Gus up here, thought Stella, he would have leapt forward.

'I came ready,' Ed said.

'And so did I,' said Coffin; he slid a small gun into his hand. 'I got this out of stock just in case. And if I miss you, Ed, don't think I didn't send a message ahead. Davenport might be outside now.'

He fired the gun straight at Ed Saxon.

'YOU DIDN'T HIT HIM,' said Stella as they drove home.

It was late at night, they had both made statements, and answered all the questions that Davenport had asked. They had agreed to come back if more was needed.

'No, I never meant to, he wasn't worth the killing, but I did enjoy the look on his face when he thought he was a dead man. He never had any bottom.'

'What about the money?'

'There won't be any. My guess is that he took money with him when he went abroad and paid it into accounts there. Laurie had been milking it. She will probably quietly disappear and live on it in comfort. Ed loved money, but more than that he resented his lack of promotion. It would have given him real pleasure to wipe me out.'

'Yes,' said Stella, 'I admit I was overjoyed when Inspector Davenport and his cohorts burst in.'

'Yes, I had the forethought to let him know where I was and to come on round. I went back to telephone.'

'I wondered what you did then... At one point I longed for Gus and his attacking teeth.'

'He did sterling work barking down below. It certainly alerted Davenport and made him get a move on.'

'Do you think Gus could hear and knew we were in danger?'

'No, I think he just wanted to join in the fun.'

'I am glad you call it that.'

They drove on in silence. They were nearly home, with the lights of the Second City all around them, when Stella said: 'I might as well tell you that the National deal coming up was a godsend. I was glad to have an excuse to come home... All these women who seem to be in your life...Phoebe, Paddy Devlin, Mary Seton...I was jealous.'

Coffin drove on. 'I knew it,' he said, a touch smugly.

STELLA WENT TO BED, exhausted, but while she slept, Coffin sat up, thinking over the events of the last few days.

Had justice been done? Would it be better if men like Ollie Deccon and Ed Saxon died? Both of them had used other human beings, which was surely the ultimate sin.

As dawn came, he went into the kitchen to make some coffee. Gus got out of his basket to come in search of food and company.

The telephone in the kitchen rang, and Coffin answered it quickly in case it should disturb Stella.

He listened to what Inspector Davenport had to say. 'Yes, thank you for telling me. Probably for the best.'

He put the telephone down and gave Gus a pat. Later he would tell Stella.

Ed Saxon had died from poison soon after being charged and detained. 'He must have had a suicide pill in his mouth,' Davenport had said. He sounded disappointed.

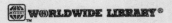

A GHOST OF A CHANCE

A SHERIFF DAN RHODES MYSTERY

BILL CRIDER

Sheriff Dan Rhodes of Blacklin County, Texas, knows that times may change, but most things can be explained with a little common sense—even the "ghost" haunting his jail. When the body of Ty Berry, the president of one of two feuding historical societies, is found shot dead in a freshly dug grave, Rhodes decides the crime is of a more earthly nature.

The outspoken head of the rival historical society becomes the second victim, putting Rhodes on the trail of a double homicide...and of course, one irascible ghost.

Available September 2001 at your favorite retail outlet.

 **WORLDWIDE LIBRARY ®**

WBC396

HEAR ME DIE
E. L. LARKIN

A DEMARY JONES MYSTERY

When private investigator Demary Jones gets a desperate message from friend Sara Garland, she begins to fear the worst. Her fears are soon confirmed when Sara disappears. Head accountant at the highly secretive Electric Toy Company, Sara isn't the only one in trouble— the office manager is a victim of a hit-and-run. Next, the eccentric head of ETC is found beaten to death.

Though the cops are convinced Sara is behind the killings, Demary believes otherwise and follows a trail of greed and desperation to a clever game where toys are more than child's play.

Available September 2001 at your favorite retail outlet.

 W⊕RLDWIDE LIBRARY ®

WELL397